THE BUSTY BALLBREAKER

A HOT DOG DETECTIVE MYSTERY

MATHIYA ADAMS

Created with Vellum

ABOUT THE BUSTY BALLBREAKER

The homeless men of Downtown Denver love watching the construction crew work...

They especially love watching the wrecking ball operator, a woman with a heart of gold. Unfortunately, the homeless men who gather around the construction site focus only on her more obvious attributes, so she becomes known as "Busty Ballbreaker," a sobriquet that she actually cherishes.

Normally she minds her own business, demolishing buildings or lifting loads of steel off of trucks. But when her friend dies in an industrial accident, Busty thinks his death was anything but an accident. Was it? MacFarland uncovers a lot of suspects, but which one of them would commit murder? Actually, which one of them *wouldn't* commit murder?

Get a Free Hot Dog Detective Novella!

About The Jovial Juror

The impossible happens! Mark MacFarland, former Denver Police Detective, gets a jury summons. He's certain he won't be selected. After all, what defense lawyer would want a former cop sitting on the jury of a murder trial? But as luck has it, he is selected to be on the jury.

But as the trial proceeds, MacFarland suspects the defendant has been framed. If so, who is the real murderer?

Click here to get this novella now!

PROLOGUE

SATURDAY, FEBRUARY 20, 0330 HOURS

HE CALLED HIMSELF THE REPAIRMAN. He only came out when things needed to be fixed, as was clearly the case right now. He was a professional who took pride in his work. When his repairs were done, no one would even know there had ever been a problem.

He moved quietly through the dark shadows towards the parked truck loaded with steel I-beams. He knew they would be unloaded in the morning, and that was when the "accident" would take place. Once that happened, one more problem would be eliminated.

This part of the construction site was deep in shadows. The Repairman knew that the site watchman, a wannabe cop named Picket, would stay in his guard shack all night. If he did venture out, Picket would stay close to the house trailers the company used as offices. Picket wouldn't venture close to the deep pit that would eventually form the foundation for the atrium of the building, nor would he go towards any of the partially erected towers that one day would stretch thirty, forty, or sixty stories up into the Denver skyline. Picket was a cautious man, a lazy man. He would stay inside the warm confines of his little security shack and let The Repairman do his job.

The load of steel had been prepped the previous evening in order to save time. The unloading plan required that the load should be rechecked, but The Repairman was confident that there would only be a cursory re-inspection. The company had a habit of taking shortcuts. It's a waste of money to do over what you've already done.

He checked the fasteners on the bundle of steel girders. As he expected, the fasteners were properly closed; they had the appropriate safety inspection tags on them. He checked the safety tags to verify that they also had been filled out correctly, then smiled. Perfect, he thought. The name on the tags was *L. Hightower*. The safety inspector had done a good job. When The Repairman was finished, it would be Hightower who took the blame for the accident.

The Repairman pulled out a wrench and began to loosen the fastener on the load restraints, concerned about how much noise he was forced to make. Fortunately, there were two crews working on Tubes A and B, twenty floors up. They wouldn't hear the noise he made, and the sounds of their tools would mask the brief screeches that came from the resistant bolts. When he was finished loosening the bolts and repositioning the wires, he looked at his work and smiled. To anyone but a trained observer, the restraint chains looked well secured.

Good job, Repairman, he thought. *Tomorrow morning, one more problem would be solved.*

CHAPTER ONE

SUNDAY, MARCH 27, 0912 HOURS

MARCUS MACFARLAND--MARK to his family and Mac to his friends--and Rufus Headley sat on the bench in Civic Center Park, staring at the dome of the Capitol Building. A strong wind blew paper cups, leaves, and dust down Lincoln Street. The streets were dirty, the piles of snow left over from a now-forgotten storm two weeks ago had morphed into piles of grey and black cinders. A bus passed, its exhaust leaving a choking bitter odor in its wake. MacFarland shivered and pulled his coat more tightly around him. Rufus hardly seemed to notice the wind.

"Sure is shiny," said Rufus. His untrimmed beard looked surprisingly neat today. His hair, though, still looked like desiccated tufts of bleached straw. As he looked at the Capitol Building, his eyes flashed with intensity, and his craggy face was crenellated with laugh lines. He shaded his eyes to see the dome more clearly. "Nice golden sheen to it."

"Affirmative," said MacFarland. "It shines that way because it is made out of gold."

"Real gold?" asked Rufus.

"As real as it gets," said MacFarland. MacFarland was a rock. Only about five feet nine inches tall, still he had the kind of hard, compact body that could burst through walls. His hair was closely cropped. His face was cleanly shaven. And, as much as he didn't like it, he had brown puppy dog eyes. Or so claimed some of the women in his life.

"Maybe we could just sort of walk around the building, see if any pieces have blown off in the wind."

"I suppose we could," said MacFarland. "I doubt very much that any of it actually blows off, though. Besides, it's so thin that it would take a large amount to be worth anything."

Rufus grunted in response, probably wondering just how thin the gold plating was.

"You know what day it is?" MacFarland asked.

Rufus furrowed his brow in deep thought. "Sunday?"

"Well, yes, it is Sunday. But more important, it's Day 650."

Rufus smiled excitedly. "That's great, boss! Six hundred fifty days sober! I always knew you could do it!"

Rufus had first met Mark MacFarland outside of a bar on Colfax. MacFarland was drunk, had been drunk for a long time, and was being accosted by a gang of young thugs. Rufus had rescued him and helped get MacFarland through years of living on the street. MacFarland finally sobered up, started attending AA sessions, got himself a sponsor (a cynical Hispanic man named Hector Spinoza), and finally was able to establish himself as a respectable vendor of America's second most favorite meal, hot dogs. At least, he had been a hot dog vendor until the middle of February, when his cart was destroyed by a man he was chasing in a high speed pursuit. The motorist was trying to get away from him and decided that hitting MacFarland's cart was the best way to end the chase. Since then, MacFarland had been without a means of selling his hot dogs. The man who destroyed his cart didn't get away ultimately, but did manage to shoot MacFarland three times, leaving him with one wound in his leg, a graze on his side, and a wound in his shoulder. Thankfully, none of the bullets had hit any major nerve, blood, or bone systems. MacFarland could now walk around without his crutches (which he hadn't used because they hurt his shoulder too much), and he could almost move his arm without feeling throbbing stabs of pain.

It wasn't a deranged customer, livid over receiving a food item that would contribute to an early death, who had attacked him, but a Chicago hit man named William Wayne Ashland. Ashland had been hired by the co-owner of a jewelry store to kill his partner and frame the victim's wife. Jerry Baker, the attorney defending the widow accused of killing her husband, had asked MacFarland to see if he could find any exculpatory evidence that might help acquit his client. It wasn't out of the blue that the lawyer, Jerry Baker, had asked MacFarland to help him. Baker knew that MacFarland was more than a hot dog vendor. At one time, years earlier, MacFarland had been a fairly competent detective working in the Major Crimes unit of the Denver Police Department. He had served in that capacity for five years, and then his life fell apart. MacFarland's wife Nicole had an indiscrete relationship with her boss, Norris Peterson. When Nicole tried to end the affair, Peterson become enraged and killed her.

Though everyone knew that Norris Peterson was guilty, the chain of custody of the evidence was tainted. Peterson was able to use his wealth to buy off the Assistant District Attorney and possibly one or more members of the jury. Nothing was proved, but when the "Not guilty" verdict came in, MacFarland lost his composure and attacked Peterson, trying his damnedest to kill the man who murdered his wife. He didn't succeed, but instead got himself thrown into jail for two months. When he was released from jail, he took solace in Jack Daniels, until finally, his friend and boss, Bob Chamberlain, had to dismiss him from the police force. For the next two years, MacFarland was lost to the world he used to know, living on the streets, drinking anything he could get his hands on. He would have died on the streets, but for the help and support of Rufus Headley.

Rufus had lived on the streets almost from the day he got off a ship after several tours of duty in Vietnam. When Rufus stepped off that ship onto American soil, he was shocked to discover that Charlie--the shadowy and terrible enemy he had fought for six years--had come home with him. Every day was one skirmish after another to avoid discovery by Charlie. Because of Charlie's perpetual presence, Rufus refused to stay in any established domicile or shelter. "Charlie knows where those places are, boss. You gotta avoid them. Best thing is to keep moving around, but if you can't do that, find a place of concealment. Me, I sleep over by the river." MacFarland was never quite certain of exactly where along the Platte River Rufus lived--there weren't too many really good hiding places there. Since Rufus' home was located right in the middle of a city, MacFarland could not imagine that Rufus got all that much privacy. Yet the man had lived along the banks of the river for years, and not once had Charlie been able to discover his place of concealment.

"I get my new wagon tomorrow," said MacFarland.

"Oh," said Rufus in a somewhat disinterested tone. Rufus knew that the wagon was a hot dog vending cart to replace the one that had been demolished by Ashland during the car chase. Since Rufus had been watching MacFarland's cart at the time it was destroyed, he felt responsible for its destruction, despite MacFarland telling him many times that it was not his fault. Even though Rufus was homeless and seemingly unemployed, he took his responsibilities quite seriously. "You do the job you're assigned as best you can," he often said, "even if that job is shoveling shit." In point of fact, Rufus did have a job. Baker had hired him to be a courier for his law firm. MacFarland suspected that actually meant that Rufus served as eyes and ears on the street for the criminal defense attorney. MacFarland was not sure what Rufus did with the money Baker paid him, nor was he entirely sure that the arrangement was totally legal. Baker was known to bend a few rules in order to get his clients out of jail. Just bend, MacFarland reminded himself. He never knew Baker to break a law. But then, he had only known Baker for a couple of months.

"Is it the same kind of cart as you had before?" asked Rufus.

"No," said MacFarland. "This one is a lot fancier. It has two umbrellas on it."

"Oh," said Rufus, finally showing some interest. "Two umbrellas. That is pretty fancy."

CHAPTER TWO

MONDAY, MARCH 28, 1000 HOURS

THE NEXT MORNING, MacFarland got up early, anxious to go pick up his new hot dog cart. Getting up early didn't do him much good, since he couldn't get his cart until the shipping company office opened up at ten o'clock.

He looked forward to this new cart. His previous cart had been relatively small, a New York style hot dog cart. It had no source of heat or electricity, so he was limited by how much hot water he could carry with him. He often got around that by having a heating element in his truck that he could use to replace the water throughout the day, but that was a major inconvenience for him. His new cart was manufactured by Kareem Carts and was easily twice the size of his old cart. It really did have two umbrellas on it, which might not be so good on Denver's windy days, but would be a great relief during the hot summer days when Mac did most of his business. His new cart had a refrigerator, generator, steamer, hand wash sink, and trash compartment. It used a propane tank, which would give him instant heat. In addition, it had a generator that would allow him to operate his grilling rollers, his steamer, a coffee maker (no longer would Rufus have to stop by a local donut shop to pick up their ritual morning coffee!), and the refrigerator. It didn't have a grill on it, so he couldn't make hamburgers, but the cart was adaptable to that option if he later decided to go that route.

He found himself waiting impatiently for ten o'clock to arrive. He busied himself by re-checking his inventory of condiments, supplies and other non-perishables that he needed for his business. Cups, napkins, storage containers, wipes, cleaning supplies, even first aid supplies. One could never be too prepared for the random cut or burn that might occur.

And, of course, MacFarland replaced his battery-operated CD player with one that could be plugged in. He would be able to listen to his language lessons without the worry of dead batteries. It took him a while to find his language CDs. The Denver Public Library had not been too pleased with him when he returned the previous set of disks scratched and damaged. The language CDs had been among the casualties of Ashford's hit and run encounter. Although he had offered to replace the damaged disks, the library said they would handle the replacement themselves.

He wouldn't need his trailer any longer, since the new hot dog cart would connect directly to his truck's hitch. That would make it more convenient for him, but it would also mean that he would have to park close by. He wouldn't be able to use the cheap lot down the street that he had been using up to now. It turned out that was a good thing also, since that half of the block had been demolished to build a new skyscraper. It would be about sixty stories tall, and for this part of town, that was a really big building. Most of the construction in Denver had been north of the Civic Center area, up towards and north of what many people called the Arapahoe Triangle. This area, where the building was going up, the Golden Triangle, had been free of a lot of construction, but that was soon to change. Hopefully, it would eventually mean more business for him, unless the city authorities got persnickety and restricted the presence of independent vendors. With every positive change in the universe, it seemed, there were corresponding negative changes. MacFarland just hoped the positive changes outweighed the negative.

At nine-thirty, he went outside and unhooked his trailer. He would have to sell it, he supposed. He couldn't keep cluttering up Pierson's yard with it. Lord knows, he took advantage enough of her generosity. When he was evicted from his apartment, she had offered him a room in her University Park house. Of course, she had plenty of room. It was a huge Edwardian house, though Pierson insisted it was not Edwardian. She claimed it was farmhouse style. He supposed she was right. She was better educated than he was. Hell, almost everyone was better educated than him. He had graduated from high school, then joined the Marines. From there he had gone into law enforcement. He wished he had gone to college, since having a degree did seem to help your advancement in the department. That really hadn't been a problem for him. He made detective after about four years as a beat cop. Somehow, being a detective came easily to him. And, up until the day he got shot, he had always thought being a detective was safer than being on the streets. Now he wasn't so sure.

His stay with Pierson was intended to be a short term solution to his housing problem, but each time he mentioned that he should go look for an apartment, Pierson insisted that he should wait a while. Though she complained constantly about his living habits--he thought he was neat, but apparently there were various standards of neatness in the universe, and his was near the low end of the spectrum--she didn't want him to move out. Since he paid very little in rent for his one room, he had little economic incentive to move out.

But he was pretty sure she would eventually complain about his hot dog stand, his truck, and the trailer all taking up space in her backyard. He would definitely have to sell the trailer. He wondered how much he could get for it.

His new hot dog trailer had been shipped from Los Angeles to Denver by truck. He located the trucking company and drove over to the large warehouse on the far side of the lot. A corner of the warehouse had windows and a door marked appropriately enough "Office."

A receptionist who looked too young to be working greeted him, verified who he was, and handed him a yellow sheet of paper. "Go through that door and someone will help you hook up your cart, sir."

He did as instructed, and after standing around for a few minutes in the cavernous warehouse, someone finally spotted him and hurried over. Muttering only "Follow me," the man took the yellow sheet and raced off towards the other side of the warehouse. MacFarland kept pace with him.

Then he saw it.

The hot dog stand looked larger in real life than it did in the pictures. MacFarland wondered if it would even fit on the corner he usually occupied. It would have to. "Should I drive my truck up to the door?" he asked.

"Yep," said the young man. "Inspect it first, and note down any damage or defects you see on the back of the yellow sheet." He handed the paper back to MacFarland, then went to open the warehouse door. MacFarland examined briefly the back of the yellow sheet, and not finding any defects, decided he ought to examine the cart. He laughed silently at his own joke. He couldn't find any defects on the cart either, certainly nothing worth the time and effort to write down. As far as he was concerned, the cart was in pristine condition. He couldn't wait until he got it back to Pierson's house so he could take off the stickers, put his own name and logo on the cart, and stock it up for tomorrow's use.

Despite the stiffness in his shoulder and the throb in his leg, life was pretty good for Marcus MacFarland, Hot Dog Vendor extraordinaire!

CHAPTER THREE

TUESDAY, MARCH 29, 0730 HOURS

MACFARLAND WAS up early on Tuesday. He had spent the previous afternoon washing, polishing, painting, and cleaning his new wagon. He thought he could have done a better job painting his logo on the wagon--*MAC'S BRATS AND DOGS*--but it was good enough. Only someone as critical as he would notice the one or two splotchy areas or the place where the paint had run and left a faint, pink drip tail. From a distance, it looked really good.

Okay, before the summer season started, he would get a professional painter to redo the sign.

He had his product cooked, loaded, and ready for transport by the time Pierson came down for her first cup of coffee.

"Damn, it will be good to get you out of the house," she muttered reaching for the coffee pot. "How's your leg?"

"The leg is doing much better. It's the shoulder that still hurts."

"Next time, don't get shot," she said with little display of sympathy. Pierson was a firm believer that civilians should stay out of police work. If MacFarland wanted to come back onto the force, she would support him wholeheartedly, but as long as he was just a hot dog vendor, she preferred that he leave all the real police work to the professionals. She did have to admit, though, that he was a damn good detective. Too bad he gave that up. "I do think your corner is still available. Someone tried to move in a week or so ago, but Jacinto chased them away."

"He's a good guy," commented MacFarland. Jacinto Gomez was another vendor who worked down the street from where MacFarland positioned his cart, although he sold tacos and other Mexican foods. Gomez was married, and from the way he described it, had a huge brood of kids to feed. Actually, he and Francesca only had four children, but that was a lot more responsibility than MacFarland had to shoulder. Gomez approached his business much more aggressively than MacFarland did, who often gave away his product to the homeless people he once knew. Even though they were competitors, they watched each other's back. MacFarland was pleased to hear that Gomez was still looking out for him.

Pierson finished her coffee and went upstairs to get dressed. "Maybe if I have a bad day, I'll drop by and see how you're doing."

A bad day for Pierson meant that no one was killing anyone else. What most normal people would actually call a good day. But Pierson wasn't normal. She was a cop. "All quiet in Denver these days?"

"Yeah. A few robberies, the usual assaults and DVs, but nothing that involves Major Crimes. You seem to have wrapped all of our recent murders up into one pretty package." When MacFarland had helped capture Wayne

William Ashland, he had been able to tie the man to four murders. It had been a good day in Denver.

"Are you complaining?" asked MacFarland. "Besides, I've found that domestic violence often leads to murder."

Pierson sighed heavily. "I just wish you would come back onto the force, Mac. Your talents are wasted doing what you're doing."

"I don't know about that, Cyn. Chamberlain tried to get me to come back, but I've been out too long. I don't think I could hack it anymore. I couldn't keep up with the competition."

She stared at him in surprise, not entirely sure what he was talking about. Physically, he was hurting now. Anyone would be after getting shot three times. But MacFarland was in as good shape as any detective on the squad. A little shorter than most of the men on the force--MacFarland stood only five foot nine inches tall, but his 185 pounds was solid muscle. Give him a few more weeks of rehab and exercise and he would be back in prime shape. Of course that rehab would be easier to get if he were back on the force.

Then it occurred to her that he wasn't talking about his physical shape.

"Are you referring to Benny?" she asked in a shocked tone. Benny Lockwood was her new partner and so far had miraculously lasted longer than any other partner she'd had since MacFarland. She suspected that Lockwood was infatuated with her, though she could not understand why. Cynthia Pierson had no regard for her looks. She had reddish-brown hair that she often tied up in a ponytail, freckles, and a hesitant smile. Though she never considered it a personal flaw, she was so much smarter than most of her peers that she often had to mask her intelligence. She had liked working with

MacFarland because he was the one partner who never tried to prove that he was her superior. They worked together very well. "Benny's just a kid," she said, then hurried upstairs.

MacFarland drove downtown, positioned his cart on the street corner, then parked his truck in one in one of the nearby lots. Finding a space was difficult, since most of the construction workers also parked there. Why did every one of them have a truck as big as his? MacFarland realized he would have to start getting here earlier if he wanted to get a decent parking space.

His first customer, promptly at eight o'clock, was Rufus, carrying his two cups of steaming coffee. "Morning boss," said the homeless man cheerfully. "It's a great day today!"

As MacFarland took the cup of coffee from his friend, he realized that he would have to tell him that his coffee service was no longer necessary. He wondered how he was going to do that. Rufus needed to feel that he had some purpose in life. He still needed to bring the first morning cup of joe. MacFarland smiled, thanked Rufus for the coffee, and took his first sip. "What do you think of my new cart?"

Rufus made a big show of walking all around it, rubbing his chin appraisingly, nodding and squinting. "Yep, boss, this is one fine piece of equipment. You're gonna tear up the hood with this baby."

MacFarland turned on his warming pans, heating rollers, steamers, and other paraphernalia. He began to explain all the attachments to Rufus who feigned interest for the first few minutes, but quickly became bored with all the details. "What's important, boss, is, does it make hot dogs?"

MacFarland smiled. "Yes, Rufus, it makes hot dogs."

Rufus left for his round of "meetings" a few minutes

later. MacFarland had never learned who participated in these meetings, nor what the meetings were about, but Rufus' presence at them was essential. MacFarland got the impression that the future of all human society would be at risk if Rufus didn't attend these meetings, so he made sure that nothing impeded Rufus' participation.

He plugged in his CD player, put on his earphones, and began to listen to his language lessons. He had fallen behind during the month of March, which had proven to be one of the most depressing months he could recall. Of course, he couldn't recall his most depressing months, when he was drunk day after day, week after week. Since he had sobered up, however, his life had entered a predictable and stable routine. The three bullet wounds he had received had disrupted that routine more than he expected. Pierson had been right. He needed to get out of the house.

He concluded that Tuesday was not the best day to restart his business. Monday would have been better, because that was the day the courts did jury selection. By Tuesday, they had selected their juries, so the number of people passing his corner was greatly reduced. Even so, he did a fair amount of business. What most pleased him, however, was when some of his homeless friends showed up. He was particularly pleased to see Kirk and Gracie.

Of all the homeless people he had ever met, Gracie was by far the most cheerful and optimistic person he had ever known. It did not seem to affect her that she and Kirk had no home, no possessions, and no hope. He was sure there were many days when the two of them had gone hungry, had shivered in the snow, or huddled under an awning to avoid one of Denver's cold drizzles. Despite all of that, Gracie kept her spirits up. Gracie seemed particularly pleased to see Mac.

"We heard you were shot, Mac! Is that true?"

MacFarland nodded. "Three times." He pointed out where his wounds had occurred. "Here in the shoulder, here in the side--that was more just a grazing shot--and here in the leg."

"Wow, you're a hero!"

MacFarland laughed. "I am not sure how much of a hero I was. I didn't exactly catch the bad guy--just chased him outside to where the police were."

"Well, everybody here thinks you were a hero," insisted Gracie. MacFarland knew that "here" was not a place, but the homeless community, part of the "invisible people" that society preferred not to see. Gracie's remark meant a lot to him.

MacFarland gave the couple some hot dogs and cups of coffee to warm them up. Kirk, true to his nature, said nothing, but nodded his thanks. As they meandered off, sipping and eating, MacFarland found himself conflicted. On the one hand, he was glad to see the couple. On the other hand, he wished that their fortune would improve enough that he never had to see them again.

MacFarland had just gotten back into his practice dialog--a rather complicated discussion about going to a cinema to watch a horror movie--when he became aware of someone he knew walking towards his corner. He looked up and smiled uncertainly.

"Hi, Stefanie," he said as his sister-in-law approached his wagon.

CHAPTER FOUR

TUESDAY, MARCH 29, 1030 HOURS

"SO THIS IS WHERE YOU WORK?" asked Stefanie. Stefanie Forester Cooper. The younger sister of the woman he had been married to.

Stefanie had the perfect looks of a top fashion model. Perfectly coifed hair, delicately arching eyebrows, full, pouty lips, she could easily pass as one of those models in a television cosmetics commercial. She was clearly the ultimate trophy wife. Unfortunately, the man who possessed this trophy was Randy Cooper, a CPA who was living proof of the truism, if you want your kid to be a CPA, drop him on his head at birth. The Coopers had two children, Kaitlyn and Ryan, both of whom MacFarland adored, and who were the main reason why he put up with Randy Cooper. Well, there was also Stefanie, who was very easy to put up with, but MacFarland tried not to think about that.

"Usually," said MacFarland. "I try to work this corner as much as I can. What are you doing down here? Jury duty?"

"No, not jury duty! Heaven forbid! No, I am here to testify for a friend in a car theft. My friend, she lives in

Denver." Stefanie paused a moment, then continued in an accusing voice. "Were you hurt or something? One of Randy's co-workers said he saw you on the news."

MacFarland nodded, trying to avoid looking at her. He hadn't contacted his sister-in-law to let her know what happened to him, and he felt just a tad guilty about keeping that information from her. Not that she would have done anything. Well, maybe she would have. She would have insisted on him staying with her. He didn't think he could tolerate a month of being around Randy, though the prospects of being around Stefanie might tilt things a different way. He blinked in disbelief. He had to stop thinking like that. She was married, for crying out loud, even if her husband was a total asshole.

"I don't think I was on the news, but they might have mentioned me. I got shot trying to apprehend a suspect," he finally said.

"What were you doing trying to catch a suspect?" she demanded. "You're not a cop anymore."

"I was trying to help a friend. And other things. The suspect came to the house where I went to kill a fucking scumbag. Guess the guy who shot me wanted to kill the scumbag too. Like an idiot, I stopped him, and I got shot for my good deed."

Stefanie stood there, her face showing her incredulity. MacFarland couldn't help but notice that even when she looked upset, she was still incredibly pretty. He reminded himself that she was Nicole's sister, and even though Nicole was dead, her spirit probably would not appreciate him lusting after her sister. "Why didn't you tell us?" she asked. She seemed to be ignoring the part where he admitted he went to kill someone. Just as well. It wasn't a good idea to go around admitting things like that.

"I didn't want to get you upset or worried," he responded. "Besides, I had a place to stay. Cynthia took very good care of me."

"Cynthia? Your former partner? Are you living with her now?" Stefanie's tone was very judgmental. "Well, that didn't take very long, did it?"

He was surprised by her comment. Was Stefanie jealous of Pierson? There was nothing going on between him and his former partner. Sure, she was an attractive lady, but for God's sake, she was his partner! "Nicole died almost six years ago." His voice quivered as he tried to suppress the emotions he felt.

Stefanie's jaw clamped shut. "Yes, you are right. It's none of my business. It's probably best for you to get on with your life."

"We're not living in sin," said MacFarland, feeling foolish for even trying to justify his life. Somehow, though, Stefanie's approbation seemed important to him. Yet, what was wrong with him living with Pierson? She was the one person who truly accepted him and tolerated his odd hours and activities. He didn't think Nicole would object to his relationship with Pierson.

Or did Stefanie prefer him living on the street, as he used to? He would never go back to that kind of life. Or was she implying that she wanted him to stay with her? If she was, why didn't she just come out and say so? MacFarland decided that he preferred his women murderous. At least he knew how to deal with them then.

Stefanie's demeanor mellowed. "I don't think anything like that, Mark. I don't care who you live with. Randy and I just want to be part of your life."

MacFarland was not sure Randy would really agree with that, and MacFarland certainly didn't want to be part of Randy's life. MacFarland thought Randy Cooper was a total asshole, but he had to admit that most of his dislike of Cooper was based on the man's undisguised contempt for him and other cops. MacFarland could never understand the basis for that prejudice. If Cooper had once had a negative interaction with the police in his past, he never discussed it with MacFarland, nor as far as he knew, with Nicole. He supposed he could ask Stefanie what problems Randy might have had with the police, but he was convinced that whatever problems the man had, Cooper was undoubtedly the one at fault. Police didn't cause people to be assholes; they just responded to the problems assholes created.

After Stefanie Cooper left, MacFarland was able to relax. There was no reason for him to feel guilty over not contacting her. After all, had she tried to contact him? Actually, he didn't know. He hadn't checked his phone messages over the past month. He wasn't sure why it mattered to him.

He spent the rest of the afternoon listening to his language CDs and serving the few customers who wanted a late lunch. He didn't see any of his usual group of homeless people. Instead, several people he had not seen before in this neighborhood made their presence known. He knew some of these individuals, from his days on the streets. He already had had run-ins with at least one of them--a man called Rolf. MacFarland had never learned the man's last name. Rolf had a reputation for rolling other homeless people. Even though most of his victims had almost nothing, even nothing was enough to incite larceny in Rolf's heart.

"So this is where you ended up," said Rolf pleasantly as he walked up to the hot dog stand. The man had the smell of creosote on him that MacFarland found mildly distasteful.

"You're a long way from home, Rolf," said MacFarland. 'Home' for Rolf was over by the railroad yards north and east of Coors Field.

"The cops are making noise on that side of town. So I opted for new vistas. How about a hot dog?"

MacFarland stared at the man, wondering what response he should make. He didn't like Rolf, never had. The man was a bully, a thief, and a predator. Rolf was the kind of man that if MacFarland still wore a badge, he would have gone out of his way to find a reason to arrest the man. Unfortunately, Rolf stayed just out of sight of the law. He preyed on those who had no power and would never have the courage to go to the cops for help.

On the other hand, Rolf was one of the invisible people MacFarland wanted to protect. MacFarland was under no delusions that any kindnesses shown to a man like Rolf would be passed on, but MacFarland wasn't the kind of man who could simply turn his back on people who had been condemned to the hell that Rolf occupied.

He pulled out a hot dog, a bun, and put them into a paper wrapper, and handed it to Rolf. "I have a lot of cop friends over here, Rolf. I think it would be better for you to take your chances back on your own turf. Get my drift, man?"

Rolf took the hot dog and glared at MacFarland. "I get your drift, Mac. Not sure you're man enough to tell me where I can stay or not, but I don't want any trouble. So to preserve the peace, I will go back to the park. Or do you own that too?"

"I don't own anything, Rolf. None of us do. Nice seeing you, man. Just don't make a habit of it."

"Yeah, fuck you too," said Rolf, walking away.

MacFarland unclenched his fists and put his headphones and CD away. Then he shut down all his warmers, burners, and electrical appliances, packed away his product, and secured his wagon for transport. Even though it was only three-thirty in the afternoon, the joy of selling hot dogs had mysteriously evaporated.

CHAPTER FIVE

FRIDAY, APRIL 1, 1220 HOURS

OTHER THAN A COUPLE of his homeless friends, there were few customers on Friday morning. Nor was the lunch crowd very large that day. So when he saw Wanda Warren, wearing an orange safety vest, heading his direction from the construction site, he was thankful that he was finally starting to get some of the work crew as customers. Up to this point, most of the construction workers had gone to Gomez's taco wagon on the other corner or to a new competitor who had set up shop across the street. Although MacFarland charged the same prices as his new competitor, even he had to admit that the owner's pretty daughter was more of a draw to the construction crews than MacFarland was. Fortunately, she only worked weekends.

So MacFarland's initial reaction to having Warren standing next to his cart was a pleasurable feeling. That soon dissipated, however, as soon as she finished placing her order. "They tell me that you are a detective," she said.

MacFarland looked at her more critically. Wanda Warren had an oval face, prominent cheekbones, narrow, deep-set eyes, a long jaw that thrust out more than was attractive on a woman. Her dark brown hair was pulled back, mostly hidden by her hard hat. She looked to be in her mid-thirties, was about five feet seven inches tall, and probably weighed about one hundred forty-five to one hundred fifty pounds. Though it was difficult to tell under her coveralls and jacket, she might have a very girlish figure. What she did have, however, was an enormous pair of boobs.

MacFarland tried not to stare at her boobs.

"Used to be," he replied. "Not anymore. Now I just sell hot dogs. If you need a detective, the police station is just across the street from your work site."

"I already talked to the police," she said as she took the hot dog from him. She walked over to the condiments section and started putting ketchup and mustard on her dog. "They're no help at all. I need someone who really knows how to solve crimes."

"What crime are you talking about?" he asked. *Maybe she's younger than thirty-five,* he thought.

"A guy at my site, my friend Mike Brady, got killed. On February 20."

"How did he die?"

Warren paused a moment. "He got crushed by falling girders. He was the guide guy when they were unloading steel girders from off a truck. He was supposed to make sure that the load didn't rotate as the crane operator lifts it up. But a cable came loose and the load fell and he was crushed. They say that the cable was not attached properly, even though it had passed inspection."

"That sounds like it was an accident," said MacFarland.

"Yeah, that's what the SRB and OSHA said." Warren shook her head. "But it wasn't any accident. He was murdered. I know he was murdered. Damn, I should have been working the crane. It wouldn't have happened then. I wouldn't let it happen."

"SRB?" asked MacFarland. He knew that OSHA was Occupational Safety and Health Administration.

"Safety Review Board. Forrester Equipment and Construction has one that investigates every accident. They work with OSHA and other agencies. They said it was a mistake by the Safety Manager, that he passed an inspection that he shouldn't have. They say he was drunk, and that's why Mike got killed."

"But you think he was murdered?" repeated MacFarland hesitantly. He was already becoming annoyed with himself for getting hooked into this conversation. Any time anyone dies, people always assume it was more sinister than it really was. Yet construction work was very dangerous. It was far more likely that Mike--what was it? Brady--had died in a tragic accident.

"Yeah, I think they wanted to shut him up," said Warren. "Because of what he knew."

MacFarland began to wonder if some of his former friends in the police department had set up Wanda Warren to play an April fool's joke on him. It was hard getting information from her. "Okay, I'll bite. What did Mike Brady know that got him killed?"

"He found out that someone in Forrester was ripping off the customer. The company has been charging for a lot more materials and labor than there actually is. It's fraud."

"Is Brady an accountant?" asked MacFarland.

"No, he was just a helper, but he was a bright kid. He was going to go into management someday, but he wanted to learn all the jobs. Had a lot of get-up and go, if you know what I mean. I told him, when he tells me about this, that he needs to be careful. If Mike says that Forrester is ripping someone off, I can believe it. It's not like Forrester is the most honest company in the world. They have mob connections you know."

MacFarland didn't know, and he seriously doubted that Forrester Equipment and Construction had any connections with the mob. There had been a reputed mob connection in Denver, back in the 1980's--the Smaldone family, who had been active for almost fifty years. But that was more than thirty years ago, and since then, the descendants of the Smaldones had been quiet, law-abiding people. Any mob activity in Denver had been taken over by organized gangs, some of which rivaled the historical mobs in organization, power, and influence. The gangs of the past thirty years, however, often exceeded the mob in terms of violence and viciousness. An industrial accident was hardly their method of dealing with a problem. MacFarland could not see any of these gangs getting involved with a major construction company's operations. Gang crimes focused more on crack cocaine, illegal gun trafficking, auto theft, home invasions, and robberies.

Once more, he suspected that the woman had been set up to play a trick on him.

"Who did you talk to in the police department?" he asked.

"I don't remember his name," Warren said. "Hell, it was a couple of months ago. But nobody's doing anything about it. I don't want Mike to die for nothing. Someone needs to find out the truth."

"As I said, Miss Warren--"

"You can call me Wanda," she interrupted.

MacFarland nodded. "As I said, Wanda, I am not with the police department, and I'm not a detective or anything like that. I sell hot dogs. That's it."

She stared at him, her expression blank and downcast. "So you're not going to help me?"

MacFarland shrugged helplessly. "It really does sound like an accidental death," he said. "I'm sorry for your loss, but there's not much I can do." He handed her his card. "But tell you what. If you get anything more definitive, give me a call anyway."

Warren nodded grimly, taking the card and slipping it into her pocket. "Yeah, so that's the way it is. Guess we'll just have to wait until I also get killed in an accident." Her voice was bitter, her sarcasm real. If this was an April fool's prank, she was doing a very good job of acting. She pulled something out of her jacket and handed it to MacFarland. "That's the copy of the review board's findings. I don't think it's accurate. They're stealing money, and they killed Mike to cover it up," said Warren one last time. "His murderer shouldn't get away with this."

As MacFarland watched Wanda walk slowly back towards the construction site, he shook his head in disbelief. He would have to find out who was responsible for this tasteless joke and get revenge on him.

CHAPTER SIX

SATURDAY, APRIL 2, 0810 HOURS

"SURE, I KNOW WHO WANDA IS," said Rufus Headley. "Except, no one ever calls her that."

MacFarland took a long sip of the coffee Rufus had brought. It was clearly better tasting than the stuff he brewed. Maybe he would have to get a better brand of coffee to serve. "What do they call her?"

"Busty," said Rufus. "On account of her big bazooms. Busty the Ballbreaker. Yep, that's what everyone calls her."

"Surely they don't call her that to her face," said MacFarland. "Seems like a pretty mean name to call someone."

Rufus was silent a moment as he considered that. "I guess it's not what you call politically correct, boss, but it is what it is. I don't ever remember anyone calling her Wanda. That's a pretty weird name too, when you think about it. Besides, her name is pretty descriptive of her. You gotta admit, she has pretty big knockers. Such a waste. She plays for the other team, you know."

MacFarland blinked. He didn't know. Rufus had once

told him that his "gaydar" was really deficient. MacFarland didn't pay much attention to a person's sexual orientation, whether male or female. Besides, his interaction with Wanda Warren—er, Busty--had been entirely professional. If anything, he had thought that her interest in Mike Brady was in part because she had some affection for him.

"Is she called Ballbreaker because of her being a lesbian?" he asked.

Rufus shook his head. "Naw, it's because of what she does. She has that wrecking ball that knocks buildings down. I usta watch her after I bring you coffee, when they was tearin' down all these buildings. She's pretty good with that ball thingie. She made short work of them buildings. A bunch of us would get together and watch her do it. We even made up some cheers, you know what I mean?"

MacFarland finally had some insight to the mysterious "meetings" that Rufus frequently had to attend.

"I thought she was pulling my leg when she came by yesterday," said MacFarland. "Put up to an April Fool's joke by some of the boys over at the station. She claimed that a friend of hers was killed because he knew something about the construction company."

Rufus tugged on his scraggly beard. "Yeah, there was a dude who got killed. Truckload of steel fell on top of him. Crushed him like a tomato. Don't know how you bury a guy who's been killed like that."

"So you know about Mike Brady?" asked MacFarland in surprise. It was not like Rufus to be up on current events.

Rufus nodded. "Happened about the same time as Gibbs got himself killed. You was kinda busy then, boss." Rufus looked around cautiously, probably checking to see if Charlie was sneaking up on him. "Didn't know the dude's name though. Didn't he usta play football?"

"Different Brady," said MacFarland. Aaron Gibbs was a young homeless man who was one of those killed by Wayne Ashland. MacFarland felt partially responsible for Gibbs' death, since he had asked some of the homeless men to watch the offices of Norris Peterson, whom MacFarland suspected of murdering Otto Freeman. Gibbs had seen Ashland coming out of the building where Peterson worked and had followed him. When Ashland discovered that he had a tail, he turned the tables, tracked down Gibbs, and killed him. Young Gibbs would still be alive today if MacFarland hadn't gotten him involved. MacFarland had been so focused on trying to solve Freeman's murder that he hadn't paid much attention to other events going on around him.

Rufus wasn't able to provide much more information than the fact that someone had been killed, though he did offer to shout out some of the cheers he and his friends had made up for Wanda's wreaking activities. MacFarland wasn't sure that he wanted to hear the cheers.

The Safety Review Board report that Wanda had given him confirmed that Brady had been killed by falling girders. The report stated that the truck arrived the evening before, on Friday, February 19, at 9:20 PM. Riley Vogel, Site Superintendent, had given instructions to prep the truck for unloading, but decided that it would not be safe to unload it that night. Hightower had done a safety inspection of the seclusion area, the truck stability, and the lifting cables attached to the load. The report went on to say that the next morning, when Hightower reported to work, Vogel detected alcohol on his breath and insisted on a Breathalyzer test. Hightower failed the test and was sent home. The work crew on site proceeded with the off-loading, but one of the lifting cables came loose and the load shifted, falling onto

Mike Brady, who was killed instantly. Subsequent examination of the cables showed no breaks, cuts, or other obvious tampering. The conclusion of the SRB was that the inspection the prior night had been inadequately performed and that Hightower was negligent. However, the SRB did not conclude that Hightower was willfully negligent, so the entire incident was classified as an accident.

Rufus had one last observation to make about Wanda. "Don't think Busty woulda let anyone make her play a joke on someone else, boss. Who would have the balls to play games with Busty Ballbreaker?"

CHAPTER SEVEN

SUNDAY, APRIL 3, 1315 HOURS

THERE WERE some weeks when MacFarland brought his hot dog stand downtown every day. Having spent a couple of years on the streets, where one day was exactly like the previous, he had gotten used to not having "time off." Once he got sober and had become a hot dog vendor, he had adopted the same philosophy about time--that it was an artificial construct designed to control people. His clocks were more practical. He got up early enough to make his product for the day, he got to his location early enough to beat the morning rush of workers scurrying to their clock-controlled jobs, he stayed until he was out of product or until he was bored with his corner, and he went back to his—Pierson's--home when he felt like it. He rarely watched television, though he was now watching more of it than he ever had, since Pierson had a huge wall screen viewer that he initially had found quite intimidating. After a while, he couldn't imagine not seeing everything nearly life-size. Not once did he miss his old tube variety television.

On this Sunday, however, he decided to stay home. He

had promised Stefanie that he would visit her and Randy, and since it was still cold outside, he decided to forego the rare tourist who braved Denver's unpredictable spring weather. He regretted that he wouldn't be there to provide at least some food for his homeless friends, but he couldn't be everywhere.

Damn, that sounded just like what he used to tell Nicole, when he came home late from work or missed an anniversary or was unable to keep a date. "I can't be everywhere, Nicole. It's the job." Was it the job now? No, he didn't really have a job. Except selling hot dogs. Okay, yeah, sure, that was a job. And it demanded a lot of his time. And according to the brochure he had read so long ago, it had the potential of making him $60,000 a year. Of course, the brochure writer had not counted on someone giving a large portion of his product to the homeless. Or on him foolishly thinking that he could solve crimes in his spare time.

He wasn't looking forward to his visit to Stefanie's house. Stefanie herself wasn't so bad. She was pretty, nice to look at, as long as he didn't look at her too lustfully. Her kids were nice, particularly Ryan, who loved to play dinosaurs or cars with him. Kaitlyn had just turned twelve, that awkward age where she still wanted the freedom of being a child yet craving the respect due an adult. He always treated her like a proper lady, and she reciprocated. She treated him with a lot of respect.

Certainly more respect than he got from her father. Randy categorized MacFarland as a loser, though MacFarland did not know why. Sure, MacFarland hadn't gone to college, but so what? MacFarland had been a Marine, which put him in a class considerably above Randy Cooper, who had never spent a day in service to his country. Like most civilians, Randy paid lip service to those in uniform.

MacFarland, however, could see right through Randy's hypocrisy. Randy was one of those who would cheer on the troops, especially when there was a war going on, yet be among the first to demand tax cuts that would jeopardize paying vets their benefits.

Randy also had a condescending attitude towards the police, what MacFarland considered the arrogant liberal bias. Randy apparently believed the police only hired the dumbest of the dumb, thugs in uniform, men and women who had been given license to dispense abuse. MacFarland had tried to explain what a typical policeman's day was like, but Randy was not interested in hearing about the hundreds of things that police did every day to make society a safer, better environment for everyone. Instead, he would recite the rare events when circumstances got out of control, and police did something that outraged the public. MacFarland acknowledged that such things happened, but they were a lot rarer than the news media would have the public believe. It just wasn't newsworthy reporting on a welfare check that found an elderly woman near death because she had fallen and couldn't get help, or a cop helping a person with a bipolar condition calm down and take the medication he needed. After the first year or so of getting frustrated and angry with Randy, MacFarland had just stopped talking about what he did as a cop. Randy was just an annoying rock in the road that he had to drive around. Someday, though, someone would have to move that rock off of the road.

"It's so good to see you, Mark," said Stefanie. "Come on in. Kids! Uncle Mark is here! Come say hello!"

Ryan ran up and hugged his leg, holding on and laughing as MacFarland stiff-legged into the house. Kaitlyn came in a much more demure manner, smiled a greeting, and then retreated back to whatever she had been doing before being interrupted. "Randy's in the TV room," said Stefanie, taking MacFarland's coat and hanging it up in a hall closet.

MacFarland nodded, thinking that it would be more newsworthy if Randy were not in the television room. He pecked Stefanie on the cheek and headed towards the room where Randy was watching a basketball game. *Great, basketball,* thought MacFarland. Randy was six feet four inches tall, while MacFarland was only five feet nine inches tall. This was another source of Randy's apparent contempt for MacFarland--the irrational bias that taller men are naturally superior to shorter men. Not surprisingly, Randy preferred watching basketball, while MacFarland, to the extent that he enjoyed watching sports, preferred football. Maybe the game would be interesting enough to keep Randy quiet, at least until dinner was served.

Randy looked up as MacFarland entered, waved a greeting, and went back to watching the game--Sacramento was apparently beating New York. "Are the Nuggets playing today?" asked MacFarland, using up his entire repertoire of sports intelligence with totally inappropriate timing.

"Later this afternoon. There's beer in the fridge. Help yourself."

Randy Cooper was an intense man, one who only found amusement in situations where his superiority over others was made evident. MacFarland always pictured Randy as a boy, holding a magnifying glass up to direct sunlight at an insect, waiting for the poor creature to catch fire.

MacFarland nodded, went over to the mini-fridge in the back of the room, and checked the contents. He found a

Diet Coke and helped himself to that. Leave it to Randy to tell a recovering alcoholic to go get a beer. *What an asshole,* thought MacFarland.

"Oh, I forgot," said Randy, realizing his mistake when he saw the Diet Coke in MacFarland's hand. "Sorry about that. Didn't mean to put temptation in front of you."

MacFarland ignored his comment and sat down, pretending to get interested in the game. Soon he found himself rooting for the Knicks, mainly because Randy was quite vocal about Sacramento's accomplishments. MacFarland had noticed that Randy wouldn't watch a game in which the team he cheered on was losing. As far as MacFarland could see, winning and losing was all part of the game. While Randy liked to cheer for the winning team, MacFarland found himself rooting for the underdog. Randy liked decisive wins. MacFarland preferred cliffhangers, decided at the last moment of the game. Of course, that also meant you only had to watch the last moments of a game to see the outcome.

A short while later, after Sacramento had built up a considerable lead over New York, Stefanie came in and announced that lunch was ready. Lunch for MacFarland was usually a simple affair, but for the Coopers, Sunday lunch was a formal dinner. The kids traipsed in from their rooms, MacFarland and Randy emerged from the man cave, and Stefanie directed everyone to their assigned chairs. It was the same as every other meal MacFarland had had at their residence: Randy at one end of the table, Stefanie at the other, the kids on one side, MacFarland on the opposite side. MacFarland supposed the kids might make a mistake one day and decide to sit on the side of the table with just one chair, so instructions were probably useful.

Conversation was light for the first few moments, then

Stefanie asked MacFarland if his shoulder was causing him pain.

He had not been conscious of the shoulder pain until she asked, then he nodded. "Affirmative, it still hurts once in a while."

"What happened to your shoulder?" asked Kaitlyn, trying to sound as adult as she could.

"He was shot, honey," said Stefanie.

Randy looked up. "You were shot? When?"

"That's what he was on the news for, Randy. You remember, you mentioned that someone at work had seen him on TV."

"You were on TV?" asked Ryan incredulously.

MacFarland shook his head. "No, I wasn't on TV, Ryan. I might have been mentioned. When we caught that man who killed Otto Freeman."

"You were really shot?" asked Randy, apparently not believing what his own wife just said.

MacFarland blushed and nodded. "Three times. Shoulder, leg, and side."

"Wow, that's great!" shouted Ryan.

"It's not great when someone gets shot, Ryan," said Stefanie sternly. "Uncle Mark might have been killed."

"I didn't mean I wanted him to get killed," muttered Ryan, somewhat sullenly.

"It's okay, Ryan, I know what you mean." MacFarland smiled at his nephew.

"In my opinion, you should stick to selling hot dogs, Mark," said Randy. "It's more your speed. You're not a cop anymore, you know."

MacFarland tried to ignore the implied insult. Sometimes it was difficult for him to maintain his temper when he was around Randy Cooper. He wanted to throw his plate of mashed potatoes right in his face, but instead he chose a different tactic. "Do you know anything about construction accounting, Randy?"

Randy shrugged. "Accounting is accounting. Some differences, but the principles are all the same, regardless of what kind of business you're running."

"How easy would it be to steal from a construction company? I mean, adjusting the books so that you can take money out of the business without anyone knowing? How could someone go about it?"

"Oh, Mark, you don't have the training to do that! But if you did know accounting, it could be done. You mainly have to defraud the customer. It's easier if you have someone on the inside in the customer's organization, because then they won't examine the books all that closely. If you can get that worked out, then there are several ways you can get money out. The most common way is to charge more for labor and materials. Unfortunately, that shows up on the construction company's books. But you could buy more material than you use, charge the customer for that material, and then just use less. Unless they have good inventory procedures, the loss won't show up on the books. Then all you have to do is sell the material on the market. You could even set up a dummy company to sell the material back to the customer who has already paid for it."

"That could be done?"

"It's all rather complicated, and there are a lot of safeguards to counter that kind of fraud. Inspectors, auditors, and others keep a close watch on all the transactions."

"How much do you think someone could make on a scheme like this?"

Randy laughed, then became thoughtful. "Depends on a lot of factors. What materials they are selling. How long they have the scheme going. How big the project is. It's easier to rip off an individual homeowner who is having a house built, mainly because they don't know much about accounting. For a larger project, it would be harder, though there is more opportunity for fraud."

"It's going to have one tower with sixty floors, I think. It's going to be a pretty big building."

"I'm not a construction accountant, so I would have to hedge my estimates. But I would think a building like that would cost between three hundred million dollars and five hundred million dollars. Of course, that depends a lot on the type of construction. Steel versus concrete, you know, union versus open shop labor. A lot of factors."

MacFarland was thoughtful. "So there would be a lot of room for graft when you're talking about numbers that big."

"I suppose so. Easily three to ten million dollars." Randy laughed. "But you would need brains to pull that trick off, Mark. You better just stick to selling hot dogs."

CHAPTER EIGHT

MONDAY, APRIL 4, 0820 HOURS

MACFARLAND WAS glad to get back to his routine on Monday morning. He vowed never to go visit Stefanie and her family again, though he knew he would not keep that promise. As annoying as Randy was, MacFarland found himself wanting the approval of Nicole's sister too much to exclude her entirely from his life. Besides, he liked the kids.

On the other hand, Randy had given him some insights to the situation that Wanda had described. While he had no evidence to convince him that any fraud really was going on, the scope of the operations made it entirely possible that what she described was not as far-fetched as he had first thought. Many murders were committed because of greed. Automatically, he began reviewing the facts that he knew about the case.

A man had died. It was ruled an industrial accident, but industrial accidents could be staged. The fact that this one had occurred in public made it difficult to believe that it had been staged, however.

The cause of the accident was an improperly secured

restraining cable. It had supposedly been inspected, but the person inspecting it was suspected of having done an inadequate job.

The review board claimed that the safety inspector had been drinking, and his drinking impaired his judgment. MacFarland could understand how that might happen, and how the individual would not be aware of what he was doing.

So far, all the facts pointed to an unfortunate industrial accident, or at most to negligent manslaughter. Certainly not murder.

Maybe Wanda was not a plant by some of his former police friends. It was entirely possible that she believed that her friend had been murdered. She just didn't have any facts to support her suspicions.

Rufus ambled towards the cart, a bit later than usual, when MacFarland saw someone about a block behind Rufus. The individual stood at the corner, watching Rufus walking down the street. Or perhaps the person was watching MacFarland. The person looked vaguely familiar, and then MacFarland placed him. It was the stranger who had rescued him from two assailants earlier in the year. January eighth, yeah, that was the date. Two men had accosted MacFarland as he was pushing his original hot dog cart back to his trailer and truck. They had done a pretty good job of roughing MacFarland up, no mean feat considering the considerable hand-to-hand combat experience MacFarland had. MacFarland had suspected at the time that the men were similarly trained, and the mysterious man--Grey Wilson--who rescued him had confirmed that he believed the two men were cops. While MacFarland was defending himself, he had cut one of the men on the jaw with his ring. Pierson had even been able to identify the assailant, using a blood sample swabbed from MacFarland's ring. It had been a Denver cop.

As for his protector, a lot of mystery still surrounded him. Grey Wilson had known who MacFarland was, even knew where he lived, as though the man had been watching MacFarland for some time. MacFarland and Pierson both suspected Wilson might be a Fed, though the FBI would not admit to any activity going on in Denver. They wouldn't even confirm that Wilson was one of their agents.

MacFarland knew that Wilson was working with someone else. Wilson had driven MacFarland and his truck to Pierson's house and left MacFarland in the front of the house where Pierson found him. Apparently Wilson's associate had picked Wilson up from Observatory Park and taken him away.

Whatever Wilson was doing in Denver, he was still doing it.

And whatever that was also still involved keeping an eye on MacFarland.

Even though MacFarland's former job had once included keeping an eye on possible suspects, MacFarland found that he didn't like it when the tables were turned on him.

CHAPTER NINE

MONDAY, MARCH 4, 0830 HOURS

BY THE TIME Rufus reached MacFarland's corner, Wilson had disappeared, so MacFarland was not able to ask Rufus if he recognized him. He did ask if Rufus noticed anyone following him, to which Rufus said, "No Charlies, but there was a friendly following me." MacFarland wondered how Rufus knew that Wilson was a friendly, but then when he asked Rufus to describe the friendly who was following him, the description was so bizarre that MacFarland concluded that Rufus was having another of his psychotic episodes.

It was entirely possible that Wilson had not been following Rufus at all, but had been keeping an eye on MacFarland the entire time. That prospect was no more reassuring than assuming Rufus had been the target.

"Keep an eye out for a middle-aged man, receding hairline, thin hair, long narrow face. He's about six feet tall, probably weighs two hundred pounds."

"Boss, I'm not any good at things like that. I can tell

when Charlie is around, but everyone else is just a blur to me. Unless he's a friendly."

MacFarland had a sudden insight. "Are friendlies the same as homeless people?" he asked.

Rufus considered the question. "Yeah, I guess they are," he said. "Damn, I never realized that before!"

MacFarland shook his head. Sometimes he wondered how Rufus survived. But these days, Rufus survived because he had a job. Jerry Baker, the lawyer who hired MacFarland to help prove his client hadn't committed murder, had given Rufus a job as a courier.

"How's that job working out, Rufus?" asked MacFarland.

"Oh, boss, it's working great!" said Rufus enthusiastically. "Mr. Baker, he's got me running all over the city, doing this and doing that. Sometimes I can't keep up with all this and that there is to do!"

MacFarland was somewhat surprised to hear that, since he didn't think that Baker had that much business. Perhaps the success Baker had had with getting the wife of a jewelry store owner acquitted of murder had led to a lot more business. MacFarland hadn't seen Baker in quite a while, so he didn't really know how busy the lawyer was. It was a good thing if Baker had gotten a lot of business from the case. *He deserves it,* thought MacFarland, surprising even himself with that realization. Normally, MacFarland didn't like defense lawyers. He had always regarded defense attorneys as part of the enemy camp, necessary to ensure justice, but often employing legalistic tricks to get guilty scumbags back on the street. Yet Jerry Baker had proven to be different. He did work to get his clients out of jail or to get the lightest sentence possible. But he knew that many of his clients deserved to go to jail. More importantly, he knew when some of this clients didn't belong in jail.

Maureen Freeman had been one of those clients.

Thinking about how he had solved that case, MacFarland found himself feeling empty. He had been alive and involved when he was working to solve that murder. Was it because he was doing what he loved? Or was it because someone--Jerry Baker--believed in him?

He didn't know, but what he did know was that he was suddenly aware that he felt very envious of Rufus Headley's relationship with Baker. Rufus had a purpose in life. A purpose that seemed more meaningful than just selling hot dogs.

CHAPTER TEN

MONDAY, MARCH 4, 0912 HOURS

FROM HIS CORNER, MacFarland could not see the construction site where Mike Brady had died, since a large parking garage blocked his view. But if he went across the street, he could see the crane that was being used to move large objects from one part of the job site to another. As he recalled, Wanda had not been the crane operator the day Brady was killed. Why did she assume that the accident wouldn't have happened if she had been on the job?

Rufus was about to walk off, but MacFarland stopped him. "Would you mind watching the cart for a bit, Rufus?" he asked.

Rufus looked a bit uncertain. "Got meetings to go to," he said. "But I guess they're not really important meetings. Okay, boss, I'll take over for you."

MacFarland knew that Rufus liked working the wagon, even though he had a tendency to give away more product than he sold. Rufus had the strange idea that a person should pay according to how well off they looked. When MacFarland had pointed out that this was a central tenet of

Communism, Rufus just shrugged it off. "Guess them Communists mighta known a thing or two." When MacFarland had asked Rufus what he had been fighting for in Vietnam, Rufus replied, "To stay alive."

Fortunately, Rufus never charged more than the listed prices on the menu, or MacFarland was certain that he would get a lot of complaints. With Rufus, a listed price was always a "not to exceed" price recommendation, so he felt very comfortable charging less than the listed price. There were some customers, however, who did point out that their hot dog only cost half as much when they bought it from Rufus compared to when they bought it from him. MacFarland would explain that they were getting a daily special from Rufus.

MacFarland walked down the street towards the construction site entrance, carrying with him a large cup of coffee, a packet of sugar and a coffee creamer. He also had a hot dog wrapped up in silver foil. He had put some mustard and relish on the hot dog. He walked towards the construction site's main entranceway. There was a large wooden fence erected around the remainder of the city block not taken up by the parking garage. A picture of the proposed building posted near the entranceway showed a large four story plaza, filled with quaint little shops. Trees and flower boxes adorned the top of the plaza. All of this was dwarfed by a series of towers that soared high into deep blue, cloud-speckled sky. Since there were very few tall buildings in this part of Denver, the building would have a commanding view of the city to the north and the mountains to the west.

A smaller sign near the entrance proclaimed that the job site had gone forty-four days without a lost time accident. Not bad, as long as all lost time accidents were created equal. As MacFarland neared the entrance, a security guard stepped out of a small shed and held up a hand. "This is a restricted area," said the guard.

MacFarland smiled and stepped back on the sidewalk. "No problem, just wanted to see what's going on down here. And to offer you a gesture of goodwill." As he handed the drink and hot dog to the guard, he examined the man carefully. He was about the same height as MacFarland, maybe an inch shorter and about ten pounds heavier. The guard had a very oval face, with short dark hair. It looked like he had once shaved his head and was just letting it start to grow back. He was wearing a green shirt, khaki trousers, and a black vest. He also had a black zippered windbreaker, open right now. MacFarland looked at the name tag pinned to the man's vest. Picket. The guard turned around when a truck blared on its horn, and MacFarland was able to see a logo for Forrester Equipment and Construction on the back of his jacket. A company guard.

The guard took the items, then backed up towards the guard shack. He made sure MacFarland was not in the way of the truck and waved the truck on through. The guard stepped into the shack, gesturing for MacFarland to join him.

"You're Mac, from the hot dog stand," stated the guard.

MacFarland nodded. "Yes, I was hoping I could drum up some more business down here. Figure you would be in the best position to suggest that the guys try out my stand for lunch."

Picket nodded. "There's two hot dog stands down at that end of the street," he said slowly. "A guy would need an incentive to go to your stand instead of the other one."

MacFarland smiled, hiding his annoyance with Picket's inept attempt at trying to shake him down. "It would be worth my while to reward someone who could direct people in my direction. At least a free meal each day."

Picket opened up the foil and started eating the hot dog. "Does taste pretty good." He held out a hand for MacFarland to shake. "Name's Marty Picket."

"Nice to meet you, Marty. When do they expect to have the building done?"

"According to the sign on the wall, about September of this year. Though if we have any more delays like we had a month or so ago, we won't make that."

"What sort of delays?" asked MacFarland.

"You didn't hear? Thought you would have, being located so close. We had a guy die here back in February. Young kid got crushed by a load of girders. Shut the place down for a week while they investigated it."

"God, that sounds awful. How'd it happen?"

Picket smiled smugly, anxious to share inside information with a stranger. "According to the safety board, it was because the Safety Inspector didn't do his job right. Signed off on the off-load set up, but he was probably drunk when he checked it out. Hightower, he's always drunk. Don't know why they keep him on." Picket smiled. "He got fired. Really, though, he should have been charged with something."

MacFarland stared out the window towards the job site as he listened to Picket. He could see Wanda inside the crane, moving a pallet containing several crates from a storage area over towards the huge pit that had been dug for the building's parking garage and foundation. He pointed towards the crane. "Is that a woman working the crane?" he asked.

Without looking, Picket nodded. "Yep, that's Wanda the

Ballbuster. Most of us call her Busty, but it's not just 'because she busts things up. You should see her in person."

"Was she around when the accident happened?"

Picket shook his head. "Nope. And if you ask me, if she had been, that kid would still be alive."

"Why is that? She have something special going on with him?"

"Busty and Brady? No way! Naw, it's cause she is always safety first. She never woulda lifted that load without inspecting it first. That's the kind of girl she is."

CHAPTER ELEVEN

MONDAY, APRIL 4, 1700 HOURS

THAT EVENING, as MacFarland was starting to shut down his wagon, he began to reconsider the facts in the case. While it still seemed that Brady's death had been an industrial accident, the idea that if Warren had been working the crane the accident wouldn't have happened made it seem more plausible that it was not just an accident. What would it take to make a murder look like an accident? *It wouldn't be that difficult*, thought MacFarland. He could easily imagine doing it. All he would need would be a safety inspector who was known to indulge more than was good for him. A crane operator who was not as safety conscious as he should be. And a victim who was new to the job.

As he imagined scenario after scenario, he discovered one major flaw in his thinking. How would he manage to get a drunk safety inspector, a novice victim, and a second-rate crane operator all in position at the same time? It didn't seem likely that such a combination could be planned.

Unless the person who planned the murder was in management.

The more he thought about it, the more convinced MacFarland became that it might be possible to create a set of circumstances that would lead to a construction accident. Maybe Warren wasn't so far off base in her suspicions.

As he was closing down his umbrellas, four teens--two girls, two boys--came up to the wagon.

"Are you shutting down?" asked a young girl. She looked to be in her mid-teens.

"I'm afraid so," said MacFarland.

"Come on, Teena," said one of the boys. "We don't have enough for both food and the bus."

"Where are you heading?" asked MacFarland.

Teena pointed vaguely towards the south. "Urban Peak. Place to sleep tonight."

MacFarland nodded, then opened up his storage container. "I might have some hot dogs left." He pulled out eight hot dogs and eight buns and assembled them, handing each of the kids two dogs. "I can open up the condiments case for you if you want," he added.

"Thanks, mister," said the other boy.

Teena smiled her thanks. "Yeah, thanks." She even took the time to shake his hand, a gesture which surprised him. "My name is Teena. With two E's, not an I."

"Pleased to meet you Teena," said MacFarland. "Stay warm tonight."

As she and her friends hurried away, Teena turned back and waved goodbye. Then they raced off, laughing, trying to catch the bus on Broadway. *Homeless at such a young age,* thought MacFarland. All four of them probably runaways.

Four more people that he would probably be on the lookout to take care of.

CHAPTER TWELVE

TUESDAY, APRIL 5, 0645 HOURS

CYNTHIA PIERSON literally growled when she entered the kitchen. "Don't even say anything, unless you have a cup of coffee for me."

MacFarland immediately handed her a cup of coffee. "My lady speaks and I serve," he said in musical tones. "Rough night?"

"Yeah," Pierson said, sinking slowly and carefully onto one of the kitchen chairs. She propped up her head with her hand. "We had a breakthrough on the drug case. Our informant was able to set up a deal and we caught the supplier. I don't think he is the supplier, though. Just a mule. The product matches some stuff we've seen out of Chicago, but we need to wait for lab confirmation of that."

"You mentioned that there might be a Chicago connection. So it's not a meth lab based here in Colorado?"

"Affirmative. So that means we might have to start coordinating with Chicago PD. You know what that is like."

Actually, MacFarland did not know, since none of his cases involved having to work with the Chicago police. He assumed that it would be like any other inter-agency case--a lot of turf issues, communications problems, and personality clashes--the kind of things that made cross-jurisdictional police work a headache.

"To make it worse, the Feds want to get involved. I have a new liaison. Norma Sykes. Why do I get stuck with the kids?"

Pierson explained that Norma Sykes was even younger than Lockwood, her current partner. The FBI agent was twenty-five years old. According to Pierson, she was a "knockout" with long brown hair and dark eyes. "Lockwood can't stop drooling over her," she said with a certain amount of contempt in her voice.

"Boys will be boys," said MacFarland, attempting to sound erudite, then realizing he couldn't sound very sophisticated spouting platitudes. He tried desperately to recover. "What is the FBI's interest in the case?"

"I'm assuming they're involved because the investigation covers multiple states. We didn't call them in, and my contact in Chicago says they didn't notify the Feds either. I think they were on top of this case all along. Just didn't bother telling us."

"Damn Feds," said MacFarland sympathetically. Pierson was about to get up to leave, but he put a hand on her arm and stopped her. "Do you know anything about an accident at a construction site?"

Pierson twisted her face in thought. "When was it? I don't remember anything recently."

"It was about six or seven weeks ago. At that site where I used to park."

"Oh, I know where you mean. It's right across from the police station. I didn't work that case. As I recall, it was just a workplace accident."

"That's what they decided it was. Could you look into it for me? See if there is a case file for it?"

"I doubt that there is," said Pierson slowly. "I'll check for you. Do you think it was more than an accident?"

"Someone does," he replied. "I'm keeping an open mind on it."

Pierson smiled, finishing her coffee. She was obviously in a better mood now. Coffee was a remarkable drug. "You have a feeling for these kinds of things, Mac. If you think it was more than an accident, then it probably was."

"That's just it," he said. "I don't have a feeling for this one. At least not yet."

CHAPTER THIRTEEN

TUESDAY, APRIL 5, 1150 HOURS

TUESDAY WAS BRIGHT AND SUNNY, an early spring day in Denver, the kind of day that fooled you into thinking that winter was over. The air smelled fresh and earthy, cleaner than the grimy air of winter. April was a fickle month, and it could be warm and pleasant one day and stormy and wet the next. Evenings still dipped down into the thirties, but daily temperatures could get into the high fifties. This looked like one of those warmer days. By eleven o'clock, MacFarland was in his shirtsleeves, greeting people on their way to and from court. Business was actually better than usual, perhaps because the hot dog stand on the opposite corner was not there today.

It was almost noon when MacFarland spotted Jerry Baker walking towards him. MacFarland automatically started getting a bratwurst ready for the lawyer. When Baker reached the wagon, the two men heartily greeted each other. "How are the wounds?" asked Baker. He felt a rare pang of responsibility for having gotten MacFarland involved in the investigation that resulted in him getting shot.

"Much better," said MacFarland. "Still can't do sprints and push-ups, at least not without a bit of pain, but I am working on getting back into shape. Pierson makes sure I get my exercise every day by making me take the garbage out. That's my rehab program. How have you been?"

"Busy, busy, busy," said the lawyer. "Getting Maureen Freeman off did wonders for my career. The TV stations ran stories for several days, which for television is a lifetime. I did try to keep your name out of it, as you asked."

"Thanks, I really appreciate that, Jerry." MacFarland busied himself wiping down the surfaces of his cart. Since this was a much larger wagon than his previous one, he found it easier to look busy now. "How's Rufus working out? You must be keeping him pretty busy these days."

Baker laughed bitterly. "I wish! I haven't seen much of Mr. Headley, Mac. He showed up one or two times, and since then, I haven't laid eyes him."

MacFarland was surprised by the news. "Really? He gives me the impression he is still working for you. I wonder what's going on with him."

"Me too. Some men just don't like responsibility."

"Or he's afraid of failing you," suggested MacFarland. "You did make it seem like a major step up in life for him. I get the feeling that Rufus likes to keep a low profile. He's not comfortable in the social circles you want him to be in."

Baker contemplated what MacFarland said. "You know, you might have something there. I tried to get Rufus to fit into my environment. Maybe it just wasn't a good fit. He may not be the right man for what I had in mind."

MacFarland shook his head. "No, I don't think that's the

right conclusion, Jerry. Rufus may be the right man, but you have to use him in the right way. Let him be what he is. Don't try to turn him into something he can't be or doesn't want to be. Rufus doesn't belong in our time or society. He is stuck in the nineteen-sixties, fighting a war that he didn't want to be part of. You can put him in a suit, but he doesn't belong there."

"But I want to help him."

"You can, Jerry. Just let him do your job on his terms. I can't guarantee that he will be more responsible, but at least give it a try."

Baker considered the idea. "I will try it. Next time you see him, ask him to come see me. He doesn't have to wear the suit."

As MacFarland watched Baker walk back towards his office, he felt a wave of shame roll over him. What kind of a friend was he, feeling envious of Rufus for having a job with Baker and missing the fact that his friend was actually not happy with the arrangement? He should have seen some sign of Rufus' true feelings, but he had only been thinking of his own problems.

He resolved to pay more attention to his friend.

CHAPTER FOURTEEN

TUESDAY, APRIL 5, 1249 HOURS

PART OF MACFARLAND'S resolve to pay more attention to his friend Rufus was a corollary resolve to drop the construction accident investigation. After all, he told himself, there is no evidence that a crime was committed. What proof was there that any kind of fraud was going on? Only the word of an untrained construction helper. What would the kid know about construction accounting?

Now I'm beginning to think like Randy.

The lunch crowd kept him busy and he didn't think about Mike Brady, not until he saw Wanda Warren walking towards him. As she approached, her jacket open, he could see why everyone called her Busty. She was clearly well-endowed.

She came up to the wagon, waited in line for other customers to get their orders, then when no one else was around, she plopped a five dollar bill down on the cart's surface. "A foot long, a drink, and some chips."

MacFarland nodded and started to assemble her order.

He could feel Warren staring at him, her gaze intense and hostile.

"Are you going to help me?" she finally asked.

"Wanda, I don't really know if a crime has been committed. I know you feel responsible..."

"How do you know what I feel?"

"I just meant that I get the impression that if you had been working that day, the accident might not have happened."

"Damn right it wouldn't have happened!" snapped Wanda angrily. "Whoever killed Brady wouldn't have dared do it on my watch. This fucking company is always trying to push us to cut corners. I don't know why that didn't come out in the safety report. That alone is a reason to call it murder."

"Actually, it would be negligent homicide," corrected MacFarland.

"I don't give a damn what it would be. It's all the same to Brady, isn't it? He's dead. Dead! And whoever is responsible is getting away with it." She snatched the hot dog from him as he held it out to her. "Besides, there is still the fraud that he discovered. Seems to me that's enough reason to suspect that he was killed because of it."

"It will be pretty hard to prove that fraud is going on," said MacFarland. "Do you actually have any physical proof?"

Warren hesitated, looked up and down the street, and then leaned closer. "I don't have anything, but Mike told me he had taken photos of two receiving manifests. For the same load of steel."

MacFarland was immediately alert. "Where are the photos?"

"On his phone, I suppose," said Warren. "How the hell

would I know where the photos are? That's what I was asking you to find out about."

"If I had some physical evidence of fraud, then I might be able to establish motive." Warren frowned as she watched MacFarland peer into the middle distance. MacFarland turned back to look at her. "Who controls the scheduling at the construction site? Is there someone in charge of it?"

Warren rubbed her chin in thought. "Scheduling is a two-step process. There's a couple of guys who do planning. At least they give us these plan sheets for each major job we're supposed to do. But that's only for the major jobs, like setting up the scaffolding, or moving materials. Then there's scheduling of people to do the jobs on the plans. Unless there's equipment involved, like my crane. Then we work on rotation."

"Was there such a plan for off-loading the truck?"

"No, that's covered by a standard procedure. We have to follow the steps defined by the Offload Procedure. And the delivery company has its own Delivery Plan."

"What steps are on the Offload Procedure?"

"I can get you a copy of it, if you need it. Some of the stuff was done the night before. It includes things like making sure the load is level on the truck. Securing the ties on the load. Setting up an exclusion zone. They set up the slinging wires the night before. And the safety inspector signed off on everything."

"This was Hightower who signed off on the set-up?"

"Yeah, Louis Hightower."

"Is he the only safety inspector?"

"No, there's two or three safety inspectors."

"Was he drunk that night?"

"I wasn't working that night, so I don't rightly know. I

can't imagine him being on the job if he was drunk. Just don't make sense to me."

"No, it doesn't, but some drunks can hide their condition. It doesn't take much to impair your judgment."

"Not Hightower. I always thought he was steady as a rock. I couldn't believe it when I heard that he was drunk that night."

"You said that there were procedures for doing this job. Who assigns people to do the actual work?"

"Could be several people. Riley Vogel is the site superintendent. He has responsibility for everything that goes on there. But actual scheduling might have been done by Leland Adams or Ryan Boyce. They are the two supervisors who were working those days. I don't know who actually scheduled the work teams that weekend."

"Which of these guys would also have access to the receiving records and inventory for the site?"

"Almost anybody in management or their staff. That's about ten people." Warren began to see where MacFarland's questions were going. "You think one of them might be the killer?"

"We don't really know that there is a killer, Wanda," cautioned MacFarland. "I am just trying to see who might be involved and who had the means of setting up an 'accident.' That would give us means and motive."

"Now we're getting somewhere!" Warren's face lit up with the prospects of bringing a bad person to justice.

MacFarland tried to calm her down. "Don't get your hopes up, Wanda. We have no proof. All of our speculations are just that. Speculations. Nothing we have would stand up in a court of law." *In fact*, thought MacFarland gloomily, *we have nothing at all.*

"Could you bring me a list of all the people who work at

the construction site?" he asked. "Maybe I can start asking them some questions."

Warren nodded eagerly. "I'll get that to you as quickly as I can," she said. She finished her lunch, tossed her trash into the waste receptacle, and headed back to the construction site.

CHAPTER FIFTEEN

TUESDAY, APRIL 5, 1634 HOURS

MACFARLAND WASN'T sure when Warren would bring him the list of names he asked for. He also wasn't sure what he would do with the Procedures documents she mentioned. Like most procedures, they were written to describe how to do the job correctly. Even so, something had gone drastically wrong. That meant that either the procedures weren't followed or someone had made a mistake. MacFarland always believed that the more he knew about how something was supposed to work, the easier it would be for him to find out what had gone wrong. For MacFarland, detective work was more than just uncovering facts. It was a process of understanding both why the crime was committed and how it was committed.

It was just after four-thirty when MacFarland saw someone coming from the construction site towards his wagon. He didn't recognize the individual, but he could tell that the person was dressed much better than the typical construction worker. *Someone in management,* thought MacFarland. White male, six feet three inches tall, probably one hundred ninety-five pounds. He walked like a pit bull--assertive, in command, ready for confrontation. Clean shaven, but with a day's worth of shadow on his face. Brown eyes, brown hair, square jaw, dimpled chin. The man had narrow squinty eyes, probably sensitive to the light.

MacFarland smiled as the man approached his wagon. "What can I get for you?" he asked.

"You're the hot dog vendor who gave some food to my security guard?" asked the man, his voice abrupt and gruff.

MacFarland hesitated, then nodded. "Yeah, I brought some stuff down. Wanted to see if I could get him to recommend my stand to the guys on their lunch break."

"Don't do it again," said the man. "I don't want any of my people accepting gifts from people like you."

MacFarland stared at the man. "I'm sorry, I didn't catch your name."

"Boyce. Ryan Boyce. I'm the supervisor down there, and I run a tight ship. I don't want any bribery going on during my watch, got it? You stay away from my job site. Or I'll have the city move you from this corner."

MacFarland did not think that Boyce could actually do that. The construction site was on the other side of the block, and MacFarland's hot dog stand was not an obstacle to their operations. On the other hand, why take chances?

"Okay, you made your point. No more free food."

Boyce seemed ready for more confrontation, but MacFarland's acquiescence took the wind out of his sails. He started to turn away, but stopped. "One more thing, buddy. Stay the fuck away from Wanda Warren!"

MacFarland was suddenly on alert. It was one thing for Boyce to tell him to stop giving food to the security guard. It was a whole different matter to tell him not to talk to a specific employee.

"I think Wanda has the right to buy hot dogs wherever she wants," he said slowly.

"Don't give me that shit," said Boyce angrily. "Wanda is a very confused girl. I know she was down here trying to get you to make trouble for us. I'm telling you now, buddy, back off! Otherwise, you will find yourself in over your head."

MacFarland smiled pleasantly. "I don't know what you're talking about, Mr. Boyce. Wanda just buys lunch from me."

"Listen, buddy, Wanda is a bit off her rocker. She sees things that aren't going on, that aren't there. All you're doing is encouraging her delusions. So just back off and mind your own fucking business."

Boyce turned away and strode rapidly back towards the construction site, MacFarland staring after him in wonder. *If anyone is off their rocker*, mused MacFarland, *it's Ryan Boyce.* While Warren's suspicions were a bit strange, MacFarland did not think they were unreasonable. On the other hand, Boyce's behavior was clearly beyond the pale of normal. Was Boyce really concerned about Warren or was he just trying to cover something up? If he had wanted MacFarland to back off, then Boyce had taken the wrong tactic. MacFarland only had one desire that was stronger than solving a mystery. That was to solve a mystery he was told not to solve.

He also wondered, if Wanda Warren was off her rocker, what the hell was she doing operating a crane? It didn't add up.

After half an hour, he shut down his wagon, hooked it up to his truck, and drove home, all the while wondering, what was it that Boyce didn't want MacFarland to find out?

CHAPTER SIXTEEN

TUESDAY, APRIL 5, 1840 HOURS

MACFARLAND DROPPED his hot dog stand off at Pierson's house, then headed back up I-25 towards Thornton. He had been able to locate Brady's address using simple social media. Brady had a Facebook page with over five hundred friends. MacFarland wasn't even certain that he knew five hundred people. Thanks to Facebook, MacFarland already knew what Mike's wife looked like. Shirley Brady was a plain-looking young woman, with long, straight blond hair, blue eyes, thin eyebrows, and a narrow nose. According to her Facebook page, she was only twenty-three years old.

The Brady's lived on Nagel Drive in a one-story ranch style house. The front yard was fenced in with a chain link fence. Paint on the house was chipping away. The screen door was loose on its hinges. MacFarland tried the buzzer, but it didn't seem to work. Finally he knocked on the door.

After a minute, Shirley Brady, holding a one-year old child on her hip, opened the door. The baby started howling as soon as it saw MacFarland. Shirley was a few inches shorter than MacFarland. She dressed like clothes no longer mattered to her. She looked haggard and annoyed, the weight of too many calamities all coming too quickly damping her down. "Yes?"

"I'm sorry to disturb you, Mrs. Brady. I was wondering if I could ask you a couple of questions."

She looked at him suspiciously. "Are you a cop?"

MacFarland shook his head. "No, I'm not. My name is Mark MacFarland. I am a friend of Wanda Warren's. She asked me to look into the situation of your husband's death."

Shirley Brady tried to calm the baby down, all the time giving him a puzzled look. "They say it was an accident. I'm supposed to get his insurance, but it hasn't come yet. Is this going to mess that up?"

"No, it shouldn't cause any delays in the insurance money," he said. "May I come in and talk to you?"

Shirley looked uncertain, but as the baby kept crying, she finally shrugged and stepped back from the door. "I don't have anything to steal."

Once MacFarland was in the house, Shirley seemed to relax. She sat down on the couch and held the baby on her lap. The baby seemed happier with this arrangement and stopped crying.

"Let me start off by offering my condolences on your loss, Mrs. Brady. I know how much it hurts when you lose someone you love."

Shirley looked up, then wiped moisture from her eyes. "Thank you. Have you also lost someone, Mr. MacFarland?"

MacFarland nodded. "Yes, my wife was taken from me almost six years ago."

"I'm sorry to hear that." She paused, then asked quietly, "Does it get easier? Over time?"

"It doesn't hurt as much over time, Mrs. Brady. The pain

just finds a deeper place to live inside of you. But it never goes away, not as long as you still love the person you lost."

Shirley was silent for a moment. "Why did Wanda ask you to investigate Mike's death?"

"I am not sure how to put this delicately, Mrs. Brady, so I will just come out and say it. Ms. Warren thinks that Mike's death may not have been an accident."

Shirley Brady said nothing, but just stared at him, her expression empty of any discernible emotion.

"You don't seem surprised by that suggestion," said MacFarland.

Shirley shrugged her shoulders. "No, not really. Though I can't think of anyone who might have wanted to kill Mike. Everyone liked him."

"Did Mike ever talk about work? Any problems at work? Or anything that he thought was going on that shouldn't have been?"

Shirley shook her head slowly, trying to think of anything that might be pertinent. "No, Mike didn't talk much about work. He did talk about his dreams, and how he hoped to get into management, but about what he did, no, not much at all. Oh, he did complain that the company didn't do a good job of training people for new assignments. They expected a person to learn from his peers, but sometimes that wasn't practical."

"Did he ever show you any documents or pictures from work?"

Shirley laughed. "No, not ever. I'm really not interested in construction, and even though that was Mike's thing, it wasn't mine. Most of my time was taken up with the baby and trying to fit school in. It's not easy, you know."

"You were going to school? Even with the baby? What were you studying?"

"I'm still going to school. I'm taking nursing classes. That's what I want to be someday. I hope that when the insurance money comes, it will be easier for me. I might try to move back closer to my mom's house, and let her take care of Amy."

"I hope that works out for you. Do you know what is holding up the insurance money?"

"No, but I talk to Mike's boss about it fairly often. He says he's putting pressure on the company to file all the reports to make sure it gets paid quickly."

"Wanda mentioned that Mike once showed her a photo or two he had taken with his phone. Do you know anything about that?"

Shirley pursed her lips and furrowed her brow. "Nope, he didn't show it to me."

"Is it possible that the photo is still on his phone? Or did he download photos from his phone onto his computer?"

"I don't know about downloading anything, Mr. MacFarland, but as far as his phone goes, it doesn't matter if the photo is still on the phone."

MacFarland was puzzled. "Why is that, Mrs. Brady?"

"Because about two weeks ago, someone broke into the house and stole a bunch of stuff. Including Mike's phone and computer and his iPad."

"What? Did you report this to the police?"

"Of course. But they said it was probably gang activity. We don't live too far from Thornton High School and the police think there is a gang of high-school kids breaking and entering houses in this neighborhood. They said there have been four break-ins in the past month."

"So you don't have his phone," said MacFarland.

"Mr. MacFarland, I don't have Mike, so I don't even think about not having his phone."

CHAPTER SEVENTEEN

WEDNESDAY, APRIL 6, 1500 HOURS

THE BREAK-IN at the Brady house could be just what it seemed: gang-related activity. When Shirley Brady finally recounted all of the items that were missing, MacFarland reluctantly agreed with the police. Most of the items were electronics gadgets that kids would take for themselves or which could easily be fenced. The graffiti that she showed him on the back of the house tended to confirm that the theft was gang-related. MacFarland took a picture of the graffiti with his phone.

Just to be sure, though, he had asked Pierson to check with the Gang unit in Vice and Narcotics to see what information Denver PD had on this gang. Since the various police departments in the Front Range coordinated intel on gang activity, the fact that the gang seemed to operate out of Thornton would have no bearing. Gangs operated across jurisdictional boundaries, and so did the police.

Even so, MacFarland had an uncomfortable feeling in the pit of his stomach about the break-in. His cop instinct told him that the missing phone and computer were just too convenient, coming just when Wanda had started asking questions about Mike's death. Unfortunately, without the phone or computer, there were no pictures, no evidence.

MacFarland tried to put the case out of his mind and focus his attention on his language lessons and serving his customers. Business was just busy enough to keep him occupied and his mind off the case.

He hadn't seen Rufus this morning, which was unusual enough to give MacFarland cause for concern. At three o'clock, MacFarland saw someone he recognized from his days on the streets. It was Ben Tyler, a black homeless man. Tyler wasn't usually found in this part of town, preferring to spend more of his time up on the other side of the Auraria Campus in the LoDo area. MacFarland wondered if the businesses in LoDo were asking the police to crack down on the homeless loitering around their business establishments. It wouldn't be the first time the homeless were brushed aside by society.

Tyler recognized MacFarland and came over to the cart. "Yo, man, is this where you been at? I heard you got respectable. Congrats, man!"

MacFarland laughed. "Hi Ben. Can't say that I am all that respectable, but I'm working on it."

"You got a place to live? I ain't seen you on the streets for a couple years now."

"I had a place, but it didn't work out. Now I am staying with my former partner."

"You living with a cop?" asked Tyler incredulously.

MacFarland laughed again. "Yeah, she keeps me out of trouble."

"Ah, yes, the lady cop," said Tyler, as if that explained everything. Apparently Pierson was well known to the homeless community.

"I thought you normally were on the other side of town," said MacFarland.

Tyler nodded. "Usually I am, but I heard there was some action over here, and I wanted a piece of it."

"Drugs?" MacFarland hadn't seen any drug activity on this side of town. That was one reason he liked doing business here. Drug users tended to be a bit too violent for MacFarland's taste.

"Naw, not drugs. I try to stay away from that, Mac." Tyler looked around, checking for potential threats. Like most homeless people, Tyler didn't like being in unfamiliar places. Better the dangers you knew than the dangers you didn't know was the prevailing philosophy of most homeless people. MacFarland also knew that Tyler did do drugs, when he could get his hands on them. So far, mostly pot, though it was unlikely that he got his legally. While pot was legal in Colorado, there was still a sizeable traffic in illicit marijuana, primarily among minors and those who wanted to avoid the high cost of commercial weed. A fair portion of the illegal weed was distributed by Colombian and Mexican cartels, who tried to undercut the cost of legal pot.

"You haven't seen Rufus today, have you?" asked MacFarland, wishing to avoid any discussion that would push Tyler deeper into deception.

Tyler rubbed his chin, trying to dredge up the memory. "Yeah, man, I did see him. He was on a bicycle. Don't know where he got that. He was over by 15th and Wazee. Don't know what he was doin' over there. Not his usual hangout, you know?"

MacFarland smiled. He hoped that this meant that Baker had found a way to get Rufus to help him. The bicycle was one of the things Baker provided to Rufus to help him with his courier duties. Rufus couldn't store the bicycle near his "hidey-hole" along the Platte River, so Baker let him store it in a closet in Baker's office building. Having the bicycle gave Rufus more mobility, and was a source of pride. Not many homeless people had bikes.

Suddenly Tyler stiffened. "Fuck, I gotta blow, man."

MacFarland looked up. "What's wrong, Ben?"

"That dude, the one coming over here. He fucked with me a while back."

MacFarland looked in the direction Tyler indicated. He recognized Marty Picket, the security guard from the Forrester construction site. "How'd he fuck with you, Ben?"

"I was picking up cans from the ground over there. The construction workers just toss them into a garbage can. Lot of them miss, and they are all over the ground. I was doing a public service, man, picking up the trash, you know what I mean? And this fucking white ass comes along and beats the crap outta me. I weren't doin' nothing wrong, man! Jus' pickin' up cans!" Tyler stared nervously as Picket came closer. "I gotta split, man."

As Tyler hurried back towards Colfax, MacFarland scowled. Although Tyler was not one of his regular homeless people, MacFarland still felt a bond with the man. Hurting Tyler was almost the same as hurting MacFarland, and as Picket approached MacFarland's hot dog stand, he felt a rising resentment towards the security guard.

Picket smiled pleasantly as he stepped up to the cart. "Good afternoon, Mac. How about a hot dog and some chips for the trip home?"

"That'll be four fifty," said MacFarland.

Picket frowned. "I thought we had an agreement. I push business your way and you give me a discount."

"I haven't exactly noticed a lot of traffic from the construction site, not on this side of the street, at least."

There had been a fair number of customers from the construction company on the other corner, patronizing his competitor. He assumed that Boyce had made good on his threat.

"Hey, it ain't my fault if Boyce has been badmouthing you! I don't know what you did to piss him off, but that ain't my fault!"

"No, but what is your fault is beating up a homeless person. You're a bully, Picket, and I don't have to serve you. So forget it, go across the street if you want a hot dog."

Picket, turning a light shade of red, stared angrily at MacFarland. "Fuck you, Mac, see if you get any business from me."

As Picket stomped off, MacFarland smiled ruefully. "Can't lose what you never had," he said philosophically.

CHAPTER EIGHTEEN

WEDNESDAY, APRIL 6, 2130 HOURS

THAT EVENING, when he got back to Pierson's house after his weekly AA meeting, MacFarland checked his supplies and prepared an order list for the coming week. He was going to run out of product by Saturday or Sunday, but he decided that he would take those days off. His shoulder was acting up again, though he assumed it was tension from having to deal with people like Picket. MacFarland was a firm believer that pain did not really exist--it was just something people imagined. Of course, after he got shot, he had to re-examine this theory. He did not believe that he had that good an imagination.

Pierson arrived home later than usual. "I've already eaten," she announced as she put her gun and badge into the drawer in the kitchen where she stored them each night. MacFarland looked up, feeling a trace guilty because he had not planned on making any dinner. Though it was never discussed, Pierson and MacFarland had divided up the household chores so that MacFarland was responsible for "unimportant" meals, whereas Pierson would be responsible for all "important" meals. Since important meals only seemed to include the holidays that Pierson never wanted to celebrate, that left MacFarland doing most of the cooking.

"And the dishes," Pierson had also reminded him one day. "You make the mess, you clean it up."

Since MacFarland paid almost no rent to stay with his former partner, he could hardly argue with her totally unreasonable terms.

Pierson looked exhausted as she sat down at the kitchen table. More as a gesture of apology, MacFarland handed her a cup of coffee. She looked at it, then finally smiled. "Thanks."

"Rough day at the office?" asked MacFarland.

"Yeah, you could say that. Damn Feds have been working on this drug case for a long time, and we only just now find out about it. What happened to inter-agency cooperation?"

MacFarland was not sure if anything had happened to cooperation, though he silently observed that Pierson was not the most cooperative cop on the force when it came to the FBI. He suspected that she had been burned by the FBI at some point in her past, though she never talked about it. Nor did he feel it was his place to pry into her affairs. If she wanted him to know why she resented the FBI so much, she would tell him.

"Speaking of cooperation," he said, "did you get a chance to look into the Mike Brady death?"

"Oh, crap, it completely slipped my mind, Mac. I'm sorry! I promise I will look into it first thing in the morning. I'll even stop by your wagon and give you a personal update."

"You just know that I have coffee now, and it's better

than that swill you drink at the station. What about that gang graffiti I asked you to look into?"

"Now that I did do. Interesting twist on that. The Thornton cop I talked to said that though they classified the break-in as gang related, the graffiti was not clearly associated with any gang they were familiar with. Same was true with our gang unit. I talked to Schwab, and he confirmed it. His opinion was that it was either a new gang or someone posing as a gang member."

MacFarland had a vague recollection of Victor Schwab. He had been working to clean up Denver's gangs for more than ten years, and probably knew more about their activities than anyone else in the department. If Schwab had doubts about the authenticity of the graffiti, MacFarland had no reason to doubt that it was painted on the house to throw the police off.

"That's interesting." MacFarland brought Pierson up to date on his interview with Shirley Brady.

"So you think the break-in was related to Brady's death?"

"That's the direction I'm headed in," he said. "There are too many coincidences for me to feel comfortable with an accidental death scenario. I really wish you would look at whatever we have in the file."

Pierson got annoyed. "I said I would do it," she said tersely. "But I've got to tell you, Mac, not every death is a murder. Even if it turns out that the company is owned by Peterson."

MacFarland stared at Pierson in stunned surprise. "What did you say? What does that mean?"

"Huh? Oh, you didn't know that? Damn, you're stupid! Forrester Equipment and Construction is one of the companies owned by Cygnus International."

The name Cygnus International suddenly set off alarms in MacFarland's head. Cygnus International was the holding company of Consolidated Colorado Properties, the company Nicole MacFarland had worked for when she was killed by CCP's president, Norris Peterson. MacFarland remembered that Detective Lockwood, Pierson's partner, had investigated the convoluted series of companies owned or controlled by Peterson. At the time, however, they had been focused on trying to determine who controlled the company that managed the Denver Crime Laboratory. That company, the Colorado Forensics Bureau, had also been controlled by Peterson. MacFarland suspected that Peterson had used his control over the Crime Lab to doctor evidence that would implicate him in a series of crimes, including Nicole's murder. Peterson was very adept at covering his tracks, and so far no one had been able to prove that he had anything to do with the problems in the Crime Lab. Even so, the Chief had wisely decided to remove Colorado Forensics Bureau as the managing company and replace it with another management company.

"Forrester is one of Peterson's companies?" repeated MacFarland, his voice quiet with disbelief. Despite what Pierson had just said, MacFarland was immediately convinced that Peterson was involved with Brady's murder. He didn't know how, but he resolved that he would find out.

A feeling of excitement came over him. *Damn you, Peterson, this time, I will get you!*

CHAPTER NINETEEN

THURSDAY, APRIL 7, 0823 HOURS

THE NEXT MORNING, as MacFarland set up his hot dog stand, he glanced repeatedly down the street towards the construction site. All he could actually see at this time was the wood fence that shielded the site from casual passers-by. Yet simply knowing that the company that was working on the site was owned by Norris Peterson gave the entire site a sinister and dark aspect. It was as though a nefarious cloud of evil had settled over the site, imbuing most of its employees with evil desires and dark souls.

Okay, maybe that doesn't include the Busty Ballbreaker, thought MacFarland. She was probably one of the few good people employed by Forrester. The fact that she was opposed to some vague wrongdoing that management was engaged in automatically gave her a halo of goodness, virtue, and purity that almost set her up on a pedestal.

MacFarland realized that his perceptions were just a tad biased, but he couldn't escape feeling a rising antagonism against Forrester and all it stood for. He had to admit that the company probably had little contact with

Peterson, but if there was a connection, he was determined to find it. He had to remind himself, however, that the worst thing a detective could do was to allow his prejudices to cloud his judgment. Let the facts speak for themselves.

Rufus showed up, somewhat later than usual, along with Kirk and Gracie. After a few minutes of idle chatter, Rufus said he had to go. MacFarland was a bit surprised, since Rufus declined his usual morning meal of hot dogs. Kirk and Gracie, however, were willing to stick around and accept the free food. "What have you two been doing lately?" asked MacFarland.

"Not much," said Gracie. "Trying to find places to sell some stuff." A slight nudge from Kirk and Gracie modified her statement. "Well, thinking about selling some stuff."

"What sort of stuff?" asked MacFarland.

"Uh, just stuff," said Gracie hesitantly, holding her hand out for the hot dog. MacFarland passed it to her and began to get a second hot dog ready. Gracie, meanwhile, put toppings on the hot dog and gave it to Kirk.

"Pretty hard to sell 'just stuff,'" said MacFarland.

"Well, it's sort of like tools or things." Gracie began to squirm as she tried to explain what they were doing.

MacFarland eyed the woman sternly. "Gracie, are you two getting involved with something you shouldn't be?"

"Oh, no, Mac, not us," she said quickly. "It's just, well, down at this construction site, they must have a lot of extra tools and things they don't need, because some of the people there get some of us to sell the stuff for them."

MacFarland looked at Gracie in disbelief. "Gracie, that doesn't make sense. Who is getting you to sell things for them? Do you buy the tools from someone?"

"No, that's the beauty of it," said Gracie, smiling

broadly. "We don't need any upfront money. We sell the tools on consignment. I think that's what they call it."

"What kind of tools are we talking about?" asked MacFarland.

Gracie shrugged. "Drills, saws, some hand tools. The only problem is, finding places to sell them. It's not as easy as it sounds. Fortunately, Bozworth knows lots of places that can buy the tools. He's got lots of connections, you know."

"Bozworth is tied up in this?"

"He got tied up in it when they asked us to sell the tools."

"What do you get out of it?"

"We get half. We have to give the other half back to the people who gave us the tools to sell. It's not always tools. Sometimes it's things like wire. Mostly stuff that they don't need at the construction site."

"Gracie, I don't think this operation is legal."

Gracie looked uneasily at Kirk, then tried to shrug. "It's not really us who is doing it. We just know that some others are doing it."

MacFarland handed Gracie her own hot dog. "I'm not going to turn you in, Gracie, but I am going to warn you to stay away from whatever is going on there. If someone is breaking the law, it's going to be people like you and Kirk who take the fall. Whoever is doing this is just using you. When someone discovers that they are missing tools or copper wire or other materials, it will be you and anyone else who is helping them who will get the blame."

Gracie looked down at the ground sheepishly. "As I said, Mac, it isn't us who's doing it. It's somebody else. We just heard about it."

CHAPTER TWENTY

THURSDAY, APRIL 7, 0915 HOURS

MACFARLAND WONDERED if he should have been more direct with Kirk and Gracie. He was certain that despite her protestations to the contrary, she and Kirk were trying to fence stolen property. He decided that the best strategy would be to talk directly with Bozworth and apprise him of the consequences of this illegal scam that they were all involved with. He was somewhat disappointed to hear of Bozworth's connection. He had hoped that the informal leader of the homeless community would show more common sense. He wondered if Pierson was aware of what Bozworth was doing.

He had a chance to ask her, less than an hour later. She and her partner, Benny Lockwood, strolled over to his cart.

"Got some bad news, Mac," she said by way of greeting.

"You can't pay for your coffee?" asked MacFarland.

Lockwood feigned a look of surprise. "You mean he expects us to pay for it? What happened to good old-fashioned extortion and police protection?"

"I think I'd actually have to get some protection for that to work," said MacFarland. "I seriously doubt that a scrawny skeleton like you would provide much protection."

"I could provide more protection than you, old man!" laughed Lockwood.

"Okay, boys, stop with all the testosterone. We're here on serious business." She looked at the menu. "I guess I'll stick with just coffee."

"Me, too," chimed Lockwood.

MacFarland poured out two cups of coffee. "So what is your bad news?"

"I looked over the police incident report and it really does look like it was just an unfortunate accident. The responding officer cited several witnesses who said that the kid was just too close to the steel girders when the chain snapped open. The load shifted, and there was nothing the crane operator could do to avoid having the loose girders swing down and crush the kid. It didn't help that the kid was standing in the restricted zone. Guess you're not supposed to be in that area when the load is being moved off the truck."

"Did you get a copy of the safety report?"

"No, the incident was closed out later that afternoon. The incident report didn't include the safety report. That came out a week later. I thought you had a copy of it."

"I do. I just wanted to make sure it was not doctored in any way. As far as the incident report, I wasn't really expecting much more. I just hoped that maybe a trained cop would have seen something that others might have missed."

Pierson frowned. "There was one comment. The officer who handled the incident, Bill Smith, did observe that there were several managers around, watching the unloading. He listed their names and titles."

"Who were they?"

"Ryan Boyce, Riley Vogel, and Norm Pelligrini. What struck me as odd was his note that Pelligrini, who is the president of the company, stated, and I quote, that he rarely visits the job site, yet he had the bad fortune to be there the day they had their first fatality."

MacFarland nodded. "I think the first two would be expected to be there. Did Pelligrini say why he was there that day? As I recall, this accident occurred pretty early in the day."

"He stated that he was there for a meeting with Vogel. Apparently Vogel is his right hand man."

"That sounds right. Vogel is the site superintendent. Who else was there?"

She handed him a paper. "I knew you would ask for that, so I made a copy of the incident report. Another five or six workers in the immediate vicinity, plus the driver of the truck. The driver was not involved in the off-loading procedure, which he stated is not uncommon for loads of this nature. The customer is responsible for moving the steel into their loading area. He just drives the truck away once it is unloaded."

MacFarland looked discouraged. "Any other comments or observations?"

Pierson smiled. Her voice was teasingly provocative. "Just one minor discrepancy, Mac."

MacFarland glared at her. "Okay, what was the discrepancy, Cyn?"

"When the cops interviewed him, the delivery truck driver--Jake Wade--said that they did the procedures for readying the truck for off-loading the night before. He had arrived late, and they didn't want to actually off-load at night, so Forrester Equipment put him up at a hotel for the night."

"So?"

"They also did the preparation for attaching the chains around the load that they would use to hoist the steel off the truck. He says that they did all the safety checks that night. Now, here's where it gets interesting. First, Wade makes no comment about whether the Safety Inspector was drunk or not. It just doesn't come up in the conversation."

"Go on," urged MacFarland.

"Second, the driver says that he was surprised that the next morning, they didn't repeat the safety check. In fact, the Safety Inspector wasn't even on site."

"Why is that significant?"

"I had the same question. I followed up with Wade by phone. I asked him why that was important enough for him to mention it. He said that something could have happened overnight that would change the conditions the load was in. He wasn't specific. He just said that his company would repeat the safety inspection if that much time elapsed. Then he said something that was even more interesting."

"Come on, Pierson! Spill it!"

Lockwood laughed at MacFarland's impatience, while Pierson gloated in being able to string him along. "When the Safety Review Board interviewed him, he mentioned that concern, but he said that it was not in the final findings of the Board's report. Wade complained to his management, but he was told that their company was exonerated and to just drop it. I also asked him if he saw anything unusual about the Safety Inspector. He said no. When I pressed him about the man--Hightower--being drunk, Wade said that he didn't get the impression that he was drunk, or he himself would have objected."

Pierson got a smug look on her face. "Now, I don't know if that helps in your murder investigation, Mac, but if I were the management of Forrester Equipment and Construction Company, I would be worried about a wrongful death lawsuit. I think you should introduce Mrs. Brady to Jerry Baker."

CHAPTER TWENTY-ONE

FRIDAY, APRIL 8, 0945 HOURS

BY FRIDAY MORNING, MacFarland decided that he had to determine once and for all whether Brady's accident was just that or something more. Fortunately, Rufus Headley did show up this morning, and MacFarland asked him to watch his cart for a while. Rufus seemed more than pleased with the responsibility. "No meetings this morning, boss. Everyone's on vacation."

MacFarland was not really sure who "everyone" was; he was not even sure they were real people. Rufus spent a considerable part of his waking hours living in an imaginary world, populated by ghosts and spirits of past warriors, friends and foes. MacFarland preferred having Rufus engaged in 'real world' activities. Even if Rufus gave away his product, MacFarland believed it was better for Rufus to spend more time in this reality than his imaginary one. Just the same, he reminded Rufus to charge the prices listed on the menu sign.

"Sure thing, boss, always do."

At nine forty-five, MacFarland was confident enough

that Rufus was sufficiently in control of reality that he could be trusted with the wagon. MacFarland headed towards the Forrester Equipment and Construction site. Picket was in the guard booth, and as MacFarland approached the entranceway, Picket came out and blocked his path.

"What do you want?" he demanded. He stood with his chest thrust out, one hand on his utility belt, the other hand resting on the top of his holster. If he was trying to be intimidating, he was doing a poor job of it.

"I want to talk to Mr. Boyce," said MacFarland politely. "Where can I find him?"

Picket blinked, and pointed towards a trailer that had been converted into offices. Without waiting, MacFarland walked past Picket and headed towards the office. He could tell that Picket was hurrying back into the guard shack, probably with the intent of calling Boyce and letting him know that MacFarland was on his way. When MacFarland reached the trailer, he climbed up the steps and pushed the door open.

The inside of the trailer was crowded with four desks aligned along one side of the trailer, file cabinets placed along the back wall, and a table in the middle of the trailer. The table was covered with blueprints and papers. A secretary sat at the first desk. She looked up expectantly at MacFarland, who simply pointed towards Boyce, sitting at the third desk down. Another man was sitting at the fourth desk. He glanced at MacFarland, but went back to his computer.

Boyce was holding a phone, which he put back in the cradle. "I thought I told you to stay the hell away from here," he said.

"I have some questions for you," said MacFarland.

"Why should I answer any questions from you?"

MacFarland smiled. "You don't want to be named in a wrongful death lawsuit do you?"

MacFarland noticed that he not only got Boyce's attention, but that of the other two people in the room. The secretary pretended to be reading a sheet of paper, while the man in the back of the room closed his computer and stared intently at MacFarland.

"I don't know what you're talking about," said Boyce. "Are you referring to Brady? That was an unfortunate accident, nothing more. We have the safety board's report on that."

"Were you there that morning, when the alleged accident happened?"

"No, I wasn't there. I came out when I heard the shouting."

MacFarland could tell by the surprised look on the secretary's face that Boyce was lying. "That's not what the police report says, Boyce. Better get your story straight. When you get on the witness stand, little things like that can come back and bite you in the ass."

"Ok, maybe I was out there. So what? That doesn't mean a thing."

"Oh, I think you'll find it means quite a bit, Boyce, when a good lawyer points out to a jury that it was your responsibility as a member management to make sure that the offload process was correctly followed. But it wasn't correctly followed, was it? You took some shortcuts that day. Whose idea was that? Yours? Or Vogel's? Who made the decision to blame the Safety Inspector?"

Boyce looked pale, but he quickly recovered his composure. "I think you've wasted enough of my time, mister. Now, get the fuck out of here. Janet, if he doesn't leave immediately, call the police."

MacFarland held up his hand, then turned towards the door. "I would think very carefully about getting a good lawyer, Boyce. You're going to need one real soon." He smiled briefly at Janet as he left, noting that she had made no move to call the police.

As he passed the guard shack, he stopped until he got Picket's attention. "I don't see Wanda today. Is it her day off?"

Picket looked towards the crane, then scratched his head. "I haven't seen her. I don't think it's her day off. Come to think of it, she didn't come in yesterday either. Not like her to miss work."

CHAPTER TWENTY-TWO

FRIDAY, APRIL 8, 1115 HOURS

MACFARLAND HEADED BACK towards his hot dog stand. Rufus snapped to attention as MacFarland neared the cart. "All done, boss?"

"Do you mind watching it a bit longer?" asked MacFarland.

Rufus looked at his wrist. He didn't have a watch, but he seemed to consult some imaginary timepiece. "Yeah, boss, I got a while before my next meeting. I can watch the cart for you."

MacFarland smiled. "Thanks, Rufus."

MacFarland retrieved in his truck and drove up towards Lincoln. When he got to Colfax, he turned right and headed east. Hightower lived in the Northeast Park Hill area. He was hoping that the man was home. He didn't have a phone number for Hightower, just an address. Traffic was heavier than he expected, and it took him almost half an hour to reach Hightower's residence. MacFarland parked in front of the house, walked past a blue, dented Chevy, and knocked on the front door. As he stood there waiting for someone to answer, he looked around. A painted gnome stood guard by front door. The neighborhood was deserted, with most people at work, most kids in school. MacFarland did not see any pedestrians, though he did see a black Suburban SUV drive slowly by the house. The driver was peering out a partially opened window, so all MacFarland could see was the top of the man's head. When the man saw MacFarland staring at him, he sped up and turned a corner, driving out of sight. After a pause, MacFarland knocked again. Another minute went by, then he heard chains being unhooked and locks turned. Slowly the door opened and a man peered out.

"Louis Hightower? My name is Mark MacFarland. May I have a few minutes of your time?"

The door opened wider. Hightower, dressed in jeans, a white tee-shirt, and sandals, propped up the door jamb. MacFarland could tell that the man had been drinking. He looked to be in his early thirties, six feet one inch tall, and one hundred ninety pounds. He had an oval face with a square chin, high bushy eyebrows, and large fleshy lips. Today he sported a two-day growth of beard. He offered his hand, a large, firm slab of flesh. "Did Wanda send you over? She said that she wanted me to talk to you."

MacFarland shook Hightower's hand, trying not to wince at the man's tight squeeze, and shook his head. "No, I came here on my own."

"Oh," said Hightower. MacFarland could discern a slight Texas drawl in his speech. "She was here on Wednesday, said she would get in touch with you. Ask you to come see me. Timing is a bit coincidental, then."

MacFarland shrugged. "Yes, it really is just a coincidence. But I am here because of Wanda. I wanted to get your impression of the accident. I'm not really sure there is anything other than accidental death here, but some things aren't adding up."

"Tell me about it!" laughed Hightower, but his tone was tinged with bitterness. "Hey, you want a beer?"

MacFarland shook his head. "Too early in the morning for me," he said. He never wanted to admit that he was a recovering alcoholic. It seemed like too much an admission of failure, even though he knew that wasn't true. He waited while Hightower went into the kitchen and came back with a PBR. Maybe it was true that he was drunk the morning of the accident. "I wanted to ask you about what happened the day of the accident."

"I can tell you it wasn't an accident," said Hightower. Despite the beer, his speech wasn't slurred or impaired. He gestured towards a couch. "Have a seat. I think someone tampered with the lifting chains."

"You examined them on Friday?"

"Yeah, Friday night. I'm about to go home and Vogel tells me that a truck is coming in late. He wants to prep it for an early morning unloading. Doesn't want to do the unloading at night, though we've done those before. I figure, what the hell, overtime won't hurt, so a bunch of us stay and wait for the truck. It gets there at about nine-twenty. We do all the standard things..."

"What are the standard things?"

"Make sure the truck bed is level, chock the truck, verify that the load hasn't shifted, put the hoisting chains on it. My only part is to sign off on the entire prep plan and make sure the connectors on the hoisting chains are secured properly. I did that. Everything was fine."

"The review board said that you were intoxicated that night."

"That's bullshit, man! I wasn't drunk that night, not

then at least. Fuck, after we had the truck secured, some of the guys and me go out and have a few beers, that's all. Hell, it was Vogel who suggested it. The next morning, when I come in to work, they give me one of those Breathalyzer tests. Say I am too intoxicated to work, send me home. How much alcohol could I have after sleeping that night? If anything, I was tired, not drunk."

"That's not when you got fired?"

"No, that wasn't until a week later. I came back to work on Monday, just to find that everything is shut down while they conduct the investigation. I was devastated when I heard Brady got killed. I liked that kid. Real bright, had a future in front of him. Wanda thinks he got killed because he had some dirt on management."

"What do you think?"

"I don't know about the dirt, but I do think someone killed him. There was no reason those chains should have come loose. I was not drunk when I examined those connections, no matter what some dumbass review board says."

"What's your relationship with Vogel?" asked MacFarland.

Hightower rubbed his eyes, then took a deep swallow of beer. "I guess we get along okay. I just do my job and try to avoid contact with him. I don't usually socialize with him. That's why I was so surprised when he asked me to join the guys for drinks. That doesn't happen very often, you know."

MacFarland could tell that Hightower was leaving a lot out of the discussion. "Isn't he your supervisor? Sounds like it would be challenging not to have contact with him."

"Vogel is a bit of a redneck," said Hightower slowly, rubbing his own neck. "I don't get the impression he likes blacks."

"Anything in particular that indicates that?"

Hightower took another sip of beer. He seemed to loosen up a bit. "Let me put it in these terms. I have a civil engineering degree from the University of Texas, and I'm stuck in a job of Safety Engineer?"

MacFarland had no idea if that was good or bad. "What kind of job should you have?"

"I applied for a job in the engineering section. Nothing was available when I hired on, so I took this job. But since then, three positions have opened up. Vogel has blocked me getting those jobs all three times. The guy has it in for me, I'd say."

"There may be other factors involved, Mr. Hightower."

Hightower laughed bitterly. "What would you know? You come from a privileged life. Try living as a black man and you will see what really goes on in this country. I'm not the kind of guy that cries prejudice every time something doesn't work out for me, but in this case, I know it when I see it. That damn fucker just doesn't want to see a black man get ahead."

MacFarland wasn't sure what to say. He didn't think that he lived a particularly privileged life, not after having lived on the streets for a couple of years. But he would never question that racism still existed in America. Whether Vogel was a racist or not was probably not relevant. What was relevant was that there was animosity between Hightower and Vogel. How that affected Brady's death, however, was unclear to MacFarland.

MacFarland decided to sidestep the entire issue. "Who would handle the safety inspection if you weren't there?"

"There's another Safety Officer, Tom Quincy. They should have called him into work when they sent me home, but they didn't. Now that there, that's something they shouldn't have done. That truck was unattended all night.

Our procedures say that we should have done a re-check on it the next morning."

"Did you see the Safety Review Board's report?"

"No, they fired me before I could see it. Vogel even told me that I might be criminally liable. Is that possible? Could I go to jail for Brady's death?"

"I'm not a lawyer," said MacFarland. "If you really were drunk when you did the inspection, you might have some liability. But I imagine the site supervisor would also have some liability in that case." He thought for a moment. "Where was Quincy on Saturday?"

"He was probably home. I was supposed to work Saturday, but like I said, they sent me home."

"Who else was at the unloading site?"

"The people you'd expect. The driver--he was off in a safety zone--me, the crane operator, Boyce, the supervisor. Oh, Vogel was there, of course. He's the one who wanted the site prep done that evening."

"Anyone else? Anyone unusual?"

"Yeah, Pelligrini. He's unusual. I'm not sure he was there to see the unloading. That would be really strange. But Pelligrini definitely was there. Norm Pelligrini is the president of Forrester. When he's around, it's usually for the ribbon-cutting photo-ops. He doesn't get his hands dirty, if you know what I mean."

"If someone were embezzling money from the company, would Pelligrini know about it?"

Hightower laughed, caught off-guard by MacFarland's question. "If that were going on, hell, Pelligrini would have to be organizing it. The guy is a skinflint, always cutting corners, trying to save a nickel here, a dime there."

MacFarland stood up, handing Hightower one of his

cards. "If you think of anything else, I would appreciate you giving me a call, Mr. Hightower."

Hightower took the card and dropped it onto an end table near the couch. "Sure thing. And say hi to Busty for me, okay? She's about the only friend I had at that damn place."

MacFarland smiled ruefully and headed out to his truck.

CHAPTER TWENTY-THREE

SATURDAY, APRIL 9, 1620 HOURS

THE NEXT MORNING, as MacFarland set up his cart, he went over the preceding day's conversations. Except for the part about him being drunk, Hightower's description of events mirrored the review board's findings fairly accurately. Hightower said that he hadn't seen the final report, but MacFarland had no certainty that was true. Someone, perhaps Warren herself, might have given a copy of the report to Hightower.

One of Hightower's comments still bothered him. When he first greeted Hightower, the man had said that he had seen Warren on Wednesday, and that she wanted Hightower to talk to him. Why hadn't she come by and mentioned that? Had she given up on MacFarland, decided that he wasn't going to help her, so she stopped confiding in him? Perhaps she realized that despite all the coincidences, there really was no crime--just a terrible accident. Someone —Picket—had said she wasn't at work either. What would keep her away from work? Where was she then?

Business began to pick up, surprisingly for a Saturday.

But this was one of those exceptional spring days in Denver when the sun shone brightly, and strong, moist breezes from the south warmed the air as it climbed up the slopes to meet the cooler air over the mountains. There would be a spring storm in the mountains, but Denver would remain dry. He didn't get a chance to think about Wanda or the accident for most of the day as tourists flocked around the Mint, the courthouse, and even the jail. He was surprised at the number of people who took an interest in the city's lock-up until a passing policeman told him that the Sheriff was trying to show the more humane side of law enforcement, so there was an "open house" at the detention center. "Christ, it's not supposed to be a resort!" grumbled MacFarland. The cop agreed with him, waving as he walked away with a free hot dog. MacFarland believed in maintaining good relations with the people who served and protected him.

"I woulda charged him double, boss," said Rufus, making a rare afternoon appearance.

"You don't like cops?" asked MacFarland. He knew that Rufus had had several run-ins with Denver's finest over the past several years.

"I like some cops," said Rufus. "I like Officer Roz. Officer Roz is pretty nice. I'd give her a hot dog for nothing. But the rest of 'em?" He shrugged.

Officer Roz--Roz Cavenaugh--patrolled the Platte River Park area. Usually she rode a bicycle, which allowed her to traverse the bike and pedestrian paths along the river. She had a reputation for being a friend to the homeless and youth she often encountered along the river. "When Officer Roz kicks you out, she does it nicely," Rufus once explained. "She makes it so that you want to leave, just to please her." MacFarland also knew that Roz Cavenaugh was one of the toughest lady cops on the force. She was sugar and spice until you pissed her off. Then the best tactic an offender could adopt was--run!

It was getting close to four-twenty in the afternoon, when MacFarland noticed one of the construction workers veering away from the crowd walking towards their parked cars. The man came up to MacFarland's cart and asked for a cup of coffee. As MacFarland filled the cup, the man asked, "Are you the guy that Busty talked to?"

MacFarland was probably sure that Warren had talked to a lot of guys, but he figured that this must involve Wanda's concern over the accidental death. "Yes, I am," he said.

"Then there's something you need to know."

MacFarland looked up and stared at the man. He hadn't seen him before, but with sixty to eighty people working at the construction site at any given time, that was not surprising. "What?"

"Wanda's in the hospital," said the man. "Someone beat the crap out of her Wednesday night." The man dropped a dollar bill on the surface of the cart and took his coffee. "You didn't hear this from me. I don't know what shit Wanda is getting involved in, but I want to stay clear of it."

The man walked away, heading for the parking lot used by the construction workers. MacFarland pulled out his phone and glanced towards Rufus.

"You need me to watch the cart, boss?"

MacFarland nodded as he punched in Pierson's cell number. "Cyn, I need your help. Wanda Warren is in the hospital. Can you find out which one?"

"What am I, you're fucking secretary?"

"Come on, I'm serious."

"I know. I just don't want you taking advantage of me."

"You know you love it," MacFarland said.

"Here it is," said Pierson. "She's at Swedish Medical Center. I have her in room 322, but check with the front desk."

"Thanks, Cyn, I owe you."

"More than you can imagine."

MacFarland drove out to the hospital, parked and hurried inside. He asked for Wanda Warren and was directed to her room. The door was closed when he arrived. He knocked softly, and pushed the door open. Wanda was sitting up in the bed, staring at a television. There was no sound, so he wasn't sure if she was really watching the screen or just staring into space. She turned to look at him as he entered. Her face lit up with recognition, but if she tried to smile, she failed. Her face was puffy and badly bruised. A bandage, looking like a turban, covered her head. From what he could see of the exposed areas of her body, she had additional bandages on her hands and arms. She was wearing a neck brace, and one of her arms was in a sling. It wasn't in a cast, at least as far as he could tell.

"Hello Wanda," he said, approaching the bed. "I just found out that you were here."

"I wanted to call you," she said slowly, as if she had trouble forming the words. "Today is the first day I could actually talk."

"Do you know who did this to you?"

Wanda tried to shake her head, but couldn't. All she could do was wave her body back and forth slightly. "It was dark, and whoever it was jumped me from behind. I do think there were two of them."

"Have you filed a police report?"

"I think one was filed when I was brought in. And then a policeman from Aurora came in and took a statement from me this morning."

"When did this happen?"

"Wednesday night, after I left Louis Hightower's house. Someone must have followed me from his house. I didn't think much about it at the time, but I did think that someone was following me. I should have been more careful. I got out to go into a 7-Eleven and when I returned to my car, I was pulled to the back of the building. I tried to scream, but I am more of a fighter than a screamer, you know. Maybe if I screamed more, I wouldn't have been so badly beaten up."

"You think someone followed you from Hightower's house?"

"That's the impression I got."

"Do you remember anything about the car? Make and year?"

Wanda tried unsuccessfully again to shake her head. "I didn't pay that much attention. I think it was a dark color, blue or black. It might have been dark green. That's all I remember about it."

Warren had seen the car at night. That would affect her perception of its color. And since she had not been focusing on the car, its color wouldn't stand out. It might have been the same car that MacFarland saw, but he had no real evidence of that. Just that feeling in the pit of his stomach. While he couldn't be certain that the car he saw was the one that followed Warren, he could be certain of one thing.

Mike Brady's death was looking less and less like an accident.

And someone did not want anyone finding out the truth about the accident.

"It may have taken me a while to decide, Wanda," he said. "But I've decided that you might be right about Brady's death. I'm going to take the case."

For the first time, Warren managed a strained smile. "Thanks, Mac. Now, what do we do next?"

MacFarland laughed briefly, then sobered up when he realized that Warren was serious. "First, you have to get well enough to get out of the hospital. And *we* won't be doing anything. I don't want you getting attacked again."

"I'm a big girl, Mac. I can take care of myself."

MacFarland gave her an exasperated look, which she ignored.

"There is one thing I meant to tell you. I probably should have told you earlier, but I didn't think it was relevant. You know that guard, Picket?" When MacFarland nodded, she went on. "He told me that the night before Mike died, he saw something strange. Vogel came to the job site at like three o'clock in the morning. Picket didn't see where he went or what he did, but he thought it was suspicious, considering what happened the next day."

MacFarland cocked his head inquisitively. "Do you find it suspicious?"

"Not really. First, Vogel will often come in at odd hours, especially when there are three shifts working. He is the site administrator, after all. Now, I don't know if there was a third shift that night, but I still don't think it that strange. I've seen him there at all hours of the day. But it might be important, right?"

MacFarland pursed his lips. "It might be, Wanda. Every little fact helps when you're trying to solve a murder."

Warren's eyes widened. "So you think it's murder, too?"

MacFarland sighed, letting his breath out slowly. "Yes, I do," he said.

CHAPTER TWENTY-FOUR

THURSDAY, APRIL 14, 1450 HOURS

DESPITE HIS PROMISE TO work on the case, in point of fact MacFarland was not able to do much at all for the next several days. Monday morning, when MacFarland started to carry his product out to his cart to load up, he discovered that someone had vandalized his cart during the night. The tires were slashed, graffiti was painted all over the cart, the umbrellas were shredded, and several of the supplementary units--the hot dog warmer, the chip display rack, the menu board--were destroyed or missing. He later found some of the items in the dumpsters in the alley. He brought his product back inside the house, deposited it on the table, and sat down.

When Pierson came down, he told her what happened. After she went out and checked the cart, she examined other areas of her property--the garage, her car and MacFarland's truck, then she checked nearby properties.

"Nothing else was damaged or touched," she announced when she returned. She called the local precinct office, which immediately dispatched a vehicle to the scene.

The officer who arrived took MacFarland's statement, photographed some of the damage, and left, commenting that it looked like gang activity. After he left, MacFarland sat down with Pierson, who handed him a cup of coffee.

"I don't think it was gang activity," he said.

Pierson didn't think so either, but she asked him why not.

"The graffiti looks very similar to what they found at the Brady house. Why would a Thornton gang be operating in Observatory Park?"

"I'll have Schwab in the Gang Unit look at the photographs," said Pierson. "But I am inclined to agree with you. Mac, I think someone doesn't want you looking into Brady's death. Maybe you should let the police handle it."

MacFarland laughed. "Based on what evidence? The case has already been closed."

"I could talk to Chamberlain, get him to re-open it."

"Let me get something more substantial to go on, Cyn. Then we can bring the Department in."

MacFarland spent the better part of three days dealing with the insurance company, repainting his cart, and replacing lost or damaged pieces of equipment. He also had to get new product, since his existing inventory expired. Wednesday evening, he sat quietly in the back of his AA meeting, wishing he could have a drink. His sponsor, Hector Spinoza, tried to cheer him up. "You're doing good, Mark. If you can get through something like this without falling off the wagon, you've got it beat. I know how strong the temptation to get a drink must be. Just hang in there."

MacFarland sighed and promised he would, thinking that he was more concerned about the temptation to knock in a few skulls. Finally, by Thursday morning, everything was back to normal. He set out once more towards his corner.

Rufus met him at seven-fifteen. "Where ya been, boss?"

"Someone tried to put me out of business," said MacFarland. "I have my little push cart for several years, and nothing happens to it. I get this monstrosity and it's damaged after two weeks! Go figure!"

Rufus scratched his head over that comment. "Boss, your first cart was run over by a car. I'd say that it was damaged too."

MacFarland laughed. "You're right, Rufus, as usual. But we're back in business, at least for now. Let's get that coffee brewing!"

The day started out slowly, then picked up as MacFarland's usual customers realized he was back. Lunch period was particularly busy as a crowd of construction workers from the Forrester job site descended on his wagon. MacFarland was surprised at their patronage, particularly since Boyce had indicated that he would try to have his employees boycott MacFarland's wagon. Apparently the rank and file employees had a mind of their own. In fact, one of them mentioned that they knew he was trying to help Warren, and that was their reason for their patronage.

By two o'clock business had slacked off enough that MacFarland was able to resume listening to his language discs. He realized that he had forgotten quite a bit, so he decided to spend a couple of days with intensive review. He was deeply engrossed in future tense verbs when he noticed a customer standing slightly behind him. He turned and regarded the man. The man was in his late fifties or early sixties, ruddy complexion, grey hair and mustache, heavy bags of tired flesh under his eyes. By his clothes, MacFarland suspected that the man was one of the homeless, though he was not someone MacFarland had met before.

"They said you would pay me," said the man.

MacFarland blinked in surprise. "Who told you that, and why would I pay you? In fact, who are you?"

"John Oswald," said the man. "The man in the guard shack over by the construction site. He said you would pay me."

"Okay, pay you for what?" Was the guard Picket? Why wouldn't Picket come and tell him himself? One explanation was that Picket didn't want his management to know that he was helping MacFarland.

"For telling you something."

MacFarland knew he had to be patient. He had no idea how long this man had been on the streets, but he suspected that the man would be easily spooked if MacFarland put too much pressure on him. "What are you supposed to tell me?"

"Oh, yeah. I'm supposed to tell you that Mr. Hightower, he was hit by a car. He was taken to the hospital."

"Hightower? In the hospital? When did the accident happen?" MacFarland stared at Oswald without clearly seeing him. First Wanda, then him, and now Hightower. Pierson was right. Someone did not want him investigating this accident.

"I don't know that. The man didn't say when it happened. You going to pay me, mister?"

He blinked, coming back to the present. "Yeah, I'll give you something, Oswald. Thanks for passing on the information." He checked his cash drawer and pulled out a twenty dollar bill, handing it to Oswald. "You hungry? It's on the house."

He assembled a couple of hot dogs for Oswald and

poured him a cup of coffee. As Oswald meandered off with his coffee and hot dogs, MacFarland picked up his phone.

"Hi, Cyn? Got a minute?" He waited while she handled whoever had been talking to her. "Yeah, I need you to check something for me. What have you got on a Louis Hightower involved in a car accident?"

"Let me check," said Pierson. "While I got you, Schwab did confirm that the graffiti is the same as what they saw in Thornton. He also says that it really is gang graffiti, just not from the Denver area."

"Where's it from?"

"Chicago. He says it's probably a resurgent splinter group of the BPSN. Not much is known about the group, not even its name. Now, here's where it gets really strange, Mac. Schwab and I were talking about this gang, and the Fed broad that's been working with us suddenly chimes in with 'Oh, I know all about that gang.' Schwab and I stand there like two dumbass clowns. What the fuck? So we ask her how she knows about them. And she tells us that the gang works with this drug smuggling cartel they are investigating. Boy, I gotta tell you, the shit really hit the fan then! Even Chamberlain got involved, wondering just what the hell the Feds knew that they weren't sharing. You would have loved it!"

"A Chicago gang that is involved with your drug smuggling group is also involved with Forrester Equipment and Construction?"

MacFarland could almost see Pierson's smug smile. "Seems so, Mac. I think you have really stepped into a big pile of shit. Oh, here is the intel on Hightower. Yep, he was involved in a hit and run accident last night. Over by MLK Boulevard. No witnesses, no cameras nearby." Pierson gave him address of the hospital where Hightower was taken.

"Thanks, Cyn, I owe you."
"More than you can imagine, asshole."

CHAPTER TWENTY-FIVE

FRIDAY, APRIL 15, 1430 HOURS

MACFARLAND WAS NOT able to get to the hospital until the next day. He made arrangements for Rufus to come back later in the morning to take care of his cart, but Rufus didn't show up until after two o'clock. "Sorry boss, meetings, you know."

MacFarland shook his head and hurried towards his truck. When he got to the hospital, he asked for directions to the ICU where Hightower was located. The nurse on duty checked a computer screen, then asked MacFarland what relationship he was to the victim. The nurse said Hightower could not see any visitors. It turned out that being a friend of the victim did not entitle him to any information about Hightower's whereabouts or condition.

As a police officer, he would have been able to get some limited information, particularly since a policeman might be trying to determine who had committed the felony against Hightower. Even under those conditions, however, the hospital would only divulge the information if it could be shown that waiting until Hightower was conscious would materially affect the investigation. Then the hospital would only divulge limited information: name and address, date and place of birth, type of injury, date and time of treatment, and a description of the patient's physical characteristics. Other information might be obtained by court orders, warrants, or other types of requests, none of which MacFarland had.

MacFarland nodded, and headed for the exit. He was about to go through the door when he happened to glance across the nurses' station. He paused, looking intently at the person he saw walking towards the ICU area. It was Riley Vogel. Vogel hadn't seen him yet, concentrating instead on trying to find someone in charge. One of the nurses on Vogel's side of the command center asked him if she could help him.

Now, what was Vogel doing in the hospital? Was the superintendent really that concerned about the welfare of all his employees, especially one that he supposedly disliked so much? Such loyalty was commendable, but hardly believable, especially given the perceived animosity between the two men.

MacFarland slowed his steps. One of the nurses at the station looked up from her desk, but did not say anything. MacFarland moved closer to the exit, making sure that the storage bins and file cabinets obstructed Vogel's view of him. The command area was large enough that Vogel's conversation with the nurse was muffled, but MacFarland did recognize the mention of Hightower's name. He assumed the nurse was telling Vogel the same thing the nurse on this side had told him.

"I need to see him!" Vogel's voice was loud enough that MacFarland had no trouble hearing it. The nurse who had spoken to MacFarland looked over at her companion, who then stood up and went to the other side of the command area. MacFarland could hear her repeating the explanation that she had given him.

Vogel did not seem happy with what she told him, but he turned and headed out of the ICU. MacFarland also left, hurrying towards his car. If Vogel came in through the other wing of the hospital, that meant he probably parked over by the north entrance. MacFarland had parked by the south entrance. If MacFarland could get to his car quickly enough, he might be able to see Vogel come out.

And then he would follow him.

MacFarland smiled to himself. It felt good to be working on a case again!

CHAPTER TWENTY-SIX

FRIDAY, APRIL 15, 1445 HOURS

MACFARLAND RACED along the hospital corridors, raising eyebrows and eliciting at least one admonishment to "watch out." But he did get to his car in time to drive to the other entrance and catch sight of Vogel walking towards his car, a yellow Tercel. As Vogel pulled out of the parking lot, MacFarland was not far behind him.

Following Vogel was not very difficult, even when MacFarland allowed several vehicles to fill the gap between them. Vogel had no idea that anyone was on his tail, and MacFarland made sure that he never got close enough for Vogel to recognize him.

Vogel was going back downtown, heading west on Colfax. When Vogel reached Park Ave, he turned right and headed northwest. When he turned onto Arapahoe, MacFarland began to get a lump in his throat. His wife used to work in this area, in the Consolidated Colorado Properties building. As MacFarland turned the corner, his anxiety became even more acute. Vogel was pulling into one of the visitor's spaces in front of the CCP building. MacFarland drove slowly by, watching in his mirrors as Vogel got out of this car and walked into the building.

MacFarland drove around the block, wanting to verify that Vogel really did park in front of the building. Once he got confirmation, he drove back to his corner. He double parked, ignoring the honks and angry looks that some drivers gave him. Rufus was still on duty--dependable Rufus!--and both men hitched up MacFarland's hot dog cart to his truck. MacFarland offered to drive Rufus over to the Platte River, and surprisingly, Rufus accepted the invitation. It was not very often that Rufus took charity in any form from anyone. Well, except for the daily hot dogs MacFarland gave him.

"You seem down, boss," said Rufus after they had gotten the wagon hooked up.

MacFarland wasn't sure that Rufus was really interested in solving Brady's murder, but he needed to discuss the case with someone. That was one of the ways he solved cases, by reviewing again and again the facts of the case. When he had been on the force, he had always used three-by-five cards to sort all the facts of a case. Other detectives preferred the grease board or a computer, but MacFarland preferred a cork board. He would pin his cards up, shift them about, change their relationship, until the pattern began to mean something to him.

Talking with someone else was not as effective, but it was better than nothing. Besides, every once in a while, Rufus Headley had a remarkably good idea or two.

"One of my suspects, a man named Vogel, went to the hospital to see a man he dislikes. The man in the hospital had been hit by a car and is in a coma."

Rufus wiggled around in the truck seat, trying to get comfortable. He was not used to being in a car, and Denver city traffic made him nervous. "Sorta like the guilty man going back to the scene of the crime?" he suggested.

"That might be one way of looking at it," said MacFarland. "Or he might be legitimately concerned about his employee. But he couldn't see Hightower, because of HIPAA restrictions."

"What is HIPAA restrictions?"

"Rules that protect an individual's medical confidentiality. I couldn't get access to him either, though if I was still on the police force, I could have at least verified that he was in the hospital. Fortunately, Cyn has access to the police report."

"Good thing she's your partner," said Rufus.

She's not my partner anymore, thought MacFarland ruefully. "Yeah. So after Vogel leaves the hospital, I follow him. Know where he goes?"

"Home?"

MacFarland laughed. "No, he went to the CCP Building. I think he went to see Norris Peterson."

"The man who killed your wife?" said Rufus in surprise. "Boss, you seriously thinking he's involved in killing this Brady kid?"

MacFarland shrugged. "I don't know, Rufus, but it sure seems that way. And if he is, I intend to get him for it."

CHAPTER TWENTY-SEVEN

SATURDAY, APRIL 16, 0830 HOURS

THE NEXT MORNING, MacFarland asked Rufus to watch his wagon again. At first Rufus expressed some reluctance, but when MacFarland said that he wanted to go see Bozworth, Rufus readily agreed. Bozworth, more commonly known as Lord Bozworth, was one of the more influential members of the homeless community. He normally plied Colfax Avenue, between Greek Town and Josephine, pushing his shopping cart of possessions up and down the street. He was a conduit of information for the homeless community, often serving as an advisor, mentor, and friend to those who found themselves on the streets. He rarely came downtown, except for Taste of Colorado and Pride-Fest. MacFarland was hoping that he would be able to locate Bozworth without too much difficulty. If nothing else, he might find someone who knew where Lord Bozworth was hanging out.

MacFarland drove east along Colfax, until he got to the I-225 interchange with no sign of Bozworth. He turned around and headed back towards Denver. This time he was luckier. He spied Bozworth sitting outside a 7-Eleven. MacFarland pulled his truck into the store's parking lot and got out. He waved at Bozworth and went over to greet him.

"Lord Bozworth! How are you today?"

Bozworth smiled at MacFarland. "Ah, the Hot Dog Vendor! I fare quite well, my friend, though I confess to having vague memories of better days. But spring is in the air, and soon all this slush and filth will be behind us. The city of Denver will blossom again, the young ladies will don scantier outfits, and old men like me will wish we were youthful again."

"I am sure the young ladies find you charming just as you are," said MacFarland.

"Surely you jest, MacFarland. It has been many a year since a pretty young thing graced my arm. But you didn't come all the way out here to banter with an old man. What can I do for you?"

"Information, Lord Bozworth."

The old man smiled, his eyes sparkled. "Information always flows better with food and beverage," he said. "Unfortunately, the servants are all off on leave, else I would offer you a fine repast. Alas, I have no vittles to offer you, my friend."

MacFarland took the hint. "Perhaps I can get some of those vittles, your Lordship. What would you like?"

A few minutes later, as Lord Bozworth slowly ate his pastry and sausage roll, MacFarland settled down on the ground next to him, sipping on a cup of coffee. After Bozworth had finished, he turned to MacFarland. "Now, my friend, ask away."

"It's about Peterson."

"Ah, yes, the scoundrel who terminated your dear wife's life. A tragic affair, and such a miscarriage of justice that such a cur should run free of the justice he deserves. What can I tell you about him that you don't already know?"

"I think he might be involved with another murder," said MacFarland.

"Indeed! This man does get around. Who has he harmed this time?"

"I don't think he did it directly," said MacFarland.

Bozworth nodded. "Men such as Mr. Peterson rarely get their own hands dirty. They use their wealth and position to influence others to do their dastardly deeds."

"Exactly. I think he is working with a man named Riley Vogel. It's possible that Vogel is the man who actually killed someone. I need to find out if he has any connection with Norris Peterson."

"Mr. Vogel, eh. This gentleman is one with whom I have some acquaintance."

MacFarland was surprised. "How do you know Riley Vogel?"

"He and I have a business relationship," said Bozworth.

"Vogel is behind the scam to sell the stolen tools?"

Bozworth looked indignant. "No one has implied that the goods are pilfered, my good sir! They are used and damaged goods that merit reclamation. We foster the thriving American economy by recycling items that have outlived their original usefulness."

"You are selling stolen goods, Bozworth!" MacFarland could not believe what he was hearing. "Don't you realize that your homeless friends will be the ones who get arrested?"

"Are you prepared to turn us in to the watch, my good friend?"

MacFarland hesitated. "No, but I don't think what is

going on is legal. I'm worried that the most vulnerable will pay the highest price if they get caught."

"A commendable concern, Mr. MacFarland, and a concern that I share. In fact, of late, Mr. Vogel has been somewhat distracted and has not afforded our business arrangement the courtesy and attention it requires. I shall endeavor to curtail the business arrangement, if that would satisfy you."

"Yeah, that would satisfy me, though I wish it had never happened in the first place. You can't trust people like Vogel, Lord Bozworth."

"You can always trust a man to follow his nature, my friend. I know Mr. Vogel's nature. I know what he is capable of doing, and how far he will go."

"And how far is that?"

Bozworth stood up and straightened out his grey coat and cap. "Mr. Vogel is easily capable of going to the extreme of taking a man's life, if it fills his pocket with lucre, Mr. MacFarland. Mr. Vogel is a very greedy man. As for the issue regarding Mr. Peterson, at the moment, my knowledge of the affairs in that part of town are somewhat out of date. Give me a couple of days, and I will procure the necessary intelligence to set your mind at ease."

CHAPTER TWENTY-EIGHT

SATURDAY, APRIL 16, 1025 HOURS

DESPITE WHAT HE TOLD BOZWORTH, MacFarland had another suspect besides Vogel. He hadn't eliminated Boyce as the potential killer, but he needed more than Boyce's disagreeable personality to implicate him. He drove back to his corner, checked with Rufus, who was cheerfully chatting with several homeless associates. MacFarland greeted everyone, then reminded Rufus to give everyone a hot dog or bratwurst. Despite the pleasant weather, MacFarland did not see any other customers around. It was better to give his product away than have it go to waste.

"Already did, boss. We're just shooting the breeze about the upcoming election."

That didn't seem likely, since MacFarland doubted that any of the individuals gathered around his cart had a legal address. He also suspected that they also had no interest in politics. What had he discussed when he was homeless? Weather. Where to get food. Where to sleep. How to avoid harassment. He had never had much interest in politics.

"I have another errand to do, Rufus. Do you mind watching the cart for a bit longer?"

"No problem, boss. We'll take good care of it." As MacFarland headed down the street towards the construction site, he could hear Rufus explaining to the men gathered around the cart that Mac was a famous detective who solved crimes the police couldn't solve. *If only that were true*, thought MacFarland.

When he got to the gate of the site, Picket came out to stop him. "I'm here to see Ryan Boyce," said MacFarland.

"Mr. Boyce isn't here," said Picket. "It's his day off."

"Where can I find him?"

"I suppose he's at home. Where else would he be?"

"Do you know where he lives?"

"I'm not telling you where anyone lives, mister. What do you want to know for anyway?"

"I'm trying to help Wanda Warren," said MacFarland. "She doesn't think Brady's death was really an accident. She thinks someone rigged the chains so that the load would slip."

Picket was silent for a moment. "There aren't many who could get away with that," he said. His voice took on a conspiratorial tone. "If anyone could do it, though, it would be Boyce. He once was a crane operator. He would know how to rig a load safely, and how to rig it so it wasn't safe. You think Boyce was involved?"

"I don't know," said MacFarland. "I would like to find out what Boyce thinks, though. After all, wasn't he the supervisor in charge of the job?"

Picket nodded slowly. "Yeah, he was. But I still can't give you his address."

"I understand." MacFarland turned to go back to his corner, then stopped. "By the way, when you get off your shift, stop by and tell Rufus that I said you could have whatever you want, on the house."

When MacFarland got back to his truck, he called up Pierson. "Hi Cyn, could you do a favor for me?"

"Another one?"

"Last one for today."

"What is it?"

"I need an address for one of the guys that works here at Forrester Equipment and Construction. Ryan Boyce."

"Mac, this is totally inappropriate!" She gave him the address anyway. "Just remember. It wasn't me who gave you the address."

"Thanks, Cyn, you're the best partner a guy ever had."

"Took you long enough to realize it, asshole."

Boyce lived in Federal Heights. MacFarland got onto I-25, headed north, and turned west onto Thornton Parkway. He followed that after it became 92nd Avenue, and then turned south into Boyce's neighborhood. Boyce was in his driveway, washing his car. MacFarland drove up and parked in front of the house. Boyce turned off the hose as MacFarland approached him.

"What the hell are you doing here?" asked Boyce, looking anxiously towards his house. The sounds of young children yelling at each other could be heard coming from the house.

"Just came for a friendly conversation," said MacFarland.

"About what?"

"Wanda seems to think that it was odd that Brady's death was ruled an accident."

"Yeah, I know all about that. She thinks it wasn't accidental."

"What do you think?"

"I think the review board found that it was negligence on the part of Hightower. If he had been doing his job, Brady would still be alive."

"I was told that you used to be a crane operator."

"Still am. My license is up to date. Just have more opportunities for advancement in management."

"That's right, you were Brady's supervisor."

"I supervise a crew of fifteen guys. So what?"

"It just seems to me that when they actually did the job Saturday morning, they should have done a re-inspection of the lifting cables."

Boyce's expression hardened, and his face became flushed. "They should have. But Vogel found out that Hightower was drunk and sent him home."

"Seems like they should have found someone else to do the inspection."

"Vogel wanted to get the load off the truck right away. It would take too long to get the other safety inspector in."

"Wouldn't you know what to look for in cable rigging?"

"Hey, don't try to lay this at my feet! What are you accusing me of?"

MacFarland held his hands up, smiling broadly and using his 'good cop' voice. "Ryan, I'm not accusing you of anything. I'm just trying to find out exactly what happened that day, that's all. But it does seem to me that you would have known how the load should have been set up for lifting off the truck. Why didn't you do an inspection? Or did you? Then it would seem to me that if you didn't find anything wrong with the setup, Hightower was wrongfully fired."

"Vogel wouldn't let me inspect it," snapped Boyce. "Besides, I told you, he wanted to get the job finished quickly. I'm certified to operate cranes, not do safety inspections. They are two entirely different things. We pay for all the time the truck and driver are on the site. If anyone was responsible for Brady's death, it was that asshole Vogel!"

"Unfortunately, being an asshole is not a crime," said MacFarland.

"If it was, then Riley Vogel would be facing life imprisonment."

CHAPTER TWENTY-NINE

SATURDAY, APRIL 16, 1210 HOURS

SINCE MACFARLAND WAS in the area where Shirley Brady lived, he called her up and asked to see her. She said she would be home at noon, and he could come over then. He stopped off at a McDonald's and got a cup of coffee. He started to review what he had learned. Then, feeling frustrated, he jumped back into his truck and drove until he found an OfficeMax. He bought some colored markers and several packs of three-by-five cards and headed back to the McDonalds. There, he began to write down the facts and details of the case, using a system that he had devised many years earlier.

Each card contained essentially one fact, event, or piece of evidence, written in the center of the card. At the top of the card, he wrote the date that the fact or event occurred. At the bottom of the card, he wrote the date that he learned of the fact and its source. Beneath the "factoid" as Pierson used to call them, he would write in pencil any questions he had about the fact.

When he finished, he had about thirty-six cards

prepared. Some of his dates and sources were approximations, since his memory of when he obtained the information or when it occurred was vague. But he would try to update the cards later. Now he had to go see Shirley Brady.

As he drove towards her house, he began to feel more in control of his life. He was getting back into doing what he always enjoyed. Amazing what three-by-five cards could do!

Shirley Brady was just pulling into the driveway when he arrived. He helped her carry in several bags of groceries as she struggled with her baby, her car seat and the diaper bag. Once inside, Shirley suggested he sit at the kitchen table as she put the groceries away. MacFarland busied himself making cooing noises at the baby, who cooed right back.

"What can I do for you, Mr. MacFarland?" she asked as she put milk and eggs into the refrigerator.

"I was just wondering if you or Mike have ever lived in the Chicago area."

Shirley shook her head. "No, we're both from Colorado. I grew up in Colorado Springs, and Mike grew up in Fort Collins. Why? What's with Chicago?"

"There is some evidence that the gang that broke into your house is based out of Chicago."

Shirley looked perplexed. "I don't think either of us have even been to Chicago. I don't see how that has any connection to us."

"It probably doesn't," said MacFarland. "I just had to check. By the way, any progress on getting the insurance money settled?"

"No, they are still dragging their feet. Riley says that there is no reason for that, and he keeps telling them to speed it up."

"Riley Vogel?"

Shirley nodded as she put away a box of cereal. "Yes, he's been very helpful since the accident."

"Were you and Mike close to Vogel before the accident?"

"No, not really. We had seen each other at last year's Christmas party, but other than that, we didn't have much contact with the Vogels."

"But since the accident?"

"Well, since then, Mr. Vogel has been quite helpful. He feels bad that the accident happened, and he wants to make sure I'm alright. He's even given me some money to tide me over until the insurance is paid out."

"That's very generous of him. How much has he given you?"

Shirley hesitated, then said, "Five thousand dollars. He says I can pay it back when the insurance money comes."

"When did he give it to you?"

Shirley frowned, trying to remember. "It was last week. Yes, Thursday. I remember, because I talked to you on Tuesday, and I was all worried about finances. It was like a Godsend!"

"He didn't demand anything from you, does he?"

"Mr. MacFarland! What a terrible thing to suggest! Riley is like a father to me! I would never do anything like that! He would never ask me to do that kind of thing."

"I didn't mean to suggest that, Shirley," said MacFarland quickly. "I was thinking more like asking you not to make any problems for the company. Like a lawsuit."

Shirley Brady was breathing heavily. Slowly she calmed down, then she sat at the table. "A lawsuit? For what?"

MacFarland slowly described some of the apparent safety oversights the company had committed, finally adding, "I think you might have reason to suspect negligence on the part of Forrester Equipment and Construction."

"I would need a lawyer, wouldn't I?"

MacFarland nodded. "I can suggest someone, a friend of mine." He handed her one of Jerry Baker's cards.

Shirley examined the card, then blushed. "I can't really afford a lawyer, Mr. MacFarland."

"I'll talk to Jerry. Tell him not to charge you unless you actually win your case. But don't accept any more money from Vogel, Shirley."

"What about the money he's already given me?"

"Talk to Jerry about that. He can help you."

CHAPTER THIRTY

SATURDAY, APRIL 16, 1445 HOURS

AS MACFARLAND SAT in his vehicle, he pulled out his stack of cards and filled out a new one. The card had the following information on it:

4/7 Thursday
Vogel gave Shirley Brady $5000
- Hush money?
- Who has $5000 laying around?
4/16 Shirley Brady

He put the cards back into his shirt pocket and prepared to drive back downtown.

On the spur of the moment, he detoured off of I-25 to get onto 22nd Avenue. He drove over to the CCP building and parked in front. As he entered the building, he told himself that he had only one intention. He wanted to confront Peterson and find out what his connection with Vogel really was. He wasn't going to get violent. Not this time. He just wanted to verify that Peterson was deeply involved in Brady's death and cover-up.

But as he entered the lobby of the building, he stopped up short. The names on the building's directory caught his attention.

There, staring him right in the face, was the name Forrester Equipment and Construction. Second Floor.

MacFarland's shoulders slumped as he continued to stare at the directory. The guard at the lobby desk looked at him expectantly, but MacFarland ignored him. He realized that all his assumptions had been wrong.

Vogel hadn't come in here to see Norris Peterson. He had come in to see his boss, Norm Pelligrini.

There was no connection between Vogel and Peterson after all. As Pierson had said, just because Peterson owned one company did not mean that he was connected to every death that occurred.

He had been walking on clouds just a few hours earlier. Now he felt like the world was falling apart. He turned, got back into his truck, and drove back to his hot dog cart.

CHAPTER THIRTY-ONE

SUNDAY, APRIL 17, 0925 HOURS

MACFARLAND AVOIDED contact with Pierson that evening. He was fearful that he would inadvertently blurt out that he had checked out the CCP building and would be forced to admit that Pierson was right all along. He didn't want to admit that his hatred of the man who killed his wife was affecting his judgment on the case. Also, as much as he appreciated her help, he really resented her smugness when she was able to prove him wrong.

Of course, he told himself, that didn't happen very often.

By the next morning, he had forgotten that he was trying to avoid talking to Pierson. For once Pierson was in a good mood. She had even gotten up early and made French toast for breakfast. "Don't go to work today," she urged MacFarland. "Let's do something fun."

Fun was not a word that MacFarland associated with Pierson, unless it included slapping handcuffs on a scumbag and dragging him off to jail. "What did you have in mind?" he asked, trying to hide his hesitancy.

"I was thinking that we might go to the gun range. I feel a bit rusty, and after your unfortunate encounter last month, I think you need some practice too."

MacFarland stared at her in disbelief. "I'm a hot dog vendor. I don't need a gun."

Pierson glared at him with a look of extreme disdain. "I'm not suggesting that you carry a gun with you when you're working. But I worry that you might be out of practice for those times when you really need to use a gun."

"Just when is that?" he asked.

"Get your jacket, gun and ammo, asshole."

Pierson insisted on driving, even though MacFarland said that his Ford F-150 would be more at home in the parking lot of a gun range. "Get real, Mac, I'm more of a redneck than you."

"That's only because you have red hair and it leaves this reddish sheen on your neck."

Pierson drove out to Aurora, to a range that she and MacFarland had used one or two times in the past. The owner of the range, David O'Neil, a man in his late sixties, was sitting behind the counter. He beamed happily when he saw Pierson walk in the door.

"Cynthia!" He came around the counter and grabbed her in a bear hug, lifting her off the ground. He was a big man, dwarfing MacFarland.

"Mac, this is my Uncle Dave. Dave, this is my former partner, Mark MacFarland."

Uncle Dave held out a beefy, powerful hand. "Name's David O'Neil, Mac. I remember you. You and little Cynful were out here a couple of times, what, almost six years ago?"

MacFarland nodded, staring at Uncle Dave, trying to remember him. He couldn't, which was strange, since Uncle Dave was not someone you could easily forget. David

O'Neil looked neither Irish nor like Pierson's uncle. He was as black as Pierson was white.

"Uncle Dave and my father met in the Army, Mac. Then they lost track of each other until they found each other in Japan and discovered that they both worked for the same government agency. I think Uncle Dave was daddy's closest friend ever."

"Neal was like a brother to me," said O'Neil. He took Pierson's hand. "You still taking down bad guys, Cynful?"

Pierson smiled. "I try, Uncle Dave. I keep fighting the good fight."

"That's my girl. But you didn't come out here to chat with me. Let's get you two signed in and on the range."

MacFarland had his Glock, while Pierson had brought her Wilson Combat 1911. "I never get enough opportunities to use this," she explained.

They spent almost four hours at the gun range, an experience that MacFarland found that he began to enjoy more and more. He wasn't as out of practice as Pierson suggested, but his shooting was not as accurate and reliable as it had been when he was still on the force. It took more than one session to make substantial improvements, but even in the four hour period, he felt more confidence in his skills. The fact that Pierson actually complimented his shooting several times was a true testament to his improved performance.

As they prepared to leave, O'Neil caught up with them. "Don't be a stranger, Cynthia. You know your daddy left you in my care."

Pierson smiled and kissed him on the cheek. "Don't you be a stranger either, Uncle Dave. You should come over for dinner some time. Mac is an excellent cook, you know."

O'Neil glanced at MacFarland, his look almost questioning whether he wanted MacFarland to be living in the same house as his 'niece.' "I'll do that," he promised.

As Pierson drove them back to her house, MacFarland had dozens of questions about David O'Neil, but he suppressed them. Pierson didn't talk much about her parents or what happened to them, and certainly had not mentioned anything about what her father did. What little he knew was limited to "my parents were killed in a car crash in 2004." Instead, he turned the conversation back to his case. He told her about his conversations the previous day. "I get bad vibes from Vogel," he said. "I also wonder why he is taking such a sudden interest in Mrs. Brady. They weren't that close before Mike's death. Why now? And where did he get that much money to just loan her? It doesn't feel right, Cyn. Would it be possible for you to look into Vogel's finances?"

"What specifically are you looking for?" she asked.

"I want to know where he got the five thousand dollars. From savings? Or did he get it from Forrester's coffers?"

"You know I can't get that information without a court order."

"Then get one."

"Mac, Brady's death is a closed case."

"Get Chamberlain to reopen it. Just a while ago you wanted to do that."

"On what basis?"

"Conspiracy to commit murder."

"We don't have any evidence of that, Mac. I can't get Chamberlain to reopen a case just because you have suspicions. I've already talked to him about it. And certainly no judge in Denver is going to grant a bank search based on something as flimsy as Vogel suddenly flashing five thousand dollars. You know how the system works. Stop trying to bypass it."

"Then I will just have to find methods outside of the system, won't I?"

"Are you going to do something that I am going to have to arrest you for? Because I will. You know I will."

"No, you won't, you love me."

"You're an asshole," said Pierson.

"That's what you tell me every day," he said.

CHAPTER THIRTY-TWO

SUNDAY, APRIL 17, 1240 HOURS

ONCE THEY ARRIVED HOME, MacFarland did not stay put. He headed back downtown and found a place to park not far from Her Bar. He went inside, sat down at the bar counter, and ordered a coffee from the young bartender. "Is Jody around?" he asked.

The bartender pointed upstairs to the upper lounge area. Jody B used this area as a game room, library, and lounge area. She liked to sit up here, often with her girlfriend sitting by her side, as she worked on her activist blog. Jody B could stay out of sight, yet still look down on the public bar area. He carried his coffee up the stairs and spotted Jody B sitting at one of the computer terminals. "Hi Jody, got a minute?"

Jody B looked up, then continued typing vigorously. "Let me just finish this, and then I will give you my undivided attention." She didn't wait for a response, but redoubled her efforts on the computer.

Jody B's current girlfriend, Bonnie Harper, looked up at MacFarland, smiled pleasantly, and then went back to reading a book. Bonnie Harper was an incredibly beautiful woman, totally self-aware of her impact on men, and totally indifferent to it. She was older than Jody B, but maintained that classic beauty that movie stars spent thousands of dollars trying to attain. Bonnie was only the latest in Jody B's long string of lovers. Few women could keep up with Jody B's energy, though Bonnie seemed to be up to the task.

MacFarland took a seat and nursed his cup of coffee. Finally, about ten minutes later, Jody B sighed, and then turned off her computer. She swung around in her chair, facing MacFarland, her brightly colored tattooed arms laced behind her head. Rumor had it that Jody B had been a biker chick. MacFarland knew her as a successful bar owner and manager.

"Mac, so good to see you! I heard that you got shot! Is this true?"

"Unfortunately, yes. But you should see the guy who shot me."

Jody B tipped her head. "Didn't the police shoot him?"

MacFarland laughed. "I did get some help in getting even with the bastard."

"Regardless, I am glad you survived. Are you still in the hot dog business?"

MacFarland nodded. "I have a new wagon. Bigger, better, brighter. But I don't spend as much time selling hot dogs as I'd like."

"Why not?"

"I'm working on a new case. I was asked by Wanda Warren to look into the death of a friend of hers."

At the mention of Warren's name, both Jody B and Harper looked up in surprise. "You know Busty?" they both asked at once, then burst out laughing.

MacFarland was surprised that Jody B would call her that. He nodded. "I understand that she is a lesbian."

Bonnie laughed. "That's putting it mildly. She's a predatory dyke," she said.

MacFarland looked from Harper to Jody B. "What does that mean?" he asked.

"Simply put, it means that Wanda is a very aggressive woman. She claims that she only wants to protect young, impressionable ingénues, but the reality is they need protection from her. I think Wanda has been through just about every girl who has come into this bar. Sometimes it's gotten so bad that we've had to ban her from coming in here. She scares off a lot of my customers."

"What is she like when she isn't here? Like, when she is at work?"

Harper shrugged, but Jody B leaned forward. "Wanda is the kind of lesbian who gives us bad press," she said. "Wanda likes to lead men on. Not hard, considering how obsessed men are with tits. Then she finds the cruelest way to dump them. Not that some of them don't deserve to be treated like shit. But deserving such treatment and actually getting it are two different things. Just because I prefer sleeping with women doesn't mean that I condone mistreating men."

"So you don't think Wanda is a very nice person?"

"She's not a bad person, Mac. She's just too pushy. Life for us is challenging enough. We don't need someone to creating more grief for us." She slumped with resignation. "Wanda is the kind of person who creates more grief."

CHAPTER THIRTY-THREE

MONDAY, APRIL 18, 1205 HOURS

THE FOLLOWING DAY, MacFarland watched as Wanda walked slowly towards him. He couldn't reconcile Jody B's description of Wanda's behavior with what he observed during the few times he had met with her. Was that because he wasn't trying to seduce her? Maybe there was more than one aspect to Wanda's personality. Perhaps there were three sides: a lesbian predator side, a man-bashing side, and a warm, friendly side. MacFarland was happy that he only really knew about the compassionate side of Warren. Very well, that was the side of Wanda Warren that he would deal with.

"Hello Wanda," he said as she neared the wagon. Her face still looked pretty bruised up, but her arm was no longer in a sling. He passed a hot dog and soft drink to her.

"You remembered what I ordered last time?" she said.

MacFarland smiled and handed his next customer their order. "I try to remember," he said. He served another couple of customers while Warren slowly ate her hot dog at the end of the cart. When the last customer left, Warren threw the remains of her meal into the waste receptacle and stepped closer to MacFarland.

"How's the case going?" she asked.

MacFarland was always surprised that civilians expected detectives to have instant success in solving cases. Some cases were easy to solve, such as when the perp was caught in the act or left obvious clues of his involvement with the crime. Cases such as this one, in which, if a crime had been committed, the police assumed it was not a crime, were a little more difficult. And while MacFarland now agreed that a crime had occurred, his conclusion was based primarily on circumstantial evidence. Real crimes got solved by teamwork, perseverance, and oftentimes, good luck. All MacFarland had going for him was perseverance. He wasn't too sure that he had any luck at all.

"I haven't solved it yet," he admitted. "I do have a couple of suspects, though."

Warren's face lighted up. "Who?"

"At first, I thought maybe Hightower was responsible, but with him being in the hospital, I now realize that someone was trying to get him out of the way. So that leaves the people who were at the job site when the accident happened. My primary suspects are Vogel and Boyce."

Warren nodded thoughtfully. "I would go with Boyce."

MacFarland suppressed a wry smile. "It's a question of evidence, Wanda. We don't pick our suspects based on how much we dislike them. But I would be interested in why you suspect Boyce. If you don't mind telling me."

Warren was silent for a moment. Then she started speaking in a quiet voice. "About four months ago, when this project first started, Boyce tried to rape me. January 5th. I remember the day perfectly. It was right after work, and I was going to go out for drinks. Boyce saw me in the parking lot, and started making advances. When he tried to push me into his car, I pepper-sprayed him. He's had it in for me ever since. Since then, I've noticed that everyone I'm friends with, he finds a way to screw them. I think he did the same thing with Mike. Except this time it led to Mike's death."

MacFarland wiped the surfaces of his wagon. "That's not evidence, Wanda. But it does lend itself to identifying motive. Did you report the assault?"

Warren turned away, looking back towards the construction site. "No, I didn't report it. I didn't want anyone to know that anything had happened."

"Why?" MacFarland could never understand why people were reluctant to tell authorities when they had problems. While it was true that many times the authorities' hands were tied, there were opportunities to prevent other crimes or greater problems.

Wanda Warren looked despondent. "I didn't want anyone to know that I led him on. I don't really want to be that kind of a person, Mac. Sometimes, though, I just can't help it."

CHAPTER THIRTY-FOUR

TUESDAY, APRIL 19, 1640 HOURS

MACFARLAND WAS FRUSTRATED. He had few leads on this case and no clear idea of how to get either of his suspects to do anything that would incriminate themselves. He briefly considered going to Vogel's house and trying to search it, but he knew that would be one of those actions that would prompt Pierson to arrest him. When he got a break from the slow stream of customers, he went to his truck and got his tablet computer. It wasn't as powerful at the computer at Her Bar, but it might do for the kinds of searches he wanted to conduct. He brought the tablet back to his wagon and started a search on Riley Vogel.

There were several internet sites that MacFarland had used when he was a detective. He no longer had access to most of those sites, but he still could conduct a significant search with the resources he had. He entered Vogel's name. After an hour of searching, MacFarland had gleaned the following information, most of it obtained from public sources and social networks.

Riley Vogel was married to Annette Porter. They had

three children and a Labrador retriever. The youngest child, Lynnette, was 21 and still lived at home while she attended the University of Colorado at Denver. Annette was active in her church and an avid quilter. Some of her quilts, in fact, had been featured in local papers, and one of them had been presented to Barbara Bush when George H. W. was President. Voting records showed that Riley was a registered Republican who had contributed to local elections in the nineties. His political activity had declined considerably after the second Bush's first term. Apparently his dislike of Obama and other Democrats did not extend to making contributions to their opponents.

A possible explanation for the decline of political involvement was a decline in the Vogel's financial well-being. Vogel had changed companies several times between 1995 and 2005. He was hired by Forrester Equipment and Construction in 2005, working on a project in Indiana for about eight months. Then for three years, he worked in the Chicago office, before finally relocating to the Denver area.

A search of LexisNexis and ProQuest turned up some interesting items. In 2004, Riley Vogel was investigated in the accidental death of a contractor--Stephen Barry--while both of them were working on a project with Brandeis Construction Company. The article cited alleged conflicts between Barry and Vogel, but no charges were filed. Nonetheless, Brandeis Construction Company decided to let Vogel go. After a period of unemployment, Vogel was hired by Forrester Equipment and Construction.

The question was, had Vogel staged an accidental death in the past? And was he staging one now?

MacFarland cut and pasted the article into a file named "Suspects. He then set up a folder that he named "Busty Ballbreaker," and saved it to his computer. He filled out a card with a notation about Vogel being implicated in Stephen Barry's death. He would have to find time to put all his notecards into the Busty Ballbreaker folder.

He did a quick search of court records, then stared at the computer with a look of grim smugness. In 2011, Riley Vogel had been taken to court by several of his creditors. He couldn't determine the outcome of the suit, and he did not find any further instances of court action. He made a notation on his notecards, closed up his computer, and stared thoughtfully at the courthouse.

MacFarland went back to listening to his language lessons, handling the occasional customer as he wordlessly practiced the dialog. He was a bit annoyed with himself for taking so long to get through this particular set of lessons. He realized, of course, that he had been neglecting his studies and resolved to spend more time with his language lessons.

At four-forty in the afternoon, Bozworth walked up to his wagon. MacFarland smiled broadly. "Lord Bozworth! What a pleasure to see you on this side of town! Where is your shopping cart?"

Bozworth smiled back. "My possessions are in the care of one of my aide-de-camps. I prefer to travel less encumbered when I have to visit yonder fair establishment." He gestured towards the detention center. "I was visiting one of my subjects, who is currently incarcerated in the city's premier holding area."

"Anything serious? Does this person need some help?"

"No, no, no need for your intervention, Mr. MacFarland. The subject in question was the object of a welfare check by the men in blue. He had not taken his medication on a timely basis and was observed wandering around in a state of dishabille. I was bringing the gentleman his medication."

MacFarland was not at all sure how Bozworth would obtain the man's medication, nor was he sure that the police would allow Bozworth to give any kind of medication to an inmate. On the other hand, perhaps Bozworth had merely delivered a prescription bottle. That would allow the police to check with the inmate's doctor and verify the medication.

"But that is not the sole reason for my presence on the west side of the Capitol Building," said Bozworth. "I have some information that might be of interest to you."

MacFarland raised his eyebrows questioningly.

"My sources inside the CCP building, after considerable efforts, have determined that the fine Mr. Vogel has never been up to the seventh floor of the building. Rather, Mr. Vogel confines his visits to his place of employment, Forrester Equipment and Construction. His interactions are solely with a rather attractive secretary in the outer office and with the somewhat dapper Mr. Pelligrini."

MacFarland nodded. "Yeah, I suspected as much as soon as I learned that Forrester had an office in the building. Well, thanks for your efforts, Lord Bozworth."

Bozworth smiled mysteriously. "Be not so hasty, my friend. There is more to my histoire. It seems that while Mr. Vogel does not interact with Mr. Peterson, Mr. Pelligrini does. Frequently, within minutes of Mr. Vogel's departure." Bozworth smiled. "I would never suspect that a man of such stature as Mr. Pelligrini would suffer to serve as a conduit of construction site gossip, but that seems to be the case."

MacFarland nodded as he considered the implications of Bozworth's news. "You've been very helpful, Lord Bozworth. How can I compensate you for your time and effort?"

Bozworth gestured towards the menu. "I do have many mouths to feed on East Colfax, and alas, your cart is rarely over there where it could do the most good."

"How about if I bring my cart over to Greek Town this coming Saturday? That will give you plenty of time to make sure all your subjects are assembled, and I can provide them some food then."

Bozworth nodded, his jovial face bedecked with a broad grin. "That would serve their needs quite adequately, I believe. Of course, I might require some sustenance to bide me over until that fortuitous day."

MacFarland was already preparing a couple of bratwursts for the homeless man. As Bozworth reached out for the meal, his eyes flashed with merriment.

"There is one other piece of intelligence you might be interested in, though you did not request it. Consider it a bonus."

MacFarland got a bag of chips and a drink for Bozworth. "A bonus, huh? What is it?"

"The man who posed as a janitor in the CCP--unfortunately, a less than adequate facilities custodian, I am afraid--was terminated. Or perhaps he left on his own. In any case, he is no longer a daily occupant of the CCP building."

"Is this the man you said was some sort of policeman?"

"The very same individual," said Bozworth. "And here is where it gets interesting, my friend. The said officer of the law has not entirely abandoned his interest in the CCP building, because he is often seen observing it rather surreptitiously. I think it is what you call, in your parlance, a stake-out."

"Interesting," said MacFarland. "You know, Lord Bozworth, you never cease to amaze me with the breadth and depth of your knowledge of what goes on in this city. Too bad you're not on the police force."

"My values are coincidental with those of the original Bobbies, though I fear current police values are often at odds with my temperament. No, I will leave modern day policing up to individuals like yourself. Nonetheless, I will continue to do what I can. It is a challenging job, my friend, but someone must do it. My city needs all the protection it can get."

CHAPTER THIRTY-FIVE

TUESDAY, APRIL 19, 1845 HOURS

"HOW'S THE CASE GOING? Did you break any laws?"

"Cyn, how can you even ask that? I always follow the law, when it makes sense."

"Remember, I was your partner, Mac. I know how you operate."

"Rest assured, I didn't do anything that would give you opportunity to put handcuffs on me. You'll have to satisfy your kink some other way."

"I did talk to Chamberlain about the fact that Hightower was involved in a hit and run and he was also a person of interest in the death of Michael Brady."

MacFarland looked up from scrubbing the pots and pans. "What did he say?"

"As you might expect, he said that's not enough to open a case on Brady, though we do have one open on Hightower, as the victim. When I told him about your suspicions, he got a lot more interested. I tell you, Mac, the Commander really values your opinion. He assigned Herbert to the case."

MacFarland nodded. Gene Herbert, one of the senior

detectives in the Major Crimes Unit, was one of the good guys. Conscientious, competent, a bit old-school in some of his ways, but otherwise, the kind of detective who would take the case seriously. Herbert and MacFarland had worked together on a couple of cases in the past--the death of a five year old girl who had been abducted and killed by a teenaged neighbor, and a bank robbery in which the teller had been shot and killed. Herbert was much better at working with the Feds than MacFarland was, which was probably why both cases were resolved with arrests and convictions.

"Good, I can work with Herbert," said MacFarland.

Pierson laughed. "Mac, sometimes you're an idiot. Gene likes you, but don't expect him to be as free and easy with case information as I am. He's getting close to retirement, and I am pretty sure he doesn't want anything to jeopardize that."

MacFarland looked indignant, then went back to scrubbing his pots and pans with more vigor. "I resent the implications of that, Cynthia Pierson."

"Don't worry, I will still feed you information. Speaking of which, we have some more intel on the vehicle that hit Hightower. Vogel doesn't happen to own a red vehicle, does he?"

"No, he owns a yellow Corolla Tercel. Why?"

"Forensics found some red paint on Hightower's clothes. They've matched it to the type of paint used on Dodge Ram and Dakota trucks in the nineties."

MacFarland nodded. Red trucks were pretty common, but at least now they knew what they were looking for.

CHAPTER THIRTY-SIX

WEDNESDAY, APRIL 20, 0810 HOURS

THERE WASN'T MUCH that MacFarland could do to find a red truck, so he went to work. He and Rufus were soon engaged in a heated argument over issues of global import.

"No, Rufus, the oceans can't rise high enough to submerge Denver."

"What about if California sinks into the ocean? Wouldn't that raise it up a whole lot?"

"I don't think California can actually sink."

"What about those polar ice caps? If they all melted, it'd make the ocean a lot deeper. I've seen a map of the world. There's more ice in Greenland than there's land in the United States."

"That's just the way the map is drawn, Rufus. Greenland isn't that large."

"The librarian said it was the most accurate and up to date map made," said Rufus in an annoyed tone.

"She was talking about the countries and boundaries."

"I'm sure it was everything about the map."

"What were you talking to the librarian for? I didn't know you ever went into the library."

"I needed to use the bathroom," said Rufus, "and it was close by. Then I got to thinking, somebody told me that Laos wasn't there anymore. They said it was Myanmar, and I never even heard of Myanmar. So I had to go see it."

"Somebody misinformed you, Rufus. Laos is still there. Myanmar used to be called Burma."

"Ah, Burma. Well, that's good news. I left some buddies in Laos, even though we wasn't supposed to be there. So where is Myanmar?"

"Didn't you find it on the map?"

"No, I saw Greenland and got to thinking about global warming and how all that water was going to flood me out of my hidey-hole."

Rufus lived in an unused drainage pipe that fed into the South Platte River. "Are you afraid of the river rising?"

"Worse than that, boss. I'm afraid the oceans will come up the river."

"It won't happen Rufus. It can't happen."

"Well, suppose Denver sinks?"

Before MacFarland could explain why that scenario also wouldn't happen, one of the construction workers from Forrester approached the cart. He was not someone that MacFarland recognized.

"Are you the cop who is investigating Brady's death?" asked the construction worker.

"I'm not a cop," said MacFarland.

"No one knows exactly what you are, but you are the person who's been asking all the questions, aren't you?"

"Yeah, I guess I am."

"Then I need to tell you something you need to know."

MacFarland nodded. "Okay, what do I need to know?"

"You need to know about Hightower."

"So tell me."

"He's not as innocent as he acts. In fact, he isn't innocent at all in all this. The guy is always drunk. I am sure he was drunk the night he did that safety check. I been cleaning up his messes for years now. So you need to back off, understand?"

"Who are you?" asked MacFarland, trying to ignore the man's aggressiveness.

"Quincy, Tom Quincy. I'm one of the Safety Engineers at Forrester."

"You're the one who should have been called Saturday morning, when Vogel dismissed Hightower. Did he call you?"

"No, he didn't," said Quincy. "If he had called me, I would have come in."

"So you weren't unavailable?"

Quincy looked confused. "I was doing things, but nothing that was more important than safety. I take my job very seriously. And I don't drink!"

"Have you actually seen Hightower drunk on the job?"

"Well, no, not really. We work alternate shifts."

"Then how do you know he was intoxicated that day?"

"I hear things. Forrester is not that big a company. People talk."

"And you believe them?"

"I know the man. I've talked to people who have gone drinking with him and seen him drunk."

"What about his work?"

"What do you mean?"

MacFarland tried to be patient. He didn't like someone bad mouthing someone else. If the person had objective information that was relevant to his investigation, then that was a different matter, but so far Quincy didn't have any facts that he could use. "I mean, how well did he do his job? Did he make a lot of mistakes? Was he normally lax in his inspections?"

Quincy shook his head. "I don't really know. I never checked his work. That doesn't mean he isn't an accident waiting to happen. Or in this case, an accident that did happen."

MacFarland nodded. "Speaking of accidents, do you know who was driving the car who ran over Mr. Hightower?"

"Why would I know that?" said Quincy angrily. "You're not accusing me of doing that, are you?"

"I'm not accusing you of anything, Mr. Quincy. I am wondering why you are here telling me not to believe anything Hightower might say. What's your angle?"

"Hightower has it in for this company. Despite all the things management has done for him, he still finds fault with the company. What does he want? His job handed to him on a silver platter? Just because he's black? I've had to work my ass off for my position. No one has given me any breaks."

MacFarland wasn't quite sure if he could believe that Quincy had spent his whole life never getting a break. Perhaps it was the acquired distrust someone who has been homeless has of those who are not deprived that affected his opinion of Quincy. Perhaps he just didn't like Quincy.

Or perhaps he just didn't like being told what he could or couldn't do.

CHAPTER THIRTY-SEVEN

WEDNESDAY, APRIL 20, 1120 HOURS

MACFARLAND WAS RELIEVED when Quincy finally left. For a few moments, neither he nor Rufus said anything. Finally Rufus spoke up. "What an asshole."

MacFarland nodded. "I wonder though, what prompted him to come see me now? Hightower, as far as I know, is still in a coma. He can't tell me anything. Did someone put Quincy up to coming and talking to me?"

Quincy's visit started a whole stream of questions in MacFarland's mind. Was there really an embezzlement scheme going on at the construction site? Was Quincy one of those involved in it? Hightower didn't seem to know anything about the fraud going on, so why would Quincy be worried about that? MacFarland knew that Hightower felt he was overqualified for the job he was doing. How qualified was Quincy for his job? Was Quincy worried that Hightower's qualifications might affect Quincy's employment? If Quincy thought Hightower was holding him back, would that be a sufficient cause for murder? He put the question to Rufus.

"I don't think so, boss. I think he's jus' one fucked-up dude."

"Maybe you're right, Rufus. You usually are." MacFarland wiped the surfaces of his cart with his cleaning cloth, then checked on his inventory. He was running low, but he should have enough for the rest of the week. If he was going to give out free food on Saturday, though, he had to get more product.

Rufus apparently did not have any meetings scheduled for today, since he hung around MacFarland's corner. He found a place to sit and lean against the parking garage, soaking up the warm spring sunlight.

MacFarland glanced at his watch. It was getting close to eleven o'clock. He turned to get Rufus' attention. "Would you mind watching my cart for me, Rufus?"

Rufus looked up from his deep reverie. "Sure, boss. Nothing makes me happier than serving the good people of Denver."

MacFarland looked at Rufus in surprise. "Really? You like serving people?"

"Well, yeah, boss, most of the time at least. I don't like serving people like that Quincy fellow. I'd send him 'cross the street."

MacFarland's original intent was to go to the Forrester Equipment and Construction offices in the CCP Building. If Quincy was concerned enough with MacFarland's investigation that he felt compelled to complain to him, what would happen if MacFarland stirred up the pot even more? Pelligrini had been at the job site when the accident occurred. Had he been there because he knew something was going to happen? Or was it, as Pelligrini explained, just an unfortunate coincidence?

MacFarland didn't believe in coincidences. If Pelligrini

was at the construction site, he was there for a reason. MacFarland intended to ask him about that. If nothing else, MacFarland intended to ask about the embezzlement scheme. He didn't expect Pelligrini to break down and confess. That sort of thing only happened in bad movies. But he did expect to shake the hornet's nest and get some reaction. Nothing made MacFarland happier than a swarm of angry hornets.

There were no spaces available in front of the CCP Building, but MacFarland found one around the corner. He parked at one of the new electronic parking meters that had been installed the previous year. The meter automatically read the electronic signature of his truck and charged his account for the parking space. It would keep track of how long he was parked in the space. He wished they had one of these meters over where he parked his truck near the detention center. He hated having to search for a parking space in the lot where the construction workers parked. There were never any spaces left!

The offices of Forrester Equipment and Construction were a hubbub of activity and noise. The office was a large open space with private rooms for the executives clustered in the middle. Lesser beings occupied desks in a maze of cubicles around the inner sanctum of executive privilege.

MacFarland headed towards the only cubicle that was in any way distinctive, since it was detached from the maze.

Bozworth had mentioned that the FE&C receptionist was quite attractive, and indeed she was. MacFarland wondered how Bozworth would know what the woman looked like, since it was unlikely that Bozworth had ever been inside of the CCP Building. MacFarland had to keep himself from staring at her. He hoped that she was more than just eye candy. Not that he objected to women using their appearance to get ahead. He just didn't agree with men who only hired a woman because she looked good.

"May I help you?" she asked as he stepped up to the desk. Her smile helped her appear even more beautiful.

"I'm here to see Norm Pelligrini," he said.

She frowned. "Do you have an appointment?" Even when frowning, she looked attractive.

MacFarland shook his head. "No. Just tell him it's about the financial scam he's running."

She pursed her lips and consulted a computer screen. "Mr. Pelligrini is not in the office at the moment. If you wish, I can set up an appointment for you. He should be back tomorrow."

MacFarland scowled and shook his head. "I'll catch him later."

MacFarland exited the office and stood by the elevator. Instead of pushing the Down button, he pressed the Up button.

He went up to the seventh floor and entered the offices of Norris Peterson. Unlike the offices of FE&C, the offices of Consolidated Colorado Properties were an oasis of silence and elegance. Light ash paneling, dark wood and leather furniture, Tiffany lamps and Persian carpets all set the tone for Peterson's empire. Peterson's secretary, Joyce Hill, looked up and smiled at him as MacFarland approached her desk. MacFarland smiled back at her, thinking this reception was almost the exact opposite of the last time he had visited this office. At that time, he had come to confront Peterson for getting him evicted from his apartment. He had no proof that Peterson was responsible, but who else could have done it? Joyce Hill had tried to keep MacFarland from seeing Peterson. This time, however, she seemed genuinely happy to see him. After all, MacFarland had saved the life of her boss.

"Is Peterson in?" asked MacFarland.

"Yes, Mr. MacFarland, let me announce you." She pressed an intercom button and whispered something into the microphone. She beamed at MacFarland. "Go right on in, Mr. MacFarland."

Peterson stood up and snaked around his desk to shake MacFarland's hand.

"Mark, I am so happy to see you!" Peterson bubbled over with apparent enthusiasm. "I never got a chance to thank you personally for saving my life."

A hit man, William Ashland, supposedly hired by Peterson's cousin Brian Newsome to kill Newsome's partner, Otto Freeman, had come to Peterson's house either to collect payoff money or to kill Peterson--no one knew for sure, since the police killed the hit man. Peterson's version was that Ashland had come to kill him.

But MacFarland knew what the truth was. Peterson had been as deeply involved with the killer as his cousin had been. The only way that MacFarland had "saved" Peterson's life was by becoming the target--he had ended up taking three bullets from the killer. Fortunately, none of the shots had been fatal.

"We both know that is not true, Peterson. If anything, I regret that I interfered with Ashland killing you. So cut the act, at least around me."

Peterson's demeanor changed almost instantly. Peterson's dark eyes bored into MacFarland, clearly expressing his annoyance and undisguised contempt. Peterson retreated to his side of the desk. "Why are you here, MacFarland?"

MacFarland felt a momentary surge of satisfaction that

he had been able to chip at Peterson's calm self-assurance. He sat down and stretched his legs in front of him, crossing his legs at the ankles. "You weave a tangled web, Peterson."

"How poetic," said Peterson, his words were spoken sarcastically. "What's that supposed to mean?"

"I know what you're doing at Forrester."

Peterson stiffened, then made a sound of contempt. "I don't know what you're talking about."

"The money you're stealing from the contract on that high rise building. The murder of Mike Brady, who discovered your little fraud."

Peterson laughed. "You certainly haven't lost your imagination, MacFarland. You're full of shit. I have nothing to do with that company."

"You own that company, Peterson. You own the building. You got the city to sell you that land. I don't know why you'd steal from yourself, but I'm sure you are. Maybe you're not directly involved, but I don't believe anything goes on in your financial empire without your knowledge, if not active involvement."

"You give me too much credit, MacFarland. I don't have anything to do with Forrester or its operations. Yes, I own the property they are building on. And yes, they are building my building. But that is the extent of my involvement with them. Now, if you are quite finished with your little rant, I would appreciate it if you would leave. Or do you want me to call the police again?"

MacFarland stood up. "No need, Peterson. Just know that I have my sights on you. You won't get away with any of this."

Peterson herded MacFarland to the outer office. "Joyce, Mr. MacFarland is not welcomed in this office anymore. If he shows up again, contact the police immediately."

CHAPTER THIRTY-EIGHT

THURSDAY, APRIL 21, 0755 HOURS

MACFARLAND WAS in a very good mood the following morning when Rufus walked up to his corner. Although he realized that he had not achieved the objective he intended when he went to the CCP Building, nonetheless, he felt satisfied with his attempts to increase consternation in Peterson's world. Despite Peterson's denial of involvement, MacFarland could not help but be convinced that the man who had killed his wife played some part in the death of Mike Brady.

Rufus arrived at his usual time, and as usual, he handed MacFarland a cup of store-bought coffee. "Ah," said MacFarland, sipping the hot beverage. "Much better than my coffee."

"Ya think so?" said Rufus. "I actually like your coffee better."

"You do, huh? Well, you know you can help yourself whenever you want some."

"One cup o' coffee is all a man needs, boss. When he

gets two cups, he gets soft. After three cups, he's spoiled. And if he drinks it all day, he might as well be married."

"That's a strange philosophy, Rufus."

"I call it my rabbit hole philosophy, boss."

MacFarland looked at his friend questioningly. "Rabbit hole philosophy?"

Rufus nodded. "Yup. When you're hiding in a rabbit hole, trying to avoid Charlie finding you, you don't have time for the luxuries of life, boss. You hafta make do with only the necessary things. The necessities of life, if you know what I mean. One cup of coffee a day. A good M-16 by your side. And God smiling down on you and not your enemy."

"You don't have an M-16 Rufus. I've never seen you with a gun."

Rufus got a panicked look on his face, then slowly calmed down. "I don't carry it into town with me, boss. Don't want to scare the mama sans away." Rufus looked around, whether for mama sans or for Charlie, MacFarland could not tell. He finished his coffee, then helped himself to a second cup.

"Where'd ya go yesterday, boss?"

"I went over to the CCP Building. I wanted to see if I could meet the man who runs the construction company down the street."

"Oh, the place where Busty works?"

MacFarland nodded. "He wasn't in, so I paid a visit to Norris Peterson."

Rufus was instantly on the alert. Over the years, he had heard a lot about Peterson. If there was one thing in the world worse than Charlie ambushing you, it was Norris Peterson and what he did to MacFarland. Rufus had never met Peterson, but he knew that if he ever did encounter the man, Rufus would do whatever he could to avenge the death of MacFarland's wife.

"At first he was very friendly," said MacFarland. "Thanking me for saving his life and all that shit. But I didn't buy it. I know that he regrets that none of Ashland's bullets killed me. He fully understands that I know that he was involved in those murders last year, and as long as I know about it, I'm a danger to him."

Rufus nodded thoughtfully. "You're smart not to trust him boss. It's like the villagers working in the rice paddies. They all look innocent enough, but any one of them could turn out to be Charlie. You can't never turn your back on 'em."

"Don't worry, Rufus. I won't ever turn my back on Norris Peterson. Not until he is dead and buried."

Rufus nodded approval. "Hey, boss, mind if I have another cup of coffee?"

CHAPTER THIRTY-NINE

THURSDAY, APRIL 21, 1150 HOURS

THREE CUPS of coffee proved to be too much for Rufus, so he headed off to attend his usual daily meetings. MacFarland put on his headphones and went back to studying Spanish, annoyed with himself that he was taking so long to get through this set of language CDs. Maybe he should just go down the street and talk to Jacinto Gomez in Spanish. MacFarland looked around at the courthouse plaza, checked the streets, then wandered up the block towards Gomez' taco stand.

"Buenos días," he said as he approached.

Gomez smiled back at him. Gomez was a wisp of a man, taller than MacFarland, but weighing a bit less. MacFarland always feared that a strong breeze would lift Gomez right off the ground. "Buenos días, Mac. How are you today?"

"Muy bien, gracias. Jacinto, you probably know that I study languages when I am working."

"Is that what you are doing? I always thought you were listening to music."

"No, languages. Trying to better myself. Right now I am

studying Spanish, and I was wondering if I could practice with you."

Gomez looked surprised. "Hey, man, I'm flattered, but there is one slight problem."

"I won't interfere with your business, I promise you."

Gomez laughed. "No, Mac, it's not that. But you see, I don't speak Spanish. Francesca does, speaks it quite well, in fact, but I was born here. Third generation American, actually. Even my parents only spoke a little."

"You don't speak Spanish?"

Jacinto shook his head. "I took it in high school. Actually believed it would be easy for me. Unfortunately, I couldn't compete with a lot of the kids who actually spoke Spanish at home. Guess that discouraged me."

MacFarland retreated back to his own cart, put his headphones back on, and began repeating the phrases he heard.

Just before noon he looked up from a quick onslaught of customers to see Wanda Warren standing a ways off from his cart. When the last of the customers wandered off, he beckoned her over. "What can I get for you, Wanda?"

"I'm not hungry, Mac," she said. "Just wanted to find out what's been happening on the investigation."

"Wish I could say that it was all wrapped up, Wanda. Truth is, I have a lot of ideas, but no real leads. I do think that something was going on."

Warren looked disgusted. "I know something was going on, damn it. I want the person who killed Mike to be caught."

"We all want that, Wanda. Sometimes these things take time. Sometimes it takes a lucky break." He shrugged. "I'm doing what I can to create that lucky break."

"What sort of things? Did you talk to Boyce? Is he still a suspect?"

MacFarland didn't answer her question. "Boyce used to be a crane operator, right?"

Warren nodded in agreement. "I've never seen him operate, but I hear that he is certified."

"Besides him, could anyone else rig that load so that it would come loose?"

Wanda laughed, waving her hand in dismissal. "Almost anyone could have done that, Mac. It's not hard to make something unsafe. That's why we check, double-check, and triple-check. I think it's more significant who gave the instruction not to do a safety check on Saturday morning. That was clearly a violation of our procedures."

"The safety report made no mention of anyone giving or failing to give that order. It just focused on Hightower's condition and how he was presumed to be drunk the night before."

"And now he's in the hospital. What does that tell you?"

"I would assume, Wanda, that it means whoever tried to kill Hightower is the same person that killed Brady."

"You got that damn straight," said Warren. Then she turned around and headed back towards the construction site.

CHAPTER FORTY

FRIDAY, APRIL 22, 1820 HOURS

MACFARLAND WAS JUST AS DISSATISFIED with his progress as Warren was. The next day, he was determined to do something about it. As the employees at Forrester were heading for the parking lot, he asked Rufus to watch his wagon.

"Isn't it time to go home?" asked Rufus.

"You can have all the coffee you want, Rufus."

"Naw, I gotta lay off that stuff, boss. I couldn't sleep at all last night. Drank too much coffee in the morning."

"You're not suited for luxury, Rufus. Can you watch the cart for me?"

"Sure, boss. Anytime. Long as I don't have to drink coffee."

MacFarland hurried over to his truck and drove around the block. He parked across the street from the parking lot used by most of the construction workers until he spotted Boyce pulling out. He allowed the car to move ahead in the traffic, then followed it as it headed north. He knew where Boyce was heading, so he did not have to stay as close to him as he would if he were tailing an unknown suspect. As predicted, Boyce went straight home, parking in the drive-way. MacFarland drove past Boyce's house, then made a U-turn and came back to park across the street.

Most of the shades and blinds in Boyce's house were open, allowing him to see what was going on. What he saw was a typical suburban, middle class family preparing for dinner and getting ready for the evening. He caught an occasional glimpse of Boyce's wife, but she spent most of her time in the kitchen, preparing dinner. Boyce disappeared for a while, then re-emerged from a back room wearing a change of clothes. He played with his children for a while, then everyone went towards the back of the house for dinner. MacFarland looked at his watch. It was five-twenty, still another two hours until sunset. Rufus would still be able to watch his wagon for him. After sunset, however, Rufus might just abandon the wagon and retreat to his hidey-hole.

MacFarland watched the house for another hour, but the only thing he saw was confirmation that Ryan Boyce led a quiet, normal family life. And, judging by the appearance of the house, his ten year old Tercel, and the general nature of the community he lived in, Ryan Boyce wasn't participating in the scam to rip off millions from the job site.

CHAPTER FORTY-ONE

FRIDAY, APRIL 22, 1830 HOURS

HE WAS ABOUT to start his truck when he saw movement in the house. Dinner had ended rather quickly. The children had disappeared somewhere inside the house, presumably for baths or homework or television. MacFarland wasn't up on children's schedules. Mrs. Boyce could be seen moving between the dining room and the kitchen, porting dishes, glasses, and serving bowls for eventual cleansing. Ryan Boyce headed back to the front room, and switched on a large flat screen television. Scratch television. The kids probably had their own TVs or computers or phones to occupy their spongy little minds. MacFarland watched as Boyce surfed the channels until he found a basketball game, at which point he stopped his surfing and settled down for an evening of athletic appreciation.

His enjoyment of the game, however, was interrupted by some muffled shouts from the kitchen. Even though the windows were open, MacFarland was too far away to distinguish more than the high pitched squeal of a woman demanding assistance. Boyce got up, stared defiantly at the television screen for a few seconds longer, and then went into the kitchen.

He disappeared from view. After a few minutes MacFarland heard the garage door open. Boyce came out, carrying two large bags of trash. He went around to the side of the house and put one bag into the green trash receptacle, the other bag into the blue recycle bin.

When Boyce first emerged from the garage, MacFarland had scrunched down to be less visible. But as Boyce headed towards the side of the house, something caught MacFarland's attention, parked inside of the garage.

A red 1997 Dodge Dakota truck.

In spite of the need for caution, MacFarland found himself staring at the vehicle, wondering if this was the one that was involved in the hit-and-run. He couldn't see the front of the truck, so he was unable to determine if there was any damage. He had to find a way to get inside that garage and check out that truck.

Boyce was coming around the corner of the house. He glanced in MacFarland's direction and then stopped, staring intently. His face clouded with anger, and he hurried back into the house.

As the garage door closed with a thud, MacFarland turned on his engine and pulled away. He didn't see Boyce peeking out a curtained window, watching him drive off.

CHAPTER FORTY-TWO

SATURDAY, APRIL 23, 0638 HOURS

DESPITE HIS RESOLVE TO go back out to Boyce's house and check on the truck himself, MacFarland decided that it would be wiser to follow Pierson's advice and let the police conduct the search. They would have the forensic teams to determine if the truck had been involved in an accident, and they would be able to arrest Boyce on the spot. When he got home Friday evening, he discovered that Pierson was on a stakeout and was unable to answer his many text messages or speak to him on the phone. When she was still not home by one in the morning, he went to bed, annoyed and frustrated.

He got up the next morning, then realized that he had promised Bozworth that he would distribute some food on Colfax. He prepared extra hot dogs and brats, loaded more buns and condiments onto his truck, and restocked his supply of soft drinks. By the time he was done, his home inventory was nearly gone. He wrote a note to himself to go shopping on Sunday and restock his inventory, then left it on the refrigerator.

Just after six-thirty, Pierson got up out of bed. MacFarland could hear her moving around upstairs, a low, steady stream of invective over no toilet paper (guess he forgot to put a new roll out after he used the bathroom), her toothpaste squirting out too forcefully (that was entirely her fault), and a final "fuck it" as she finally came downstairs and entered the kitchen.

"Rough stake-out?" he asked sympathetically. Stake-outs were one part of the job he did not miss. Lousy coffee, long, tedious hours, and too much temptation to eat junk food. Nope, he didn't miss them at all.

"Yeah, but we caught the bastard." Pierson headed over towards the coffee-maker and poured herself a cup. Good thing he had remembered to make coffee.

Capturing a perp probably meant that Pierson was actually in a good mood. Fantastic! "I have a favor to ask," he said.

She gave him a nasty look. "You're out of favors, Mac."

"This is a good one, Cyn, one that you will like."

Pierson frowned. "You want help moving out?"

MacFarland blinked in surprise. "You want me to move out?"

Exasperated, Pierson rolled her eyes. "No, asshole, I was trying to make a joke. God, what an idiot you are in the morning! What's the damn favor?"

"I found a red truck that might have been used in the Hightower hit and run."

Pierson was suddenly awake and intent. "Where? What makes you think that it is the right vehicle?"

"It's a '97 Dodge Dakota, and it's owned by someone at Forrester."

"You think someone Hightower worked with tried to run him over?"

MacFarland nodded. "Hightower was the one person who could mess up their 'accident' explanation for Brady's death. I think they tried to kill him, but they failed."

"Who owns the truck? Where is it?"

"It's owned by Ryan Boyce, a supervisor who works at Forrester. He lives up in Federal Heights. I can text you his address. How soon can you get a warrant?"

"A warrant won't be a problem. Any other indications that it was Boyce who hit Hightower?"

"Do you mean, have I examined the truck?"

"I'd be surprised if you hadn't."

"Well, I didn't. I'm playing by the rules, Cyn. I don't want to mess up this arrest and conviction."

Pierson stared at MacFarland in mock surprise. "My God, who are you and what have you done with Mark MacFarland? Is this a permanent change, or were you just too dru--" Pierson stopped abruptly, then turned a bright red. "Oh, Mac, I'm sorry, I didn't mean to say that."

MacFarland waved off her apology. "Cyn, I am 677 days sober. I have it as much under control as one can expect. I can take a joke every once in a while. Now, what about getting that warrant?"

Pierson got her cellphone from the drawer where she stored her gun and badge and speed-dialed Benny Lockwood, her partner. "Where are you, Benny? Still? Well get your sorry ass to the station. We need a warrant. The Hightower hit and run. Yes, that's right! What? You're breaking up, say again. I'll explain when I get downtown. Give me fifteen minutes. Shit, that long? I might as well get the fucking warrant myself." She ended the call and glared at MacFarland. "Partners! Totally useless!"

As Pierson hurried upstairs to finish getting dressed, he hoped that she wasn't speaking about him.

CHAPTER FORTY-THREE

SATURDAY, APRIL 23, 1055 HOURS

MACFARLAND WANTED to go with Pierson and Lockwood, but Pierson put her foot down. "I don't want civilians, even you, Mac, messing up this bust. Besides, it's not even my case. I am just helping out a fellow officer."

MacFarland realized that he couldn't go with them anyway, since he had to drive his truck up to Colfax. He had forgotten to tell Rufus Headley about his change in plans, so he stopped off near his corner to see if Rufus had shown up. By a strange coincidence, Rufus was actually sitting on a bench near the courthouse. MacFarland called him over.

"Change in plans today, Rufus. Hop in." Once Rufus was in the truck, MacFarland explained what he planned on doing that morning.

"Lord Bozworth got ya to do this?" asked Rufus, unable to conceal his incredulity.

"Affirmative," said MacFarland.

MacFarland drove east on Colfax until he spotted Lord Bozworth standing at a corner on the opposite side of the street. Bozworth indicated that MacFarland should pull into a largely empty used car lot. He drove down a side street, pulled into the empty lot, and parked at an angle. He and Rufus got out and greeted Bozworth.

"I feared that you might not remember our rendezvous," said Bozworth.

"Boss is a man of his word," said Rufus sharply. "If he says something, you can count on it."

"I can only stay for a couple of hours though," apologized MacFarland.

Bozworth smiled. "That should be plenty of time, my friend. I've notified my associates that they should come early in the day."

MacFarland and Rufus then got to work, turning on the heating rollers, the bun steamer, and making sure the condiment containers were full. It wasn't long before a slowly increasing stream of individuals started showing up. MacFarland and Rufus were soon quite busy dispensing hot dogs, bratwursts, chips, other snack foods, and drinks to the dozens of people who showed up. Most of the individuals were strangers to MacFarland, though there were way too many who recognized him from his own days on the street. Some individuals, similar to Rufus, had spent so long on the streets that they felt uncomfortable in shelters or homes, so they literally slept on benches or on the sidewalks. The majority of the individuals they encountered retreated to shelters at night; many of the families that showed up found temporary housing in the motels along Colfax. Almost all of the individuals wanted to get off the streets. Most of them wanted jobs. All of them wanted security.

When MacFarland had been on the street, he had rarely gone without some food, though it was also rare that he didn't feel hungry. Food was available to those who lived on the streets. Many organizations provided free meals to the disadvantaged. But those who had no homes often had to hunt down their food, going to the places where food was distributed. If an individual had a car, this was no great problem. But for people who had only their feet for transportation, walking miles from one place to another was a challenge, especially when hunger made them lethargic, depressed, and fearful to take the steps necessary for their own survival.

Some organizations countered this by bringing food to the needy. MacFarland was quite familiar with the large green food trucks that visited many Denver neighborhoods, providing food to those who needed it. As good as these programs were, they often missed out on the more extreme elements of the population--the long term homeless, the very young, those who were new to privation and didn't know where to get their next meal.

MacFarland was surprised at how many people knew Rufus. Even though Rufus spent most of his time on the west side of the city, he knew scores of people who lived along "Cold Facts"--the name given to Colfax by those who wandered up and down the street. Of course, there had been a period of time when Rufus lived along Colfax. MacFarland found it depressing that so many of the people from that long ago were still here.

It was nearly ten o'clock when the flow of customers slowed enough that Bozworth finally decided that his "Food for All" event was over. "It appears that many of those now approaching your food mobile are actually capable of paying for their victuals, yet you continue to hand it out without receiving compensation," observed Bozworth.

"Wouldn't be fair to discriminate," said MacFarland. "I

don't ask anyone whether they can afford to pay. I just provide."

"Very commendable of you, my friend. But you have more than fulfilled your obligation to me. I and my associates thank you most graciously."

"I might try to do this more often, Bozworth. I forgot what it's like on Colfax. Thank you for the opportunity to be of service."

MacFarland and Rufus closed down their cart and prepared to drive back towards the west side of Denver. "Back to our home base, boss?" asked Rufus.

MacFarland nodded. He was not sure how much product he had left, but he would keep his wagon open until he ran out.

His corner was still available when he drove up. He unhooked his cart, then searched for a place to park. The parking lot was full. He was glad that Rufus had stuck around, because street parking spaces were hard to find. Finally he found one close to the library. As he walked past Jacinto Gomez's cart, he asked why there were so few parking spaces available.

Jacinto pointed towards the U.S. Mint. "They are having some brouhaha over there. Minting a special coin or something. It's brought in a lot of tourists, even the news media." To prove his point, he gestured towards a Channel 9News truck parked on the street. "I am hoping they come over here afterwards. I would like to meet that pretty new reporter they have."

MacFarland was not sure what new reporter Gomez was referring to, but he wished him good luck in getting to meet her. As he walked towards his cart, he promised himself that he would try to watch the news more often.

MacFarland was pleased when he reached his cart to

find that Rufus had already set up all the burners, heaters, and warmers. As the first customer came over to the cart, Rufus cheerfully helped get the man's order. MacFarland noted that Rufus was wearing the plastic gloves that he provided in an attempt to ensure more sanitary operations. MacFarland didn't get much opportunity to watch Rufus actually handle operation of his cart, but what he had seen today was quite reassuring. MacFarland smiled and put on his headphones.

He hadn't gotten very far in his language lesson when the daughter of his cross-corner competitor came over to his cart. She greeted him cheerily. "Hi, my name is Felicity. Felicity Davenport. I don't think we've ever really been introduced, Mister...?" Felicity stuck out her hand, smiling broadly.

MacFarland stared at the pretty blond-haired girl. She looked to be about sixteen. He glanced over at her father, who waved and smiled. Then MacFarland took her hand and shook it. "Mark MacFarland," he said. "I'm pleased to finally meet you, Felicity. I apologize for not introducing myself sooner."

"That's alright," she said. "We haven't been overly friendly on our side of the street. That's Sydney for you."

"Sydney? You mean your dad?"

"Sydney Morgan is my step dad, NOT my real dad. I mean, Sydney used to be cool. An honest-to-effing-god rocket scientist, you know, at Lockheed Martin? But he's been a real downer ever since he got laid off and became a lame hot dog seller..." She trailed off and backpedaled in a different direction, speaking quickly. "Uh, I mean, not that there's anything wrong with being a hot dog seller. That's cool too. Actually, I've been helping him out a lot since he started this a couple months ago, and it's kind of fun. It IS a great place to meet hotties." She flashed a brilliant smile, gazing off into the middle distance at the remembered hotties, clearly excluding MacFarland from that category.

"There's nothing wrong with good, honest work," said MacFarland. "Lockheed Martin, eh?" With the government cutbacks in defense spending, no wonder he was out of a job. "I can understand why he doesn't find this as challenging."

"Life's tough and then you die," she said brightly. "Nice meeting you, Mr. MacFarland. I better get back, since the lunch crowd will be starting up soon. Though there aren't that many people here on Saturdays. Maybe with it getting warmer, business will pick up." Felicity turned and hurried across the street. MacFarland watched her hurry back to her stepdad's cart. He could see why their cart drew so many customers. Her enthusiasm was contagious.

"Mac?"

He turned, surprised that Wanda Warren had been able to sneak up on him. He must have been paying too much attention to Felicity. *My God*, he thought, *I'm turning into a dirty old man!*

"Wanda! It's good to see you." Warren didn't look very happy. "What's up?"

"I have some bad news," she said.

"Bad news? What happened?"

"Louis Hightower is dead," she said. "He passed away during the night."

CHAPTER FORTY-FOUR

SATURDAY, APRIL 23, 1545 HOURS

MACFARLAND WAS NOT REALLY SURPRISED. He hadn't been able to see Hightower at the hospital, but from comments made by Benny Lockwood, who had gotten a chance to review the Incident Report of the accident, Hightower had sustained rather severe injuries. It was remarkable that he hadn't been killed instantly. When MacFarland asked Wanda if she knew what he had died from, she could only reply, "He was hit by a fucking car, Mac!" That didn't tell him much more than he already knew.

Wanda wandered back to the work site, which she said was closing down for the rest of the day in memory of Hightower. MacFarland thought that was a kind gesture on the part of management, but Warren pointed out that most people would just stand around talking about Hightower's death anyway. When MacFarland had asked if the company had a day off after Brady's death, Wanda's response was disturbing. "No, they killed Brady. Why should they honor him in any way?"

MacFarland brooded over Hightower's death for most

of the afternoon. Then, at a quarter to four, Pierson and Lockwood drove up, double parking in the street. Lockwood stayed in the car while Pierson got out and came over to Mac's cart.

"Was it Boyce's truck that killed Hightower?" he asked, not waiting for Pierson to speak.

Pierson gave him a puzzled look. "Hightower died? Shit. That ups the crime to manslaughter. And to answer your question, fucking no. We didn't even find a truck. Furthermore, a search of Boyce's DMV records doesn't show that he ever owned a red truck. We totally struck out, Mac."

"Maybe he got it painted."

"Mac, listen to me. No fucking truck. None registered, no truck there."

"I don't understand that," said MacFarland. "I saw the truck in the garage last night."

"Well it wasn't fucking there this morning!" Pierson had a difficult time keeping her tone from sounding annoyed.

Lockwood glanced over, concerned at hearing his partner raise her voice.

"I don't know what you saw, Mac, but when we questioned Boyce and his wife, they both claimed that they knew nothing about a red truck. We even questioned the neighbors, and no one reported seeing a red truck. Except one guy who lived across the street."

"Well, there, that should mean something."

"No, it doesn't," said Pierson sullenly. "When we checked the guy out, it turns out he has red-green color blindness. He insisted that he can tell the difference between a red truck and a green truck, but how reliable can he be?"

MacFarland shrugged. "There must be other people who saw the truck. Hell, it was parked in his garage. He must have opened the garage door hundreds of times. Someone must have seen it. You need to go back and talk to more neighbors."

"I'm sorry, Mac, but unless you have something else, we're through. Let me talk to Chamberlain. Maybe now that Hightower is dead, he may give this a bit more priority. But without any evidence, we can't go after Boyce anymore."

Pierson got back into the car and Lockwood drove off towards the station.

MacFarland stared at the receding car. He had tried to follow the rules and look where it got him. He now realized that Boyce must have seen him watching his house the previous evening and realized that he had to get rid of the red truck. MacFarland was convinced now of two things.

First, he was almost certain that Boyce had been the one who had tried to kill, and finally succeeded in killing, Louis Hightower. Did that also make him the killer of Mike Brady?

And the second thing he was convinced of was that following the rules was not always a good idea. From now on, he would follow his own rules.

CHAPTER FORTY-FIVE

SATURDAY, APRIL 23, 1600 HOURS

AT FOUR O'CLOCK, MacFarland headed down to the construction site. He didn't like leaving his cart unattended, but Rufus had left for the day. MacFarland just hoped that none of the Denver Mint crowd showed up looking for hot dogs. Not that he had many left.

The main gate to the construction site was closed. As Warren had said, the site closed down for the rest of the day. He went over to the guard shack and knocked on the door. Marty Picket opened the door.

"Nobody's here," he said. "They all went home because of Hightower's death."

MacFarland nodded. "I know. Wanda told me. Sorry to hear the news."

"Yeah," said Picket. "Do you know if they caught the bastard that ran him over?"

"Not as far as I know," said MacFarland. "I'm not exactly in the loop on these things anymore."

Picket looked surprised. "I was under the impression you still worked closely with the cops. I mean, even though you're a hot dog vendor, you always seem to have cops stopping by your stand."

MacFarland was not aware that cops came to his stand with any great regularity or frequency, but he let the comment pass. Picket seemed to be friendlier than usual, but perhaps it was because he was going to be spending the night alone. "You put in some pretty long hours," he said.

Picket shrugged. "I work a four day week, usually ten hours a day. I try to work Thursday through Sunday nights."

"I've seen you here on other days," observed MacFarland.

"I cover other guy's shifts. Try to get as much overtime as I can. The company is willing to pay time and a half as long as they don't have to pay benefits for another employee. Stupid policy as far as I can see, but hell, if it means more money in my pocket, who the hell cares?"

As someone who had never had a job that paid by the hour, MacFarland could only nod in agreement. As a hot dog vendor, he often had ten hour days, six days a week during the winter months. In summer months, he often worked twelve to fourteen hour days, as he tried to take advantage of the longer hours of daylight. He hated to think what his income would be if he calculated his earnings based on the number of hours he worked.

"So you work every weekend?"

"Just about. I like it that way."

"As I recall, you were here the weekend that Baker got killed."

Picket decided that the conversation might go on for longer than he originally anticipated. He sat down and motioned for MacFarland to take the other chair. Putting his hands behind his head, he leaned back in the chair. "Yes, I worked that weekend. Didn't see the actual accident, though. My shift was up just as everyone was coming in to do the unloading."

"Wanda mentioned that you saw something strange early in the morning. Mind telling me what it was?"

"Busty said it wasn't so strange, but I thought it was. I saw Vogel come in to work real early in the morning."

"How early is real early?"

"Like three o'clock in the morning."

"What was Vogel doing?"

"That's just it, that's what made it strange to me. Busty is right, it's not odd for Vogel to come in at odd hours, but if it is at night, usually he goes over to the construction site office. I can see the lights go on in there if he is inside. But not that night. No lights, not in the office at least."

"Where was he?"

"Hell if I know. My job is to keep people out of here who don't belong. If someone who is supposed to be here comes onsite, it's not my job to babysit them."

"No, I don't suppose it would be. But possibly you remember something else about that night. Something that seemed out of the ordinary?"

"I know what you're trying to do," he said in a conspiratorial voice.

"What am I trying to do?"

"You're trying to get me to tie Vogel into Baker's death. Well, sorry buddy, no can do. Vogel's an asshole, don't get me wrong, but he ain't no killer. The guy's strictly a company man. In tight with the bosses, follows the company line. He wouldn't do anything to get the company in trouble."

"What if the company was involved in something illegal? Would Vogel be the type of guy to turn them in, or would he turn a blind eye to it?"

Picket considered the question carefully. "I've known Vogel for maybe two, three years. Can't say that we're all that close, but I would say that if he thought the company was doing something wrong, he would just clam up. Don't know if that makes him a criminal or anything. He just has a lot of loyalty to the people who gave him a chance."

MacFarland realized he had to get back to his wagon, but he had become engrossed in what Picket was telling him. "What do you mean by that? How did the company give him a chance?"

"It's no secret. Vogel got fired from his last job. He got picked up by Forrester when he was desperate. The company has moved him around a bit, using him in critical jobs. Vogel and Pelligrini are quite close. Some say too close. I don't know. But I do know that nothing goes on here without Vogel and Pelligrini both being in agreement on it."

MacFarland was thoughtful as he hurried back to his cart. He was pleased to see that nothing had been done to it. Then he heard Sidney Morgan call out to him from across the street. "I kept an eye on it for you, Mac," he shouted.

"Thanks, I appreciate that!" MacFarland responded.

He shut down his wagon, locked up his bins, then waved good-night to his new acquaintances across the street. "I'm going to get my truck," he shouted. "I should be back in a couple of minutes."

"No problem, Mr. MacFarland. We'll be here for another hour," yelled Felicity.

He waved and hurried away to retrieve his truck. He returned about ten minutes later and pulled up to connect his cart to the trailer hitch. As he was hooking up the electrical cable, he had a sudden realization. The witness who lived across the street from Boyce said that he had seen a red truck in Boyce's garage. The police discounted his testimony because they were focused on the color of the vehicle and the witness wasn't reliable when it came to color.

What they should have focused on was that the witness said he saw a truck in the garage. It didn't matter what the color was! The important question was, where was that truck now?

CHAPTER FORTY-SIX

SUNDAY, APRIL 24, 0830 HOURS

MACFARLAND TRIED to tell Pierson about his interpretation of the neighbor's testimony, but Pierson tired of arguing with him. "If we can't trust his testimony on the color of the vehicle, what makes you so sure that we can trust his statement that it was a truck? What if he was just repeating back to us what he heard us asking about?"

"Who did the interrogation? You? I can't imagine you making that kind of a rookie blunder." He regretted his snide tone almost immediately.

Pierson looked away. "It was Lockwood. He corrected himself on subsequent interviews, but I still wouldn't trust the guy's statement. I think he was probably high on marijuana."

"You think everybody is high on marijuana."

"These days, just about everybody is. The point is, forget it. We didn't find the truck. When would he have time to dump it anyway? You claim you saw the truck the previous evening. His wife says there was no truck, none of his neighbors saw a truck driving away from the house. It's a dead lead, Mac. Now, I am going to the gun range. I feel a compelling need to destroy something. You want to come with me?"

MacFarland wondered if he was one of the things she wanted to destroy. "Uh, thanks, but no. I need to replenish my supplies. My donations to the poor yesterday pretty much cleaned me out."

"You can get stuff on Sunday?"

"Yes, of course. I know a place."

MacFarland watched Pierson go off to her gun practice, wishing that he had planned his day better. He was about to leave for the wholesale house when his phone rang. He looked at the name on the screen. Stefanie Cooper, his sister-in-law. *Damn,* he thought.

"Hello Stefanie, what's up?"

"What are your plans for the day?"

"I have to go replenish my supplies."

"Oh, how long will that take?"

MacFarland sensed that he should be on the alert, but he wasn't quick enough. "Just a couple of hours." As soon as he uttered the words, he realized he should have said "all day."

"Good, then I want you to come over here for lunch. The kids really miss you, and I have someone I'd like you to meet."

"I really might take longer," he said nervously. *She wants me to meet someone?* "Who do you want me to meet?"

"Don't worry about that. Just get over here before noon. I will be very disappointed if you let me down, Mark."

MacFarland spent the next two hours purchasing his meats, buns, napkins, paper hot dog trays, condiments, and supplies. He took them back to the house, stored the perishables in the refrigerators, and finally looked at the clock. Eleven-thirty. Maybe if he was lucky, he would get a flat tire on the way to Highlands Ranch. Or have a load of steel girders fall on him.

As luck would have it, he didn't get a flat tire. In addition, traffic flowed very smoothly, and he found himself pulling into the Cooper driveway at a few minutes after twelve. Stefanie met him at the front door.

"Mark! You're right on time! Come on in." Stefanie gave him a peck on the cheek as he entered. He had a wild impulse to just grab her, bend her backwards, and kiss her passionately, but he held his emotions in check. He often had secret impulses like that, and so far he had successfully resisted every foolish urge he felt.

He followed Stefanie into the living room. He could hear the children upstairs, or at least Ryan, playing. Kaitlyn was at the age where she played more quietly. Randy, as usual, was in the TV room, watching something on his wide screen. MacFarland didn't notice there was a woman in the room until she stood up to face him.

He stopped and stared at her. She was shorter than he, probably only five feet four inches tall. He estimated her weight at one hundred twenty pounds. She had long brown hair, parted on her left side, framing a narrow face. Large dark eyes sparkled at him, and when she smiled, she looked part angelic and part devilish. MacFarland was not sure how a woman could look both innocent and naughty at the same time, but this woman certainly pulled it off.

"Oh, Mark, this is my best friend from college, Laura Miller. Laura, this is my dear brother-in-law, Mark MacFarland."

MacFarland was momentarily unable to move or speak,

but Laura quickly crossed the room and shook his hand vigorously. "I'm so pleased to meet you, Mark. Stefanie has told me so much about you!"

"She has?" he said, feeling a bit foolish. "What is there to tell about me?"

"Mark is terribly modest," said Stefanie. "Come, let's all sit down. Mark, what can I get for you? Coffee? Tea?"

"Just water would be fine," he mumbled, still unable to stop looking at Laura. If she was the same age as Stefanie, that made her only about thirty years old. Probably too young for him. But maybe not. Certainly not the devilish part.

Laura sat down and Stefanie nudged MacFarland to sit next to her. He sat awkwardly, wanting to stare at her, but also embarrassed at being so obvious.

"Stefanie says you have your own business," said Laura.

Ah, here it comes, thought MacFarland. As soon as she learns that I am just a hot dog vendor, she will lose any interest in me. As if she had any interest to begin with. "You could say that," he said. "I own a hot dog cart. I sell hot dogs and brats over by the courthouse."

Laura nodded. "Is that a seasonal business? I mean, do you operate it in the winter?"

"It's seasonal to the extent that more people are on the streets during the summer months, but I work all year long. Where I am located gives me an edge, because the court is open all year long. I started selling coffee just recently." He wasn't sure why he added that comment. Perhaps selling coffee made working in the cold winter months more sensible. *God, I'm an idiot!*

"Mark used to be a policeman," said Stefanie, returning with MacFarland's glass of water. "He quit that after Nicole got killed." She smiled in a motherly way at him. "I think he took her death so hard."

"A policeman! Wow."

"Actually a detective," said MacFarland. "I worked in Major Crimes."

"Wasn't that dangerous?"

Before MacFarland could say that it was actually less dangerous than being a patrolman, Stefanie burst in. "Actually, since he has been selling hot dogs, his life has gotten much more dangerous than when he was on the police force. Earlier this year, he was shot three times!"

"Oh my God, really?"

MacFarland was about to point out that the wounds were largely superficial when Stefanie went on to describe how he had single-handedly freed a woman who had been wrongly accused of murder. The more Stefanie described his exploits, the harder he found it to stop her. After all, Laura did seem to find his exploits exciting. He thought perhaps Stefanie was exaggerating just a bit. But as Pierson always said, "Mac, when others are tooting your horn, just learn to keep your mouth shut." The look Laura Miller gave him--a mixture of awe and admiration--in turn excited him. Yep, definitely her devilish side. He kept his mouth shut.

Finally, he was able to turn the conversation away from him and back towards Laura Miller. MacFarland asked her what she did for a living.

"I'm a massage therapist," she said.

"I could sure use one of those some days."

Laura smiled, gently touching the back of his hand. "Maybe that could be arranged, Mark."

MacFarland felt his heart pounding. Was she suggesting what he thought she was suggesting? He was about to find out, when Randy wandered into the room.

"Ho, hot dog man! I heard you were coming over! Are you still losing money with that useless business?"

MacFarland tried to avoid looking at Randy Cooper. There were times when he thought there was no justice in the universe. It was always the wrong people who got killed. Those who really deserved killing kept on breathing.

CHAPTER FORTY-SEVEN

SUNDAY, APRIL 24, 1719 HOURS

BY THE TIME MacFarland left the Cooper residence, he was depressed. Not only had he failed to make a good impression on Laura Miller--she had actually laughed at a lot of the jokes Randy made at his expense--but he had been unable to exchange contact information with her. It didn't matter. He wasn't going to sully the memory of Nicole by going out with the first pretty face he encountered.

Although it had been six years since he encountered a pretty face.

And she did have a lot more than a pretty face to offer.

As he was driving out of Highlands Ranch, he also remembered to kick himself because he had not gotten anything done on the Brady case. Well, he could correct that omission. He headed over to Broadway and drove north. When he got to Evans, he continued onwards instead of turning east. Perhaps he could get hold of Boyce and find out from him what happened to the truck.

When he arrived at the construction site, he parked across the street. He went up to the guard shack and knocked on the door for Picket. When the door opened, it wasn't Picket who greeted him, but a different guard.

"I thought Picket was on duty," said MacFarland. "Is he around?"

"Nah, Picket didn't show tonight. Just me."

"Doesn't Picket work the weekend night shifts?"

The man laughed. "Maybe he does, maybe he doesn't, but guess what? Sometimes people get sick. What can I do for ya?"

"I wanted to talk to Boyce."

The guard laughed again. "It's Sunday, man, the shirts don't show up on Sundays. Try tomorrow."

MacFarland frowned, then turned and headed back to his truck. He was under the impression that there always was someone from management on the site. Was the guard just brushing him off, or was something going on?

This was turning into one of those days you just wish you could do over. He headed south on Broadway, wondering what else could go wrong.

CHAPTER FORTY-EIGHT

SUNDAY, APRIL 24, 1900 HOURS

WHEN MACFARLAND GOT HOME, he was surprised to discover that Benny Lockwood was sitting in the kitchen, drinking beer with Pierson. An empty pizza box sat on one side of the table. MacFarland had not known Pierson to spend much time socializing with her partner. Was he here on police business, or was he simply pursuing Pierson? MacFarland was well aware of Lockwood's protective puppy-love feelings for Pierson.

"Sorry we didn't save any for you," said Pierson as MacFarland came in. "There's coffee in the coffee pot, if you want to join us."

MacFarland nodded, going over to get a cup out of the cupboard. So, it was more a social visit than police work. He sat down at the table. "It's okay, I'm not hungry."

Lockwood leaned back in his chair, sipping his beer. "How's your new case going?" he asked.

MacFarland tried to detect if there was any irony or scorn in Lockwood's voice. He couldn't tell if Lockwood was mocking him or not. He also wasn't sure if he had forgiven Lockwood for having screwed up the questioning of the neighbor. If he had made that mistake when he was partners with Pierson, she would have been on his case for weeks. Of course, he was a much nicer partner than Pierson. "I thought I had a lead with the red truck, but as you know, that didn't pan out. This evening I stopped by the construction site to see if Picket, the guard, had any record of red trucks owned by any of the employees. I thought there might be a chance that Picket might have seen Boyce in a red truck."

Lockwood looked interested. "And?"

"Picket wasn't there. Guess he's sick today."

There was a moment of silence, then Lockwood said, "I did go out to Federal Heights again today. Pierson said that you suggested that we should just determine if Boyce had any kind of a truck regardless of color, so that's what I did."

MacFarland raised his eyebrows questioningly.

"Sorry. It still didn't lead to much of anything. The color blind neighbor insists that Boyce did have a truck, at least until last week. But it also turns out that the witness has had a lot of problems with Boyce."

"What kind of problems?"

"The neighbor is gay, and Boyce has threatened him several times. Says he is a bad influence around his kids."

"Did any of these threats result in calls to the police?"

"No, never got that serious. But it does throw some doubt on the motives of the witness."

"What about other neighbors?"

Pierson was becoming impatient. "For crying out loud, Mac, we already checked with the neighbors! Give it a rest. Your lead sucked. I don't know what you saw in the garage, if anything. You shouldn't even have been out there. If Boyce had found you on his property, he could have shot you. The guy practically has an arsenal in his home."

"I was never on his property," said MacFarland defensively. An arsenal? MacFarland wondered what constituted an arsenal in Pierson's mind.

"That's not the point. Mac, you're not a cop anymore. Stick to selling hot dogs and leave the police work to us." She stood up, prepared to leave the room. "Come on, Lockwood, let's go do some serious drinking."

Lockwood rose as she stomped out of the kitchen. He looked at MacFarland sympathetically. "She stuck her neck out for you on that red truck search. I think she feels like she's lost a lot of credibility with the Commander."

MacFarland remained sitting in the kitchen long after Pierson and Lockwood left the house. He was not sure how to react to Pierson's outburst. There had been many times, when they were partners, where one or the other of them had pursued a false lead. It was part of police work. If every lead worked out perfectly, the police would solve every case and no one would get away with murder. Pierson knew how the world worked. Police work was messy, and success depended on perseverance, teamwork, and luck. There were no sure things when it came to solving crimes.

If she was still his partner, she never would have acted like that. He began to wonder if Lockwood was turning her against him. It occurred to MacFarland that nothing would please Lockwood more than making sure Pierson and MacFarland never discussed a case again. Why was she having beer and pizza with him? It was so totally out of character for her. The more he thought about finding them together, the more convinced he became that Lockwood was trying to cut in on his relationship with Pierson.

What a fucking snake in the grass, thought MacFarland angrily.

CHAPTER FORTY-NINE

MONDAY, APRIL 25, 0810 HOURS

BY THE NEXT MORNING, MacFarland had recovered from his disappointments and frustrations of the previous day. MacFarland was the kind of individual who could let minor annoyances slip from his mind. The exceptions, of course, were the cases he was trying to solve. He would mull over the details of cases repeatedly, staring at his cards, shuffling them to see if new patterns emerged. Even now, as he waited for the coffee to finish brewing and as Rufus helped put hot dogs on the heating rollers and buns in the steam oven, he was flipping through his cards.

"Boss, somebody told me on Saturday that we shouldn't feed hot dogs to the poor people."

MacFarland wasn't really paying attention and had to ask Rufus to repeat what he said. "Why shouldn't we?" he asked.

"This person said that hot dogs wasn't very nutritious. Poor people needed better food."

MacFarland thought about that. "When you're hungry, Rufus, and someone offers you something that isn't very nutritious, but tells you, wait a few days and maybe someone will offer you something better, what do you do?"

Rufus shrugged. "Beggars can't be choosers, boss."

"That's one way of looking at it. There's a scene in the Bible where a woman who only has two pennies, yet she gives them to the offering box, whereas rich people are putting in lots of money. Who gave more?"

Rufus smiled. "I know that story, boss. Jesus says that she gave more because she gave all she had, while the rich people gave what they didn't need."

MacFarland smiled. "I'm not equating us to the poor woman. But I think it is important that we do what we can. We have hot dogs. We don't have the nutritious foods that it would be best to give the hungry. Maybe someday we both will be rich enough to give better food. When the homeless actually can choose between really nutritious food and our measly hot dogs, then I will stop offering un-nutritious food. But right now, they don't have a choice."

"No, boss, they don't." Rufus put some more brats onto the heating rollers.

MacFarland was about to go back to reviewing his cards when he happened to look up. He stared down the street at a man in a blue pea coat and grey slacks. Even though the man was almost a block away, MacFarland recognized him as Grey Wilson, the man who had mysteriously saved him from being seriously hurt by two muggers.

"Watch the cart, Rufus," he said as he started racing down the street. Wilson watched him for a moment, then took off at a rapid pace down the street. MacFarland was gaining on the older man when Wilson ran up to a car parked on the street. He opened the door and jumped in. The car sped off, but not before MacFarland was able to recognize the license plate.

They were federal government plates.

And MacFarland was pretty certain that the woman driving the car matched descriptions of Norma Sykes.

Was Grey Wilson a federal agent? What the hell is going on, MacFarland asked himself. He would have to ask Pierson if Sykes had a partner. If she did, why hadn't Pierson ever told him about the man?

CHAPTER FIFTY

MONDAY, APRIL 25, 0830 HOURS

MACFARLAND DIDN'T GO IMMEDIATELY BACK to his cart. Instead, he continued on down the street, hoping to catch a further glimpse of the car. Unfortunately, the car continued on up to Broadway, disappearing from view. MacFarland stared after if for a moment, then walked around the block.

He approached the entrance to the construction site. He didn't think that he would find Picket working today, but perhaps a man who was so desperate for overtime would switch shifts. The least he could do would be to find out when Picket would be back to work.

There was a different guard at the front gate. MacFarland introduced himself. The guard said his name was Jon without an H Murphy. When MacFarland asked about Picket, Murphy claimed not to know him. MacFarland described who Picket was. Then the guard nodded. "Oh, I know who you mean. I think he got fired. When he called me in this morning, Vogel told me that the previous guard had missed two days. That's grounds for dismissal around here."

"I thought that Picket had called in sick yesterday."

"That's news to me. There's no record of it in the logbook. Was he a friend of yours?"

"No, not really. He was just somebody I wanted to talk to."

Murphy smiled ruefully. "When I got hired yesterday, I was told that keeping your trap shut was an important qualification for keeping your job around here."

MacFarland looked up in surprise. "You were hired yesterday? On Sunday?"

"Yeah, so what?"

MacFarland didn't respond, but turned to walk back to his wagon. He had gotten only twenty yards down the street when he heard Wanda Warren call his name. He stopped and turned to greet her.

"Hi, Wanda. Did you have a good weekend?"

She ignored his question. "Did you find out any more about who killed Hightower?"

"Still working on that. One of those times when my lead didn't work out." MacFarland furrowed his brow. "This is an odd hour for you to be out. Early lunch hour? Come on down to my cart. I'll get you a cup of coffee."

Warren followed him, frowning as she explained her early break. "No, they've gone and fucked up the schedule. They were supposed to pour the cement for the four main pillars on Wednesday, but Vogel moved the schedule up. I can't get my crane in position to move steel until the damn cement pump truck is out of the way. I hate it when they change the schedule like that. There's twenty of us, all just standing around like dog turds on a shoe."

MacFarland smiled. Other people's scheduling problems didn't really concern him, except there might be more business today with more people like Wanda standing around. Even as that idea took shape, something bothered him. "I had the impression that Vogel and the management of Forrester were so concerned about keeping costs low. Isn't this expensive, keeping a bunch of workers standing around?"

Warren greeted Rufus as they reached the wagon. "Damn fucking right it's expensive. I guess cement is in short supply, so they have to pour when they have the cement available. Not even our regular supplier though. Doesn't make any sense to me. But what do I know? I'm just a fucking crane operator."

"I know the feeling," laughed MacFarland. "But sometimes, it's nice to be out of the loop."

Warren mellowed, and finally smiled. She was much prettier when she smiled. "Guess you're right. Hey, how about that cup of coffee? Might as well just enjoy my idle time."

Rufus hastily poured her a cup of coffee and handed it to her in a surprisingly deferential manner.

"How will you know when to go back?" asked MacFarland.

She pointed towards the construction site. "See that red pipe moving around up there? That's the feed pipe on the Putzmeister 70Z. When they put that mother away, then I can get back to work. As long as it's extended, they are still pumping concrete. It'll be hours before I can do anything."

"Maybe Vogel will send you and the others home."

Warren shrugged. "Maybe. Right now he's too busy making sure they get the cement poured. Never seen him so anxious to get a job finished." Warren sipped on her coffee. "Say, what was this hot lead that didn't work out?"

"I thought that Boyce owned a red truck, but it turns out that he doesn't."

Warren rubbed her chin, coaxing the memory to the forefront of her mind. "I've seen him with a red truck, but you're right. It's not his. He borrowed it from a cousin of his or something. He used it to lug firewood down from the foothills. Offered to give me some firewood, but I live in a stupid apartment without a fireplace. What would I do with firewood? I think the asshole just wanted a reason to find out where I lived."

MacFarland stared at Wanda in surprise. "His cousin's truck? No wonder we couldn't find anything registered to him! Do you know the name of this cousin?"

Warren shook her head. "No, of course not. I try to have as little to do with Boyce as I can. I take it that this is an important breakthrough?"

MacFarland wanted to give her a hug, but he stopped himself just in time. There was no telling how Busty would respond to his excitement. He contented himself with smiling broadly. "Wanda, you don't know just how much help you've been!"

CHAPTER FIFTY-ONE

TUESDAY, APRIL 26, 0945 HOURS

MACFARLAND WAS FEELING FRUSTRATED and annoyed with Pierson.

When he told her that the truck might be registered to one of Boyce's relatives, she told him that she didn't have time for wild goose chases. He then got into a heated argument with her, said some things that he already regretted (and he hoped that she likewise regretted what she said, though he suspected she wouldn't), and separated with no promise to look into any of Boyce's relatives. He planned on going over to Boyce's house and asking his wife about the truck, but first he wanted to find out why Picket had been fired.

Picket lived in the part of Aurora they called Saudi Aurora, mainly because there was nothing out there but fields and prairie dogs. MacFarland asked Rufus to watch his wagon, which Rufus reluctantly agreed to. "Do you have someplace else to be?" asked MacFarland.

"I got my meetings to go to," said Rufus sullenly.

"Rufus, you don't have any meetings. Please just watch my cart for me."

"I do so got meetings," muttered Rufus as MacFarland headed off for his truck. "Important meetings."

MacFarland drove east on Colfax. Traffic was heavy this morning, in both directions, which never made sense to MacFarland. Then, after a half hour of creeping along, he passed a construction zone that funneled both directions of Colfax traffic into one alternating lane. Why didn't they just put up a detour, he wondered?

It was almost nine forty-five when he pulled up in front of Picket's house. MacFarland didn't see a car in the driveway. The garage door was closed, so Picket's car was probably parked inside. He went up to the front door and knocked. After waiting a couple of minutes, he knocked again. The door slowly opened. A bleary-eyed woman, wearing a dirty white bathrobe, answered the door.

"Yes?" she said.

"Hello, I'm looking for Marty," he said.

"Marty? Whaddya want with Marty?"

"I'd like to talk to him," he responded. He could smell booze on her breath. The odor brought back bad memories.

"He ain't here."

"Where is he?"

"Hell if I know. Probably at work. Probably out drinking. Probably out whoring. Who the hell knows where the damn fucker is? He's often gone for days at a time."

"Does he have two jobs?"

"What the fuck are you talking about? He's only got one job."

"You mean at Forrester Equipment and Construction?"

"Yeah, that's where he works."

"I was told he was fired."

"Fired? What the hell are you talking about?"

"He hasn't been there since Saturday night, Mrs. Picket."

She stared at him in disbelief. "I ain't seen him since Sunday. What day is today?"

"It's Tuesday, Mrs. Picket."

"Damn," she said, leaning unsteadily up against the door jamb. "Where the fuck is that bastard? Where the fuck did the time go?"

CHAPTER FIFTY-TWO

WEDNESDAY, APRIL 27, 0910 HOURS

MACFARLAND WAS CONVINCED that something was going on at Forrester Equipment and Construction, but he wasn't sure what. First Brady dies in an accident. Then Hightower gets killed in a hit-and-run. Now Picket goes missing.

There were too many coincidences for this to be just random unrelated events. If the events were related, what was the common denominator? Just the company. The company and the rumor that people in management were embezzling money.

MacFarland spent the night reviewing his notecards. Five of the cards stood out:

- *Bozworth says that Vogel is behind the tool selling scam.*
- *The new guard says that Vogel claims Picket called in sick.*
- *Vogel changed the schedule in order to pour cement.*

- *Boyce thinks Vogel is responsible for Brady's death, since Vogel was calling the shots.*
- *Picket was fired on Monday for missing work, but his replacement was hired before he was fired.*

Everything was leading back to Vogel. He had a question about the last factoid. Who fired Picket? The guard said Picket missed two days, but MacFarland knew he was there Saturday. So it had to be Sunday and Monday. Didn't the security guards report to Vogel? Although he had no confirmation, MacFarland was fairly certain that it must be Vogel who was behind Picket's dismissal. Call it his cop instinct, but he felt that Vogel was deeply involved in this.

But was he responsible for Hightower's death? That part didn't make sense, since everything pointed towards Boyce for that one.

Rufus hadn't shown up this morning. MacFarland was afraid that his insistence that Rufus watch his cart yesterday had offended the homeless man. Those meetings of Rufus' had to be imaginary! Who did Rufus know who would actually attend a meeting? He was fairly sure that Rufus wasn't going over to Jerry Baker's office to do errands for Jerry. Rufus headed in the exact opposite direction when he went to his "meetings."

Then it occurred to him that Rufus would do exactly that, especially if he didn't want the Viet Cong trailing him to headquarters. Had MacFarland been unwittingly screwing up Rufus's chances for gainful employment?

He went across the street to where Sidney Morgan had his hot dog stand. Felicity wasn't there, of course. She would be in school at this hour. "Hi Mr. Morgan, could I ask a favor of you?"

Sidney Morgan stared at him blankly. "What sort of favor?" He ran a hand nervously through his receding grey hair.

"I have to go down the street for a while. If any customers come to my cart, could you call them over here? Tell them I will be back in an hour or so and you will be able to take care of their needs."

Morgan nodded uncertainly. "Yeah, sure, I guess I could do that. You're MacFarland, right?"

MacFarland nodded, extending his hand. "Yes, I am. And I really want to thank you for helping me out."

"No problem. Guess that's what neighbors are for."

MacFarland smiled, then hurried down the street towards the construction site. He noticed that the cement pump truck was gone. Wanda's crane was busy moving steel girders into a staging area for a tower crane to move up where they were needed. The steel skeleton of the building was already ten stories tall. He didn't stop at the guard gate but walked purposefully towards the construction offices.

Vogel was sitting at the first desk. As MacFarland entered, he looked up, a look of surprise that transformed into an angry scowl. Vogel was a beefy man, with slabs of flesh slapped onto his face. He had a barrel chest and a ballooning stomach. *This man is a killer?* thought MacFarland incredulously. Although MacFarland and Vogel had never actually met, Vogel acted as though he knew exactly who MacFarland was.

"How did you get past the guard?" he demanded, standing up and starting to come around his desk. Did the man think he was going to physically remove MacFarland from the office? "This is private property. You have to leave."

MacFarland had to get Vogel out of the office, and short of grabbing him by the collar and dragging him out, he could only think of one way to get him out of sight of the other occupants. "I know what you are doing here. I have the proof. I have pictures, Vogel."

Vogel stopped short. "I don't know what you're talking about," he said hesitantly.

"I can send them to the cops. I am sure they could figure out what to do with them." MacFarland smiled. "Or perhaps we could find a more private place to discuss what I might do with them."

Janet stared wide-eyed at the two men. "Should I call the police, Mr. Vogel?"

"Shut up, Janet," snapped Vogel. He pushed past MacFarland. "Come outside," he ordered.

MacFarland smiled at Janet and followed Vogel out of the trailer.

Vogel, who was two inches taller and twenty pounds heavier than MacFarland tried to push MacFarland up against the wall of the trailer. MacFarland grabbed Vogel's finger, twisted it back, and using the man's pain as leverage, got his arm twisted behind his back. MacFarland swung the man around and shoved him face first against the trailer. "Don't try any tricks like that, Vogel. Now, I want some answers."

"Ahhhh, you're hurting me!"

"I'm going to hurt you more if you don't talk to me. Who put you up to it?"

"I don't know what you're talking about," whined Vogel.

MacFarland pulled Vogel's arm up higher. He didn't want to do any real damage, so he merely gave it a couple of quick tugs, just enough to create a lot of pain, but not enough to tear ligaments. Vogel yelped again, this time attracting the attention of a couple of men walking towards the deep pit that would eventually be the underground parking garage of the building. The two men hesitated, then one of them pushed the elbow of the other, and they hurried on towards their destination.

"You know what I'm talking about," said MacFarland.

He knew better than to put words into Vogel's mouth. The problem with using pain to elicit information is that the perp often told you what you wanted to hear, just to stop the pain. The vaguer the questions, the more likely the suspect would admit to something that was true. Vogel should have no idea what kind of pictures MacFarland had. He wondered just what pictures would cause Vogel to panic.

"I'm not the one responsible," said Vogel, a tone of desperation in his voice.

"Responsible for what?" demanded MacFarland. He kept the pressure on Vogel's arm, just to remind him that he could increase the pain in the blink of an eye.

"The embezzlement. That's all Pelligrini's doing. You have to believe me!"

"But you're part of it, aren't you? You get a piece of the action, don't you?"

"Yes, yes! Stopping twisting my arm! I'll tell you everything I know, just let me go!"

MacFarland released the pressure slightly, but didn't let go of Vogel's arm. "Go on, talk. It can't just be Pelligrini who's involved. I know you're involved in more than just embezzling."

"Okay, so I get a piece of the action, but it's just a small piece. Pelligrini and Peterson, they're the ones who run everything. Pelligrini does the price fixing and Peterson does the money laundering. I don't know more than that, I swear!"

"You're a lying piece of shit, Vogel. Who was responsible for killing Brady? He found out about your scheme, didn't he? And you had him killed."

"You can't pin that on me! The Safety Board--"

"I know what the Safety Board said. But the Safety Board got it wrong, didn't they? Who gave the order to waste Brady?"

"It was an accident, I tell you!" Vogel stopped. Both he and MacFarland could hear a police siren screeching in the distance, but drawing closer. "You better let me go! You have nothing on me. You don't have any pictures! Let me go, and I won't tell the police anything."

MacFarland pushed Vogel hard against the wall, released his arm, and stepped back. "I'm watching you, Vogel. I know you arranged that accident for Brady. I know you had Hightower killed. I'm putting the pieces together. Watch your step, got it? And tell Pelligrini and Peterson that their days are numbered also. The net is closing in."

MacFarland was halfway back to his cart when he saw the squad car pull into the construction entrance. He smiled. He didn't think Vogel would say anything to the police. And while he wasn't sure that all the pieces fit together as nicely as he had suggested to Vogel, he hoped that putting pressure on Vogel might reveal more pieces of the puzzle. Soon, everything would fall into place.

CHAPTER FIFTY-THREE

WEDNESDAY, APRIL 27, 0930 HOURS

MACFARLAND WAS NOT at all sure how reliable Vogel's statements had been. MacFarland had never been a strong advocate of brutal interrogation tactics, for he was well aware of the mixed results they delivered. On the other hand, he was not above using force if the circumstances required quick response.

Most of the time, however, it depended on the suspect as to whether force worked. The more experienced and committed the suspect was, the more likely that he would be able to modify his responses to throw the police off the trail. The less experienced the suspect was, the more likely that force or the threat of force would bear viable results. All too often, force worked well on people who would talk under other forms of interrogation.

Pierson, who was much better at interrogation than he was, never used force to obtain a confession. She preferred to use psychology and subterfuge to get the suspect to spill his guts. With her, it worked. Of course, most of the things she did worked. She was just a damn good cop. Or just maybe, most guys liked confessing to a pretty woman.

In this case, Vogel's statements confirmed what MacFarland already suspected. He didn't believe Peterson when he had claimed that he had no interaction with Forrester Equipment and Construction. Peterson was the kind of man who had his fingers in every pie. While he didn't like to get his own hands dirty, he did make sure that he knew what was happening in his vast economic empire. It was one of the traits that Nicole had been fond of describing--how incredibly knowledgeable Peterson was of all the minutiae of his organizations.

That sort of thing seemed to impress Nicole.

Rufus was standing near the hot dog wagon when MacFarland returned. "You're not open today, boss?" Rufus asked.

"I had things to do, Rufus. I wasn't sure if you were coming."

"Oh, I'm here alright. I got my meetings out of the way first thing. Want me to set up the wagon for you?"

"That would be great, Rufus! I have to go someplace else."

"Where're you going to, boss?"

"The CCP Building. I think I have the dirt on Peterson I need to get him to do something stupid."

Rufus stared, wide-eyed. "Really? You gonna take the bastard down finally, boss?"

"I hope so, Rufus, I sincerely hope so." MacFarland handed Rufus the key to the cash drawer, then headed resolutely towards his truck.

Maybe this time, he would be able to shake Peterson's tree enough to get the fruit to fall.

CHAPTER FIFTY-FOUR

WEDNESDAY, APRIL 27, 1005 HOURS

IT TOOK MacFarland a lot longer to get from one side of Denver to the other side. He also had problems finding a parking space close to the Consolidated Colorado Properties Building. He eventually parked several blocks away and walked back towards the building that housed Norris Peterson.

As MacFarland was about to enter the building, he felt a hand on his shoulder. He spun around rapidly, assuming a defensive posture but ready to go on the attack. The man who had stopped him anticipated his move and jumped back, holding his hands up defensively. "Whoa, there, fella! Let's not get over excited!"

MacFarland stared into the face of Grey Wilson, the man who had once saved him, then mysteriously disappeared. "You," he said in an accusing voice. "You've been following me!"

Wilson smiled broadly. Even with a wide smile, Wilson's face was elongated and worn, with indecisive eyebrows and droopy eyes. If Wilson had been vegetable instead of animal, he would have been an old, weathered tree that had withstood far too many storms. "Guess I have. May I ask what you're doing over here, instead of watching over that nice hot dog stand you have?"

"I don't think it's any of your business what I'm doing."

Grey put his hand gently on MacFarland's arm. "Let's go get a cup of coffee, okay?"

MacFarland looked angrily at Wilson's hand on his arm. "Why should I go with you?"

Wilson sighed loudly. "I suppose I could just arrest you. But I would rather work with you. And right now, I need a cup of coffee. It's been a long night."

MacFarland glared angrily at the man, then allowed his countenance to soften. Maybe coffee would loosen Wilson's tongue. It could be a chance to learn what part he played in this case. "I don't know where there is a coffee shop around here."

"Two blocks over," said Wilson. He pulled a small object out of his pocket and spoke into it. "Do you want to join us?"

MacFarland heard a woman's voice respond, "Meet you there."

As they walked away from the CCP Building, MacFarland carefully examined his escort. "You're FBI, aren't you?"

Wilson nodded. "Yes, though I've been trying to maintain a low profile. You make it difficult to remain hidden."

MacFarland nodded. "Were you posing as a janitor in this building a while back?"

Wilson seemed surprised that MacFarland knew that, but slowly nodded. "Yes, I needed to get access to the building when no one was around. Doing a bit of janitorial work seemed like the best approach."

"What were you looking for?"

Wilson smiled, then pointed to a small breakfast bar. "That's where we're going."

Wilson didn't seemed inclined to answer MacFarland's question, so MacFarland shrugged and followed the older man into the restaurant. Wilson went to a table near the back--a policeman's table--that provided a view of the back of the CCP building, the street, and most of the customers, while still keeping one's back to the wall. Wilson took the best seat, allowing MacFarland to take the next best seat. They had no sooner sat down then a young woman hurried over to the table, pulling off her coat and dropping it on a chair next to Wilson.

"Mr. MacFarland, this is Norma Sykes, my partner."

MacFarland looked at Norma. This was the first chance he had to see her up close. Mysteriously intense, with burnt sienna hair, dark brown eyes, a thin oval face, and a wide smile that flashed in his direction but didn't really include him. She looked to be twenty-five years old, five foot eight inches tall, and probably somewhat under one hundred and forty pounds. So this was the Norma Sykes who was working with Pierson. Pierson had never said Sykes was this attractive.

Norma held out her hand. "Did you guys order anything yet? I'm famished!" After shaking MacFarland's hand, she waved for the waitress who hurried over to their table, notepad in hand.

"I'd like a Number Two," said Norma. "And a glass of orange juice and lots of coffee."

The waitress looked towards MacFarland. "Just coffee for me."

Wilson glanced at the menu, then handed it to the waitress, who put it back with the other menus at the end of the table. "I'll have two slices of toast, some strawberry jam, an order of bacon, and one fried egg, well-cooked. And coffee also."

"This is a surprise," said Norma, looking at MacFarland and smiling. This time her smile did include him. "I feel as though I know you so well, yet this is the first time we've actually met."

"I found him about to enter the CCP Building," explained Wilson.

Sykes shook her finger accusingly. "Naughty boy! I can't imagine you doing anything good inside that building, Mr. MacFarland."

MacFarland was getting frustrated with Sykes' condescending attitude. He also didn't like someone he didn't know treating him in such a familiar manner. "Just what is going on here? Why is the FBI snooping around the CCP Building?"

Wilson and Sykes looked at each other briefly, then Wilson nodded ever so slightly. "We're part of a larger investigation into racketeering and fraud," she said. "We're based out of Chicago, but Mr. Peterson is heavily involved in the case we're investigating, so we've been assigned to Denver. I work as liaison with the local police departments and Grey does a lot of the undercover work."

"How is Peterson involved?" ask MacFarland.

Wilson shook his head. "We can't really discuss that, Mark. As far as you're concerned, he might just be a material witness."

"As far as I'm concerned, he's a killer."

Sykes put a reassuring hand on his arm. He was caught off guard by the intimacy. "We know about the incident with Nicole, Mr. MacFarland. That was a travesty of justice, I can assure you. But our interest in Norris Peterson goes way beyond murder."

"Does Pierson know what you're doing?" MacFarland asked Sykes.

Sykes shrugged, then sat back as the waitress brought over their orders. She waited until the waitress had finished putting all the dishes out and poured coffee for everyone before she spoke. "Detective Pierson believes, quite correctly, that she and I are part of a drug trafficking task force. As we said, we're involved in a much larger investigation."

"But you can't really discuss any of the details with me," said MacFarland in a surly tone.

Norma Sykes smiled broadly. "Oh, you know us so well!"

"So what do you want with me?" asked MacFarland.

Grey leaned forward, concentrating on the task of spreading jam on his toast. "We want you to sell hot dogs, MacFarland. Stay away from Peterson. Don't mess up our case, understand?"

"I think Peterson is responsible for the death of Mike Brady," said MacFarland.

Wilson shook his head. "He may have been complicit, but he didn't order this death."

"But he is involved with the embezzlement," insisted MacFarland.

Wilson shrugged indifferently, as he started to eat his egg and bacon. "We are still trying to determine the extent of Mr. Peterson's involvement with a variety of things."

MacFarland tried a different tactic. "Do you know about the money laundering?"

Neither Sykes nor Wilson batted an eye, yet it was apparent to MacFarland that he had caught them off guard. "What do you know about money laundering?" asked Wilson slowly.

MacFarland took a wild guess. "I know that Peterson is involved in that part of it."

There was a moment of silence as Wilson and Sykes busied themselves with their food. MacFarland wasn't sure how long the two agents had been working together, but they had a rapport that was remarkable. Almost as good as when he and Pierson worked together.

Finally, Sykes put her fork down. "Mr. MacFarland, it's like this. We can't stop you from finding out who was responsible for the death of Michael Brady. We'll concede that one to you. But please, focus your attention on that problem, and let us take care of Peterson."

"And if I don't?"

Wilson's voice was heavy and threatening. "If you don't, you will find yourself facing an obstruction charge. We can play pretty nasty if we have to, Mark. We'd rather play nice with you. Just don't test us."

MacFarland looked from one to the other, then stood up. "I'll think about what you said." Then he turned and left the restaurant.

CHAPTER FIFTY-FIVE

FRIDAY, APRIL 29, 1716 HOURS

MACFARLAND WAS in a grumpy mood on Wednesday night after he got home from his AA meeting. When he saw Pierson, he asked her about Norma Sykes and Grey Wilson, but Pierson was in an even more pissy mood than MacFarland. "I don't want to talk about the Fucking Bunch of Imbeciles!" she snapped. "Just leave me the hell alone."

"You know, you get more flies with honey than with vinegar," said MacFarland, trying to be helpful.

"That's bees, not flies! You get flies with shit, and that's all I get from those imbeciles!"

Maybe it was because of Pierson's mood, but for most of Thursday, MacFarland was also in a grumpy mood, snapping at Rufus, demonstrating impatience with customers, and losing all interest in his language lessons. After an hour of being told that he was doing everything wrong, Rufus had finally torn off his plastic gloves, threw them on the ground, and said he was going off to find Viet Cong sympathizers. "They'll be easier to get along with than you," he said sullenly as he walked off.

“There are no Viet Cong sympathizers in Denver!” shouted MacFarland.

“Shows what you know!” shouted back Rufus.

By Friday, MacFarland’s mood had improved considerably, primarily because he had decided that the Feds would have to lock him up before he stopped working any angle of his case. Okay, he might not be able to go to Peterson’s office to confront him, but they didn’t say anything about his home. He could catch the man at his home. Or on the street. Or at his club. MacFarland smiled broadly. There was no way the FBI was going to interfere with his pursuit of Norris Gilbert Peterson!

His mood remained positive for most of the day. He even spent a few minutes across the street getting to know Sidney Morgan a little better. Morgan specialized in a wide variety of flavored hot dogs, including a variety of regional style dogs: Kansas City style, Chicago style, Boston style, New Jersey style. MacFarland was particularly interested in what Morgan described as an Oki dog--served on flour tortillas, covered with chili and pastrami. "It is particularly popular on Okinawa," said Morgan. “Hence its name.”

As MacFarland went back to his own wagon, he began to realize that perhaps his competitor did more business for reasons that went beyond the attractive looks of his pretty step-daughter.

MacFarland was shutting down his wagon when he noticed Wanda Warren walking resolutely towards his corner. He greeted her cheerfully, despite the worried look on her face. "Something bothering you, Wanda?"

"I think they’ve killed Picket," she said.

MacFarland stared at her in surprise. He knew instinctively that the "they" were the mysterious party or parties who had presumably killed Brady. "What makes you think that Picket was killed?" he asked. He realized that he had dropped the ball on following up with Picket. The man was missing, yet MacFarland had not done anything to locate him. He had been so focused on the information provided by Vogel that Peterson was involved in the embezzlement scheme that he had let Picket entirely slip from his mind. Damn, what kind of a cop was he? That was the problem. He wasn't any kind of a cop.

"I don't have any evidence," said Wanda testily. "Just believe me, Mac, when I tell you that I am sure of it."

"I'm not doubting you Wanda. I've learned that you have pretty good instincts about these things. I just want to understand how you got to this conclusion."

"Okay, here's what I know. Picket hasn't been around for a while. He was supposed to be at work yesterday, but he didn't show up. So I ask around. They say he's been fired. Well, that's pretty damn strange. No one gets fired at that damn place. Fired for what reason? For not showing up! What the hell? So I called his wife and that drunken bitch hasn't seen him in almost a week."

This confirmed the information that MacFarland had since Tuesday. "When did you call her?" he asked.

"Yesterday. When he didn't show up. That's what got me concerned."

"I didn't realize you were close to Picket," said MacFarland.

"Why? Because I'm a lesbian? I can't have male friends?"

"I didn't mean it like that, Wanda. I just didn't know that he was the type of guy you hung with."

"We don't hang. We just have a drink together once in a while. Sometimes it gets lonely drinking by yourself. Even Picket can be good company some of the time."

MacFarland nodded. "I share your concern that Picket's disappearance is odd. But that in itself doesn't prove that he was killed. His wife told me on Tuesday that he often is gone days at a time."

"I don't know anything about that, but I wouldn't trust anything she says. Okay, how about this? On Monday, they changed the cement pouring schedule."

"Yeah, you mentioned that on Monday. Why is that significant?"

Wanda leaned in closer so that she could whisper conspiratorially to MacFarland. "They were supposed to pour the bottom parking floor foundation, but instead, they pour those four towering columns. Why'd they do that?" She didn't wait for MacFarland to respond. He didn't have a response anyway. "I'll tell you why. Because Picket's body is in one of those towers. They buried the damn fucker in cement."

CHAPTER FIFTY-SIX

SATURDAY, APRIL 30, 0830 HOURS

MIKE BRADY'S death might have been an accident or it might have been murder. Unfortunately, there was no way to use the facts of the incident to prove murder. But if Marty Picket's body was indeed encased in one of the cement towers on the construction site, that clearly was homicide. It would go a long way to proving that the "accident" three months earlier was probably not truly an accident.

The problem was, until they found a body, it would be hard to prove there was a murder.

He trapped Pierson in the kitchen on Saturday morning. He described the circumstances of Picket's disappearance and Warren's suspicions. Pierson listened, then pursed her lips. "We don't have any record of a John Doe showing up in the morgue or in any hospitals. I will run his name and see if anything has come up. You say he lives in Aurora? I'll have to check with them too. The best I can do other than that, Mac, is to issue a BOLO."

A 'be on the lookout' is better than nothing, thought MacFarland. "Can we get a search warrant?"

"For what?" asked Pierson.

"For the construction site."

Pierson gave MacFarland one of her standard looks of disbelief. "Get some evidence that he's really a victim, Mac. We don't have probable cause to go onto the site. And given who owns it, I can just imagine the fireworks that might follow if anyone finds out you are involved. I'll do what I can, Mac, but I can't bend the rules, even for you."

"When we were partners, you used to bend the rules, Cyn."

Pierson looked hurt by the comment. "That's not true, Mac. I was the one who made sure you followed the rules. We made a good team because you caught the bastards and I made sure they got convicted."

"Does that mean we're still a team?"

Pierson shook her head in disbelief. "You're an asshole, Mac. We'll always be a team. Though God alone knows why."

MacFarland took his wagon downtown and after he arranged for Rufus to take over, he headed back out to Aurora to talk to Picket's wife. He knocked on her door and waited patiently for her to answer. It took several knocks before she finally opened the door. She was leaning against the door jamb, dressed only in panties and a bra. If a woman was going to dress like a Victoria's Secret commercial, she could at least have an attractive body. Or clean underwear. She squinted in the bright morning light.

"Whaddya want?" she asked.

"I was wondering if you had any news of Marty, Mrs. Picket."

"Oh, fuck, him again? Why is everyone so interested in Marty? Does he owe you money?"

That gave MacFarland an idea. "No, but as a matter of fact, I owe him some money."

Mrs. Picket blinked several times and tried to focus on him. "How much?"

"Twenty bucks."

"Lemme see if he's here." She turned into the house and shouted "Marty!" After a few minutes of shouting, there was no response. "Gimme the money and I'll give it to him."

"It would be best if I gave it to him myself," said MacFarland. "Does Marty have any relatives or friends he might stay with?"

"Naw, no relatives. He's got a brother who lives in Oregon. Friends? Maybe Pete."

"Pete? Do you have an address?"

"Whaddya think I am, the fucking phone book? I don't know where he lives."

"Do you know his last name, at least?"

"Rodriquez. Yeah, that's it."

He was about to turn and leave when she reached out and grabbed his arm. "Hey, you want a blow job? I can do ya for twenty bucks."

He pulled his arm away. "No, not today," he said, walking away from the house. As he climbed back into his truck, he wondered if Marty Picket had just gotten smart and left Colorado searching for a better life.

CHAPTER FIFTY-SEVEN

SUNDAY, MAY 1, 1000 HOURS

MACFARLAND DID NOT TAKE his cart downtown on Sunday morning. Instead, as soon as he could, he called up someone from his past. "Eric? This is Mark MacFarland."

Eric Logan had been on the force during the same time period MacFarland had been on it. Logan had retired a couple of years ago, long after MacFarland had been dismissed from the force in disgrace. He wondered if Logan would even speak with him.

"MacFarland? My God, I never expected to hear from you again! How are you doing?"

"Six hundred and eighty-five days sober," said MacFarland. "I take it one day at a time. But I have a good business, I'm almost self-sufficient."

Logan chuckled. "I also hear that you're still fighting crime," he said, unable to hide his amusement. "Except I thought you told me once that you left Patrol so you wouldn't get shot."

"I admit, selling hot dogs is a bit more dangerous than I thought. I think being a cop is something that's in your blood. I still get involved in trying to solve crimes, mostly those that the police can't solve or seem to have forgotten."

Logan became serious. "Are you working on something now?"

"Yes, Eric. And I need your help."

There was a pause on the other end of the phone. Finally Logan said, "You know where I live? I'm north of Castle Rock. The easiest way to find me is to take South Parker Road."

MacFarland wrote down the address and said he would see Eric Logan in an hour.

MacFarland had worked with Eric Logan several times in the past, though calling Logan in to a case usually meant that you were dealing with a corpse. Logan managed one of the cadaver dogs, and their job was to find human remains. MacFarland and Logan had always gotten along, but they had not been particularly close. Logan was a lot like Pierson--a cop who went strictly by the book. On more than one occasion, Logan had indicated that he didn't always approve of MacFarland's less than orthodox techniques.

Logan lived in a ranch-style house set back from South Parker Road. The house was set up on a hill, overlooking a gently rolling slope that led down to a pond. Clumps of trees surrounded the pond. Behind the house was a set of low buildings nestled in a fenced in area. MacFarland assumed that was the kennel where Logan kept his dogs. A split rail fence enclosed a large open area surrounding the house. An Open Road RV sat in the driveway. A Honda Civic was parked next to that. MacFarland pulled in behind the Civic and walked up to the house.

The door opened even before he knocked. He was greeted by a tall, bald man with smiling blue eyes and a large German Shepherd who wagged his tail excitedly.

"Lucy told me you were here," he explained, inviting MacFarland inside.

MacFarland shook Logan's hand, then leaned over to rub Lucy behind her ears. Lucy carefully sniffed MacFarland, then resumed wagging her tail.

"Can I offer you something to drink? Coke? Coffee?"

"Water would be just fine," said MacFarland.

Logan gestured for MacFarland to follow him to the kitchen where he got a glass of water from a filter pitcher in his refrigerator. Lucy followed, then planted herself comfortably on the floor, watching the two men for a moment, then resting her muzzle on her paws and feigning sleep. The two men sat down at the kitchen table. Logan still looked more like an ex-Marine than an ex-cop. In top shape, hair still closely cropped, eyes always alert. He was the kind of man who always expected good situations to turn bad and was always ready for that contingency.

"Can Lucy still find bodies?" asked MacFarland.

Logan looked over at Lucy fondly. "Yes, she can. She's getting old, and because of the wound, she can't move as well as she used to, but her nose is still top notch as ever."

"The wound? What happened to her?"

"She got shot by a guy who had buried a little girl on his property. I am sure you're aware that Lucy is a badged police officer. Shooting her is a felony, like shooting a human cop. The guy would have been put in jail just for that. Fortunately, Lucy had already found the location of the girl's body, so the scumbag is serving a life sentence for murder and concurrent time for shooting an officer. Lucy was already nine years old when she got shot, and it took a long time for the wound to heal. So she got retired. I was allowed to keep her, since I had worked with her most of her life."

"She looks like she gets around pretty well now."

"She has good days and she has bad days. On her good days, she likes to remain active." He smiled. "I guess she has cop in her blood too. We do some private freelance work. She still loves to find cadavers."

MacFarland nodded, looking over at the sleeping dog. "I'd like her to help me find a cadaver."

"Where do you think there's a body?" asked Logan. "And why do you think there's a body? And if there is a body, why aren't the police involved in the case?"

"Wow, a lot of questions!" said MacFarland. "First, I think the body may be on a construction site." He went on to explain the accident to Mike Brady, Wanda's suspicions about the nature of his death, the death of Hightower, and now the disappearance of Picket.

"And this woman, Wanda Warren, thinks Picket might be buried in cement on the construction site?" asked Logan.

"Yes. She thinks the construction schedule was changed in order to hide the body. I admit it's circumstantial."

Logan nodded. "It's quite a far-fetched story, Mark. I can now see why Chamberlain wouldn't be involved yet. It's also a big leap to tie all these deaths and disappearances together."

"The one connection is the construction site. And the probable embezzlement that's going on." MacFarland was about to mention the FBI involvement in the case, but he decided to keep that information private.

Logan nodded. "So, what do you want me to do?"

"I was hoping you could see if your dog could find Picket's remains."

Logan held up his hand to silence MacFarland. "You came to me because you think since I'm not on the force anymore that I would just do this? Well, think again, Mark.

First, Lucy is a certified HRD dog. I won't do anything to jeopardize her certification."

"HRD?"

"Human remains detection. As I said, I am not going to do anything to jeopardize that certification, and going onto private property without permission or a search warrant could do that. Second, this is a construction site. Suppose Lucy finds Indian remains instead of your security guard. That might get the entire construction project put on hold as various groups fight over an Indian burial site."

"Could Lucy find something that old?"

"Absolutely. Lucy helped locate the remains of an Army and Indian skirmish that happened out near Kiowa back in the 1860's. That's not the issue. The point I am making is that we won't do anything that is illegal or improper."

"So what do I have to do to make it proper?"

Logan shrugged. "Get permission from the guy who owns the property for us to do a search, and Lucy and I will be happy to help you."

MacFarland relaxed, smiling happily. "I think I can manage that."

CHAPTER FIFTY-EIGHT

SUNDAY, MAY 1, 1615 HOURS

IT DIDN'T TAKE LONG for MacFarland to convince Norris Peterson that it would be in his best interests to cooperate with an "informal" investigation of the construction site.

MacFarland was fairly certain that Peterson was not involved in this particular murder, at least not directly, and Peterson wasn't stupid enough to hide a body anywhere that could lead back to him. MacFarland was banking on Peterson being so certain that there wasn't a body at the site that he would be willing to risk cooperating with the police.

When MacFarland ended his call, Logan looked at him reproachfully. "This is not a police operation. I can see that you're still up to your old tricks."

"I did say it was an 'informal' investigation," said MacFarland. "If there's no body, what harm is there?"

Logan smiled grimly. "You're a piece of work, Mark. Let's go see if we can find a body."

MacFarland drove Logan and Lucy up to Denver. As

they headed north along I-25, Logan called up Chamberlain.

"Hi Bob. Yes, it's Eric. It has been a long time, hasn't it? Say, I have a favor to ask of you. I'm going up to a construction site with Lucy right now. If she finds anything, we can get a search warrant from her nose. MacFarland thinks a body may--yes, that MacFarland. Is there another one? Now, calm down! I think he's on to something. Yes, yes, I know, but we both know he was one of your best detectives. Of course I'll keep him on a leash. If Lucy finds anything, I'd like you to move on it rather quickly. Huh? Yeah, we have permission. Oh, it won't be hard to find. It's right across the street from you." He turned to MacFarland. "You made a recording of that call, right? Yes, we have Peterson giving us permission to go onto his property. As far as we know he's the owner. Sure, go ahead and verify it. It'll take us another half hour to get there. Yes, yes, I said I'd keep him under control. Bob, I used to train attack dogs. I can control MacFarland. Okay, see you there."

MacFarland was not pleased that Logan had called the Commander, but he wasn't surprised. Logan had a reputation for making sure that cases he was involved with ended up with convictions. As he once boasted, "Lucy is one of the most valuable assets the police department has. We don't want to waste her talents with sloppy work."

As they reached the construction site, Logan got another call. "Good," he said. "If your officer can get him to sign the consent form, then that would be better. Yes, we're going onto the property now. I'll give you a call if we get positive results."

The guard at the gate must have received a call from Peterson already, because he waved MacFarland's truck onto the site. MacFarland drove over to the construction office and parked. He, Logan and Lucy got out of the truck. No one was working on the site, though the guard came out to see what they were doing.

"What happens now?" MacFarland asks.

"I talk with Lucy, and then she gets to work." He knelt down and put his hands on each side of Lucy's head. She licked his nose. He whispered something to her, and then she bounded away from him. She raced around the job site, then ran down the ramp that led down into the deep pit that would eventually become the underground parking garage.

A crisscross pattern of rebar on the floor of the pit made moving around challenging for the dog, but Lucy persevered, nose close to the ground, moving back and forth. As she got closer to one of the cement columns, she became more and more excited. When she was just a few feet from the column, she lay down on the ground, her paw outstretched before her. Logan pulled out his phone and set it on record.

"The time is four-fifteen, tentative positive results, on my way to verity." He, MacFarland, and the guard climbed down the ramp into the pit, then stepped awkwardly towards one of the four columns where Lucy still lay on the ground. "What have you got, Lucy?" asked Logan as he arrived.

Lucy patted the ground with her paw, right next to the edge of the cement column.

"Where is it, Lucy?" asked the handler.

Lucy stood up and placed her nose against the concrete, about eight inches off the ground. Logan marked the spot with chalk, then pulled a rope out of his pocket and waved it above Lucy's head. She jumped up and got a grip of the rope with her teeth. She and Logan then began a short, strenuous game of tug-o-war, which Lucy finally won. She wagged her tail, then brought the rope over to Logan's feet and dropped it on the ground.

"Good girl," he said, then spoke into his phone. "Positive results found in cement column, southeast corner of construction site." He stopped recording, then dialed Chamberlain. "Bob? Affirmative. We have positive results. Get the warrant and your men over here. The body seems to be encased in cement, so I don't think it's going anywhere."

Logan petted Lucy's neck and turned to MacFarland. "It seems your information was correct, Mark. There's a body in that pillar."

CHAPTER FIFTY-NINE

SUNDAY, MAY 1, 1900 HOURS

THE POLICE ARRIVED JUST after six in the evening on Sunday night. Chamberlain was with them. He briefly greeted MacFarland, then spoke quietly with Logan.

One of the officers asked the guard to get out of the pit, since this was now officially a crime scene. They got the warrant rather quickly, then stretched tape around the column.

As they were doing that, Logan had Lucy check the rest of the site, but no other bodies turned up. MacFarland wanted to stick around to watch the police exhume the body, but Logan insisted he had to get back to his dogs. MacFarland felt obligated to drive Eric Logan and Lucy back to their house, even though Chamberlain was willing to assign a squad car to drive them back.

"Thank you for your help, Eric," said MacFarland as Logan and Lucy got out of his truck.

Logan smiled and shook MacFarland's hand. "You've always been a bit unconventional, Mark, but I trust your instincts. Almost as much as I trust Lucy's."

MacFarland smiled broadly. "That's pretty high praise, after seeing Lucy in action! I appreciate your confidence."

"Just catch the perp who killed whoever is in that cement," said Logan.

MacFarland nodded. "I intend to," he said.

He drove back to the construction site, which was now lit with floodlights and crowded with police and police vehicles. MacFarland also saw several of the Forrester management team standing around.

At first the police, who had taken over guarding the entrance of the site, refused to let him onto the site. MacFarland asked them to check with Chamberlain, who waved him over. MacFarland parked his truck and went over to where Chamberlain was standing with a couple of officers. MacFarland recognized one of the plainclothes officers. Alan Iverson, one of the detectives MacFarland used to work with.

Iverson was the detective who messed up the chain of custody of evidence in the trial of Norris Peterson. He was one reason why Peterson got away with the murder of MacFarland's wife. Of all the detectives who could be assigned to this case, Iverson was the last one MacFarland wanted to see.

"What made you suspect there was a body here?" Chamberlain asked him as he neared the group.

"A tip from one of the employees who works here. She said that the schedule was arbitrarily changed, and she suspected that a missing person was buried in the concrete. The victim is probably a man named Martin Picket, a security guard who used to work here."

"How long has he been missing?" asked Iverson.

MacFarland refused to look in Iverson's direction. "Picket has been missing for a week."

"Is there a missing person's report on file?" asked Chamberlain.

"I doubt it," said MacFarland. "His wife is an alcoholic who doesn't seem to have the best grip on reality. As far as the company is concerned, Picket just didn't show up for work and was terminated." He looked around. "Are you going to try to get the body out of the cement?"

"We're going to do that tomorrow," said Chamberlain. "One of the engineers here said that just breaking into the column might cause it to fall. We're just going to secure the site for now." He looked questioningly at MacFarland. "You have any idea who might have done this?"

MacFarland looked from Chamberlain to Iverson, then back. "No, sir, no idea whatsoever."

CHAPTER SIXTY

MONDAY, MAY 2, 0600 HOURS

WHEN MACFARLAND GOT to the construction site early on Monday morning, Iverson reluctantly let him cross the police barrier so he could watch the excavation. Iverson went over to Vogel, who was shocked at the number of police on his job site.

"We'll let your men stabilize the column and remove it down to the mark near the base," said Iverson. "We'll take over from there. If there are any remains, we have to make sure it is removed very carefully."

As soon as the first shift arrived, Forrester management identified a work crew that could demolish the cement column. About a dozen men, some armed with pneumatic drills, others with sledge hammers and shovels, attacked the column. The rest of the work crew stood around, kept back by the police tape, watching curiously. Eventually, after an hour or so, Vogel gave instructions for his supervisors to send everyone home who was not directly involved in demolishing the column.

As the construction workers tore into the column and

removed most of the concrete, crime scene investigators kept a close watch. Finally, after about a couple of hours of chipping away at the concrete, one of them called a halt to the activity. He went over and carefully examined the cement near the base. He looked up towards Iverson. "We've got tissue," he said.

After that, CSI employees took over the tedious job of removing the cement and extracting the body. At nine-twenty in the morning, Pelligrini arrived at the scene and began shouting for the police to leave. MacFarland watched as Iverson went over to the man and made it clear that this was a crime scene and if Pelligrini didn't cooperate, he would be arrested for obstructing an active investigation. When it became apparent, a few hours later, that there really was a body buried in the cement, Pelligrini responded with unrestrained shock.

"How could there be a body there? We just poured that cement earlier this week! We checked everything! This is an outrage. Vogel, tell them!"

Vogel insisted that it was impossible for a body to be there. When it became apparent that the victim might indeed be Marty Picket, Vogel expressed even greater surprise. "What was he doing around the job site?" he demanded of everyone standing around him. "He must have fallen into the wet cement after it was poured!"

MacFarland wasn't about to speculate how Picket had gotten buried in the column, nor how improbable that scenario was. Nor did he point out that Picket supposedly had been fired. He would wait for the CSI lab and the coroner to complete their examination and verify that it was Picket.

As for the idea that Picket might have fallen into a column filled with wet cement, MacFarland seriously doubted that Picket's body would sink to the bottom of the column. If the body was found at the bottom of the tower, it was because it was there from the beginning, and the cement was poured on top of it.

Iverson was talking to Pelligrini. MacFarland edged closer so he could listen in on their discussion.

"We regard this as a crime, Mr. Pelligrini," said Iverson.

"I promise you," said Pelligrini, "we will do everything we can to help you capture this poor man's murderer."

"We don't know that it's a murder yet," said Iverson. "We will need to get the body completely out, examine it, and then we will be able to determine the cause of death."

"I promise I'll do everything I can to help you, officer."

"Detective," said Iverson.

"Yes, of course, Detective. Now how soon can you get this body out of here so my men can get back to work?"

CHAPTER SIXTY-ONE

MONDAY, MAY 2, 1515 HOURS

THEY FINALLY COMPLETED the extraction of the body by three-fifteen, a lot faster than MacFarland had expected. Although there wasn't much he could do while the technicians were getting the body out of the cement, he stuck around anyway, mainly to watch the people at the construction site. MacFarland was convinced that one or more of them were involved in Picket's death, and he wanted to see which of them might express undue interest in uncovering the crime.

Unfortunately, he was not able to discern any distinctive behavior that might give away feelings of guilt or panic. He did observe that both Boyce and Vogel kept to themselves, close to the management offices. After fruitlessly trying to get Iverson to give him a time estimate of when the police would be finished, Pelligrini left the job site.

Iverson spent part of his time watching the technicians chipping cement, and the rest of his time interviewing people around the job site. When MacFarland tried to join him, Iverson made it clear that he didn't want MacFarland listening in. MacFarland spotted Wanda Warren outside the perimeter of the crime scene, so he went over to her.

"You were right," he said simply. "Picket was buried in the cement."

"You think Boyce did it?" asked Wanda.

MacFarland shook his head. "I really don't have any idea. I am hoping the CSIs can figure out something that might give us a clue."

"Was he alive when he was buried?"

"I don't know," said MacFarland. "I sincerely hope not. The body was in a prone position, so it was unlikely that he was conscious. But, I am not the expert. Let's just wait and see what the real experts tell us."

As the body was transported by stretcher up to a waiting ambulance, Iverson came over to where MacFarland and Warren were standing.

"You're the person who thought the victim might be buried in the cement?" asked Iverson.

Warren nodded. "Yeah, it seemed strange to me that they changed the cement schedule. That got me suspicious."

"I'll have to have you come down to the station," said Iverson. "For questioning."

"I don't know anything," Wanda said. "I just told you everything I know."

"Look, Miss. We can make it easy or we can make it tough. Which will it be?"

"Go easy on her, Iverson," said MacFarland to the detective. Turning towards Warren, he added, "They just want a statement from you, Wanda. Nothing serious."

"I'll determine how serious it is," snapped Iverson. "She's the only one who had an inkling that the victim was buried in that thing. That sounds mighty odd to me. Right now, she's my prime suspect."

MacFarland was dumbfounded. "You can't be serious! Get your head out of your ass, Iverson. She just put two and two together and came up with four. That doesn't make her a suspect."

"MacFarland, get the fuck out of my crime scene. If I find you butting into my case again, I will have you arrested. Chamberlain put me in charge of this investigation, and if I say she's a suspect, then God damn it, she is!"

As MacFarland stared in stunned silence, Iverson called a uniform over and asked him cuff Wanda Warren and take her over to headquarters.

CHAPTER SIXTY-TWO

TUESDAY, MAY 3, 1000 HOURS

MACFARLAND WAS furious with Iverson's actions. That night, he complained vociferously to Pierson.

"Look Mac, we both know Iverson is an asshole. Let me talk to Chamberlain tomorrow. I'm sure Bob won't support Iverson's heavy-handed approach. But you do have to admit, you and Iverson rub each other the wrong way."

"He's a jerk. Of course he rubs me the wrong way. Why did Chamberlain give him this case anyway?"

"Iverson has the lightest caseload."

"Big surprise!"

"The truth is that Chamberlain doesn't expect Iverson to solve the case."

MacFarland was flabbergasted. "Who does he expect to solve it?"

Pierson stared at him blankly. "You."

MacFarland was not sure if she was mocking him. "Are you being serious?"

Pierson went over to him and grasped his hands in hers. "Mac, you have always been one of the best detectives I've ever known or worked with. Chamberlain knows that too. He has a lot of confidence in you, probably more than you have in yourself. You've had a few bad years. I don't know what it was like on the streets, but I can't imagine that it made you feel good about yourself. I wouldn't be surprised if Iverson told you to stay away from the case at Chamberlain's orders."

"I thought you said that Chamberlain has confidence in me."

"He does. I do. Most of us do. He just doesn't want you getting your investigation corrupted by Iverson's. He wants you to go your own way."

MacFarland stared at her in disbelief. "God, I thought I was fucked up. If you guys are what passes for normal, the world is really in a mess."

She kissed him lightly on the cheek. "The world is really in a mess, Mac. We need you to help set it right."

Tuesday morning came and MacFarland drove his wagon to his corner. Rufus greeted him hesitantly. Once upon a time, MacFarland had given Rufus a cell phone, so that they could stay in touch with each other. But after a few days without charging, the phone was useless. Rufus had traded it for cigarettes from one of the kids at Urban Peak. "Lot's going on at the construction site," said Rufus. "Only thing is, they're all closed down for now. All that because of you, boss?"

"I guess you could say that, Rufus," said MacFarland. "But the real credit goes to Wanda."

Rufus smiled. "Busty doesn't ever forget her friends, boss. She's a good person to know."

He called up the station to find out what happened to Warren. Although Iverson had brought her in for questioning, she was not held. After giving her statement, she was released. MacFarland tried to call her on his phone, but she did not answer. He spent much of Tuesday trying to locate her, even going down to Her Bar on Colfax, but no one had seen her.

MacFarland considered what Rufus had said about Wanda. Some people found Wanda Warren overbearing and aggressive, even belligerent. Yet time and again, he saw evidence that Rufus was right. She was the kind of person who didn't abandon her friends. She would stick by them and fight to protect them. He wondered if he had friends like that. Then he had to admit, that he did. Rufus had taken care of him during the years he had been a homeless drunk, and even now, remained loyal to him. Pierson was like that too, though she would be the first to deny she had a soft spot for him.

"If you see Wanda today, Rufus, tell her that I'm looking for her."

"Sure thing, boss. Where're you heading now?"

"I want to talk to Mr. Vogel. I want to find out exactly who changed the cement pouring schedule and why."

MacFarland checked to see if Vogel was at the construction site, but Janet said that she hadn't seen him all morning. Was he sick? She didn't know. All she knew was that it was terrible what happened to poor Mr. Picket.

There wasn't much activity going on at the construction site, although the police tape had been removed. Most of the construction site was deserted, with a minimal management team present. A crew was working on demolishing the tower that had held Picket's body. MacFarland assumed that they would have to rebuild it. He checked to see if Wanda was operating the crane, but it was someone else.

"Has Wanda Warren been in today?" he asked Janet.

Janet wiped her eye, shaking her head no. She hadn't

come in either. What about Boyce? No, he wasn't in today either. Most of the management team would be out for the week, or over at the main offices trying to re-plan the project.

"Do you have an address for Riley?" asked MacFarland.

Janet nodded, checking a Rolodex on her desk. She wrote down the address and handed it to MacFarland. "Are you going to check to see if he is okay?" she asked.

MacFarland nodded.

Janet smiled. "It's good that he has friends like you, especially during a time like this."

MacFarland smiled grimly, not really sure he was Riley Vogel's friend. "We all need friends when bad things happen," he said.

He drove out to the address Janet had given him. MacFarland knew Vogel drove a yellow Tercel, but he didn't see any sign of the car. He parked in front of the house and went up to the front door. He pressed the doorbell and waited.

After a minute, the door opened a crack and he could see a woman with short brown hair, brown eyes, and a pointed chin staring out at him. Her eyes were bloodshot, and streaks of tears had ruined her mascara. He tried to recall her name. Oh, yes, Annette.

"Mrs. Vogel? Is Riley home?"

"Who are you?" she asked.

"My name is Mark MacFarland."

"MacFarland? You! You're the one who's ruined our lives! You! You! Get out of here, get away from our house! I'm going to call the police!"

"Please, Mrs. Vogel, tell me where your husband is. He didn't show up at work today and people are worried."

"He didn't show up because of you, you bastard! It's all

your fault. He's gone! I don't know where he is. He just took a bag of clothes, said that you had ruined his life, and that he had to leave."

"Where did he go?"

By now Annette Vogel was crying profusely. She started coughing and MacFarland was afraid she was going to choke. "I don't know where he is," she sobbed. "I don't know what's going on? What have you done to him?"

"Mrs. Vogel, did your husband have anything to do with the death of Marty Picket?"

Annette Vogel stopped sobbing long enough to stare at him blankly. Then her gaze hardened into a look of hatred. "My husband would never kill anyone," she hissed, her chest heaving with emotion. "Get the fuck away from my house!"

CHAPTER SIXTY-THREE

WEDNESDAY, MAY 4, 0650 HOURS

"VOGEL SEEMS TO BE MISSING," said MacFarland as soon as Pierson came downstairs the next morning.

"He's one of your suspects, isn't he?"

"Until he disappeared, he wasn't my prime suspect. But now I am not so sure. Is he guilty because he disappeared, or is he innocent because someone has buried him in a column of cement?" He poured Pierson a cup of coffee. She took it with a smile of thanks. "I wish you had run the financials on him back when I asked."

She looked at him plaintively. "Mac, back then, who knew what was going on? Now you have a bona fide murder. That changes everything. I think I can talk Iverson into requesting a bank check. We might turn up enough to do a more thorough investigation."

"You know, Picket might still be alive if we had been able to pin something on Vogel three weeks ago," he said, with a short laugh.

Pierson set her cup on the table and glared at MacFarland. "Don't try to lay that blame at my feet, damn you. I told you we couldn't go after his financials because we didn't have a case. I think that's a pretty low blow, Mac."

MacFarland was surprised at how strongly Pierson reacted. He hadn't been seriously blaming her. He knew that the financial trail wouldn't have changed the outcome. There wasn't even any proof that Picket had been killed by Vogel. It was only speculation that Vogel was missing because of the murder. In fact, the more he thought about it, the more he began to suspect that Vogel may have also been killed.

"I apologize, Cyn. I didn't mean it as a criticism. I can't find Vogel, and his wife thinks it's my fault he has run. Hell, I don't even know if he is actually running. Suppose he's dead? I can't believe he's in hiding because of me. I don't know what his wife meant. How did I mess anything up? It doesn't make sense. Maybe something else spooked him. Or he could be running because he is involved in the embezzlement scheme, which is a very real possibility."

"You're fairly certain there is an embezzlement scheme going on?"

"Yes, absolutely. It's not just me that thinks that. I think Grey Wilson and Norma Sykes are pursuing a racketeering case against Peterson and probably Pelligrini. Of course, they don't share anything with me. Have they said anything to you?"

Pierson shook her head, apparently accepting MacFarland's apology. "I don't know anything about a RICO case. I haven't had any contact with Wilson," she said. "Agent Sykes wouldn't confirm that she and her partner met with you. She wouldn't even confirm that she had a partner. I really hate interagency cooperation. Especially when the other agency doesn't cooperate!"

"It could be worse," said MacFarland.

Pierson looked at him cautiously. "How could it be worse?"

"You could be doing this because you really need a job. As it is, you do it for the sheer fun of catching and shooting scumbags."

Pierson shook her head. "You really are an asshole. But asshole or not, you're still my partner. I'll get the financials myself."

CHAPTER SIXTY-FOUR

FRIDAY, MAY 6, 1300 HOURS

MACFARLAND SPENT most of afternoon at his hot dog cart, disinterestedly listening to his language lessons, sorting his evidence cards, and discussing with Rufus as many of the elements of the case as Rufus seemed interested in hearing.

Surprisingly, Rufus was a good barometer of how important a clue was, oohing and ahhing as a card caught his attention. If Rufus asked questions about it, MacFarland would study the card, then set it aside. There were times however, when Rufus seemed lost in thought, spaced out, and distant. After MacFarland had gone through all his cards, Rufus asked for a second cup of coffee.

"Two cups today, Rufus? Is this the start of the high life for you?"

"You're making me work, boss. I need some energy drink."

As MacFarland poured out a cup of coffee, Rufus summarized what he had heard.

"Ya got three murders it seems. Mike Brady. Louis

Hightower. And Marty Picket. All three of them is part of one big crime. All you gotta do is figure that crime out, boss, and your case is solved."

"I think I know what that crime is," said MacFarland. "I think someone was embezzling from the company and committing fraud. The question is, who?"

"Well, you got it right there, boss," said Rufus.

"Where?"

Rufus pointed at the small stack of cards that he had oohed and ahhed over. "Here, this one."

MacFarland picked up the card Rufus pointed at. It read:

Before 2/19

If anyone is embezzling, Pelligrini would be involved--he's always cutting corners.

4/8 - Hightower

"You think Pelligrini is the killer?"

"Oh, I don't know that, boss. But I think he is the one committing the one big crime."

MacFarland nodded, deep in thought. "Yeah, you might be right. The problem is, how do I prove it?"

Rufus laughed, finishing off his coffee. "Ah, boss, that's your problem. You're the detective. I'm just a homeless man who sometimes sells hot dogs."

As the sun started descending on the mountains, MacFarland had gotten no further in proving that embezzlement was going on. He longed to have access to the computers in the police department. He considered going over to Jody B's bar to use her computer, but he would have to hack into several databases that he didn't have authorization to use. It would be too easy for someone to trace activity back to her computer. He wondered if he should get his own computer, though he was not sure how he would be able to afford it. He could barely afford the tablet computer he had.

He was lost in the details of configuring his imaginary computer system when he noticed that Lockwood and Pierson had pulled up next to the curb. Pierson rolled down the window. MacFarland stepped closer to talk to her.

"Two pieces of news, Mac. Some good news, some bad."

"What's the bad news?"

"We didn't get much on the financial search on Vogel. The FBI stepped in and said that we could get any information we needed from them."

"And what did they provide?"

Pierson gave him a look of disgust. "Nothing, of course."

"And the good news?"

"We got some preliminary results from the body," she said. "You'll be pleased to learn that your favorite CSI is the person working the case."

"Annabel?" he asked. Colleen Annabel Beltane was a CSI technician who had discovered a crucial piece of evidence in MacFarland's last case. She had been wrongfully discharged by the company that employed her, until MacFarland had shown that she had actually solved the case. MacFarland had been instrumental in convincing Chamberlain to bring her back to Denver and reinstate her. Beltane and MacFarland had never actually met, but their mutual regard had remained high.

"Yes. Picket was hit on the head with what looks like a tire iron. She found traces of chrome plating, yellow paint, rust, and grease on the wound. No clear fingerprints, though, just partials. The coroner also confirms that Picket was already dead before the cement was poured."

"Do they have any idea how long Picket had been dead? When he was actually killed?"

Pierson shook her head. "They are still working on that. The coroner thinks the victim was killed shortly before the cement was poured."

MacFarland nodded. He was relieved that Picket was not alive when the cement was poured. His face began to shine with excitement.

Pierson looked up at him. "Damn it, Mac, you have that look! You know who killed him!"

MacFarland smiled. "I have my suspicions, Cyn, but nothing definite."

Despite Pierson's threats that she would make him sleep in the backyard, MacFarland refused to name whom he suspected. The truth was, while there was only one individual who could have changed the cement schedule, there were still two individuals who could have killed Picket. "Iverson's on the case," he said. "He'll solve it soon enough. Annabel's given him all he needs."

Lockwood, listening intently, nearly choked trying to suppress laughter. Pierson gave him an angry glance, then looked at MacFarland. "You are not a very good team player," she said.

"Took you this long to figure that out?"

It was after eight o'clock in the evening when MacFarland finally headed home. He was feeling discouraged as he backed his wagon into its parking space. Perhaps that was why he didn't see the man standing in the shadows. As he finished unhooking his wagon, the man stepped out of the shadows. MacFarland recognized him immediately.

"Vogel! We've been looking for you."

Vogel kept looking around nervously. "MacFarland, you've got to help me!"

MacFarland barked a short laugh. "Your wife said that I was the reason for you running."

"I had to tell her something. I couldn't tell her the truth."

MacFarland stared at Riley Vogel. It was difficult to read his features in the deep shadows. "What's the truth, Mr. Vogel?"

"They're after me," he said. "I'm sure they are going to kill me."

MacFarland was surprised. This was not what he expected. "Who is after you? Who's going to kill you?"

"I don't know their names," said Vogel. "I just know that Pelligrini brought them in from Chicago. They're vicious, MacFarland! They take pleasure in hurting people. Fuck, just to be part of their organization, you have to kill someone."

"Are you talking about the Chicago gang that is operating here in Denver?"

"You know about them?" asked Vogel incredulously. "They call themselves the Sons of BPSN. I don't know any more about them, except they work for Pelligrini."

"What do they have to do with you?"

Vogel looked around again, backing further into the shadows. "They drove by my house. I saw them. The first time I didn't realize who they were. The second time, they had the window of their car opened, and I saw them. One of them raised an arm and fist, like he was threatening me. I saw the tattoo, and I knew who they were."

"You could recognize them from a tattoo?"

"I knew about them from when I lived in Chicago. Back in 2008. That's when the gang reformed. With backing from Pelligrini's organization. They're here to kill me."

"Why are they here to kill you, Mr. Vogel?"

"That's the way Pelligrini works," said Vogel desperately. "He--"

Vogel fell silent. MacFarland was about to ask him what his problem was when he heard it too. A large vehicle was driving slowly down the alley. Although it was still light enough to see, the shadows in the alley were deep enough that MacFarland would assume the driver would have turned on his lights. The fact that the vehicle was driving without lights put MacFarland on the alert. He peeked around the corner, not surprised at seeing a large, black Suburban SUV slowly moving in his direction. He pulled back, then took out his phone. He had just finished dialing 911 when he sensed a movement behind him. Too late, he saw Vogel's arm coming down with a large rock in it. He tried to dodge the blow, but Vogel succeeded in hitting him on the side of the head.

As darkness engulfed him, he thought he could hear the 911 operator saying, "What is your emergency, please?"

CHAPTER SIXTY-FIVE

SATURDAY, MAY 6, 1100 HOURS

"DID I JUST WAKE UP?" asked MacFarland early Saturday morning.

"No, you've been slipping in and out of consciousness for several hours," said Pierson. She was sitting next to him on his bed. She wrung out a washcloth and placed it over his forehead.

"What happened?"

"You tell me. Apparently you called 911, and when you didn't respond to the operator, she sent a squad car over to check on you. They found you lying out by the alley."

MacFarland tried to sit up, wincing at the throb in his head. He pushed past the pain and took the cloth away from his head. "I found Vogel in the back waiting for me. I didn't realize he knew where I lived."

She tried to get him to lie back down, but he waved her off. She relented reluctantly, helping him sit up. "What did he want?"

"He wanted my help. He thinks the gang that vandalized my cart and robbed Brady's house is out to kill him."

Pierson showed her surprise. "Really? That gang from Chicago?"

"Yes. We should let Victor Schwab know who they are. Apparently they are an offshoot of the BPSN. Vogel says they call themselves the Sons of BPSN. They resurfaced about five to eight years ago. And get this. They have ties with Pelligrini's organization."

"Forrester Equipment and Construction?"

"I'm assuming so," said MacFarland. "Unless Vogel was implying some broader organization."

"I think I'm beginning to see how Wilson and Sykes fit into this. What happened to Vogel?"

"I'm not sure. He hit me with a stone from the yard. You got to get rid of those stones, Cyn. The Sons of BPSN were driving down the alley. I was busy calling 911 and trying to get a read on their license plate when he surprised me."

"Do you think the gang picked up Vogel?"

MacFarland shrugged. "I have no idea," he said. He started to get up, but Pierson put her hands on his shoulders. "Where do you think you're going?"

"I'm going to find out if the gang has Vogel," he said.

"You're not going anywhere," she said firmly.

He tried to gently push her aside. "Cyn, I have to do this. I owe it to Brady and to Wanda."

She let him push her back, then she reached for his shirt and pants. "Well, if you're going, I'm going with you. Whenever I let you out of my sight, you get shot or banged on the head."

MacFarland smiled at her as he got dressed. "Just like the old days," he said.

"Not quite," she snapped back. "In the old days, I was in charge. But trust me, we're getting there."

They took Pierson's car, since she didn't think it was a

good idea for him to drive. "I don't think it was serious enough to give you a concussion," she said. "You haven't shown any symptoms of one, but I don't want to take any chances."

MacFarland knew better than to argue with Pierson. "Where to?" she asked once they were in the car.

"The CCP Building."

She gave him a questioning look, but started the car and drove over to University. She took University to First, then over to Speer. She turned on Lincoln, and drove up to Lincoln until it rejoined with Broadway, then turned right onto Arapahoe. On the way, he explained who he was after. "I'm surprised you're not after Peterson," she said. "Do you really think Pelligrini will be in his office today?"

"As long as his construction site is shut down, he's losing lots of money. He needs to stem the flow of money, and that means office work. Besides, I don't get the impression he's the kind of guy who does his own dirty work. After all, if he's really responsible for helping to rebuild one of the most notorious gangs in Chicago, he likes to work through others. He's like Peterson in that respect. Money is his weapon. So I think he will be working his ass off to get the money flow going again." He smiled broadly. "Besides, I called up this morning and verified from his secretary that he would be there."

Pierson found a parking space in front of the building and they got out to go into the building. They had gotten as far as the elevator before they were assaulted from two different directions. Agent Sykes came out of an office in the back of the lobby and Agent Wilson came in through the front door.

"I wouldn't go up there," said Wilson.

MacFarland stopped and glared at Wilson. "Why am I not surprised to find you here? Still protecting Peterson?"

Sykes smiled at Pierson. "Hello, Detective. Has he gotten you involved with this too?"

Pierson stiffened, frowning at Sykes. "We're pursuing an active murder investigation, Agent Sykes." She glanced over at Wilson. "So this is the partner you never talk about. Pleased to meet you, Agent Wilson."

"Please, call me Grey. No need for us to be all formal here. But we can't let you go upstairs, MacFarland. I asked you to stay away from here."

"I'm not here to see Peterson," said MacFarland. "I am here to see Norm Pelligrini."

Both Sykes and Wilson froze abruptly. They glanced at each other, and Wilson shook his head. "Detective Pierson, perhaps we should all return to the Headquarters building to discuss this," said Sykes.

Even though Sykes stood two inches taller than Pierson, Pierson stretched to her full height. "Why don't we discuss it right here, Norma." The tone and emphasis Pierson used in saying the agent's name clearly indicated that there was little love between these two.

MacFarland found himself in the unusual role of being a peacemaker. "We believe that Pelligrini is involved in the murder of Marty Picket, a guard who used to be employed at Forrester Equipment and Construction. We would like to question him about his role, as well as his association with the Sons of BPSN."

Sykes tried to hide her smile, but Wilson's tone was grim. "We would like to know more about what the SBPSN is doing here in Denver, but I can assure you that they haven't murdered anyone."

"Yet," added Pierson, her tone icy and constrained.

Wilson nodded. "I'll concede that. The four that we think are here are a very dangerous group. But we've had eyes on them, and they didn't kill Picket."

"What about the attack on Wanda Warren?" asked MacFarland.

"We didn't know they were here when that happened," admitted Wilson. "We are coordinating with your Gangs Commander."

"Then you know where they were last night," said Pierson.

Wilson lowered his eyes. "No, not last night. We lost track of them a couple of days ago."

Norma Sykes put her hand on MacFarland's arm. "Listen, Mark, Pelligrini didn't kill Picket. Talking to him isn't going to help you catch the killer, but it would really jeopardize our case against him. I admit that he is complicit, but he is not the killer."

MacFarland looked down at her hand, then returned her stare. "If he's not the killer, who is?"

Sykes smiled, looking like a love-struck teenage girl. "I think you already know who the killer is, Mark. Go get him."

A few minutes later, as Pierson and MacFarland climbed into her car, she let out a string of epithets. "What the fuck was that? She looks at you goo-goo eyed and you turn into a puddle? God, Mac, get your damn brain out of your pants!"

"But she's right," said MacFarland. "I do know who the killer is."

"Then perhaps you wouldn't mind letting me in on your little secret?"

"I think the killer is Ryan Boyce."

CHAPTER SIXTY-SIX

MONDAY, MAY 9, 1010 HOURS

MACFARLAND AND PIERSON went to Boyce's house early Sunday morning. There was no sign of the car in the driveway, and no answer at the door when they knocked. A child's tricycle was overturned in the driveway. The Sunday paper lay on the front porch of the house.

Pierson checked with a neighbor who said that the family often went to church, but he hadn't seen them that day. MacFarland tried to peer in through the windows, but all the curtains were drawn and the blinds closed. His suggestion that he try to break into the house was met with a sour look from his partner.

"I can't do that," said Pierson. "We have no probable cause, no warrant."

"I'll do it."

"Yeah, and then I will arrest you for breaking and entering. Let me get hold of Iverson and get a warrant. If this guy is the killer, Mac, do you want him going free because someone like Baker points out to a jury how many laws you broke to catch him?"

MacFarland didn't answer her question because he was pretty sure Pierson wouldn't like his response. But he followed her advice, and they returned to Pierson's house.

If Pierson expected Iverson to obtain a warrant, she greatly over-estimated his enthusiasm and his initiative. As evening approached, he had still not obtained one. When she complained to him, his response was that her evidence was too flimsy. When he heard that it was MacFarland's belief that Boyce was the killer, Iverson burst out laughing. "Are you still listening to that dumbass hot dog vendor, Pierson? Get serious! We've already got a suspect."

Pierson was surprised to hear this. "Who?" Pierson put the phone on speaker so MacFarland could hear.

"Jon Murphy. We found the tire iron in his car. We have him dead to rights."

MacFarland got a look of disbelief on his face. He mouthed the words, "No way," while Pierson tried to shush him. "You're certain it's the murder weapon?"

Iverson sounded smug. "Absolutely. No clear prints on it, but we did find blood that matched Picket's. It's the murder weapon all right."

"What was Murphy's motive for killing Picket?" asked MacFarland.

"Is that MacFarland there with you? Well, since you helped find the body, I'll tell you. One of the oldest motivations in the world. Greed! Murphy wanted Picket's job. We have a statement from Boyce that they couldn't hire Murphy since they already had their gate guards. So Murphy must have decided to take matters into his own hands."

"Murphy confirms that?"

"Are you kidding? He's already lawyered up."

"What color car did Murphy own?"

"Dark green, why?"

"The wound had yellow paint flecks in it. The tire iron probably was in a yellow car."

Iverson laughed. "That's why it's a good thing you're not a cop anymore, MacFarland. Always jumping to conclusions. The yellow flakes could have come from anywhere. You can't prove a case with assumptions, you know. Stick to selling hot dogs, MacFarland."

Iverson hung up. MacFarland and Pierson sat staring at each other, then both burst out laughing. "I'm glad you don't take his comments seriously," said Pierson.

MacFarland stopped laughing and smiled grimly. "If someone like you or Chamberlain said that, I probably would take it more seriously. But I know where Iverson is coming from, so I don't even think about his comments. But he has a point. I've been thinking that the deaths of Brady, Hightower, and Picket were all related. But we know Hightower was hit by a red vehicle. Maybe the tire iron doesn't belong to a yellow vehicle, but just has yellow paint on it, as Iverson suggested. Does the killer have two cars?"

"Or are there two killers? Maybe these murders aren't as closely linked as you think."

MacFarland shook his head. "No, the murders are linked, but they may not have been done by the same killer. I think we have several killers, all working towards the same end."

MacFarland mulled over that idea most of the night. Were there two or more killers? Were the crimes related, or had someone used the opportunity of Brady's death to seek resolution of a personal vendetta? That didn't make sense to him, since Brady's death had been ruled an accident.

When he woke up the next morning, Pierson had already left. He found a note from her on the kitchen table, informing him that she would check on the search warrant. She warned him to stay away from the case.

Yeah, sure, he thought.

The construction site was finally operating at full capacity once more. More than a hundred men scrambled on the towering skeletal steel structures of the building. MacFarland could see the north tower and the south tower. The connecting mezzanine, which would eventually be devoted to shops and eating establishments, was only partially completed. They still had to re-pour the destroyed pillar that formed one of the corners of the four story roof of the central area. It would be an impressive building when it was done, rivaling anything on the Sixteenth Street Mall, and clearly marking the opening of the Golden Triangle as the place to be.

Once Rufus was in place, ready to serve hot dogs and brats to the onrush of potential jurors hurrying in to do their civic duty by serving on a jury, MacFarland went over to the construction site. There was a new guard at the gate, who refused to identify himself. "Everyone who talks to you gets killed or arrested," he said. MacFarland was not sure if the man was speaking in jest, but he couldn't deny the truth of the man's statement, at least for security guards. The guard did tell him, however, that Boyce had not yet come to work.

MacFarland headed back to his wagon. Rufus was talking to a young teenage girl, one of the four youths MacFarland had given food to the previous month. "Teena, right?" he said. "With two E's, not an I."

She smiled at him. "Yes, that's right. You have a good memory! I was just telling Rufus about my good luck."

MacFarland smiled. "Good luck? What happened?"

"I have a job for the summer! I am going to help take

care of homeless kids up at a summer camp in the mountains. It doesn't pay that much, but I will have room and board the entire summer. I should be able to save all the money I make. Isn't that great?"

MacFarland agreed that it was, then asked Rufus to watch over his cart a bit longer. "Be sure to let Teena have whatever she wants," he said.

"Sure will, boss. But I gotta tell ya, she can really gobble up them hot dogs!"

Rufus and Teena both laughed as MacFarland got into his truck. He drove up to Federal Heights and slowly approached Boyce's house. The house looked the same as it did the previous day. The tricycle and paper were still where they were yesterday. Not a good sign. MacFarland parked in front of the house and went to the front door. After knocking several times and ringing the bell with no response, MacFarland went to the side of the house. He went into the backyard and tried the back door. It was unlocked. He slid it open and stepped into the house.

"Boyce? Hello? Anyone home?" The house was deep in shadow, with all the curtains and drapes closed. MacFarland went over to a wall switch and flipped the lights on. His eyes widened as he saw Boyce, sitting in an over-stuffed chair facing the television. He was clearly dead, his head shattered by a large caliber bullet that left his brains scattered on the wall. A .357 magnum revolver lay on the floor near Boyce's outstretched hand. Clearly, Iverson had not gotten the search warrant. MacFarland pulled out his phone, dialed 911 and gave the operator his location. While he waited for the police to arrive, he checked the rest of the house. He felt nauseated when he found the wife and two children lying on the floor of the children's bedroom, also shot at relatively close range.

MacFarland heard the police sirens approaching the house. He went to the front door, opened it, and held up his hands. "I'm not the shooter," he said as several Federal Heights police officers raced towards him, their pistols drawn. "I'm the person who called 911," he added. "There's one body in the living room, three more in the back bedroom."

They cuffed him anyway as they examined the crime scene. One of the officers, a sergeant, came over to him and began to question MacFarland. MacFarland explained who he was, what had prompted him to check on Ryan Boyce. "Call Robert Chamberlain of the Denver PD and he will tell you who I am." The sergeant pulled out his phone and called his department for their crime scene staff. Then he got around to calling Chamberlain.

The Federal Heights crime scene staff arrived just before Iverson also pulled up. Iverson identified himself and explained that Boyce was a person of interest in a case he was working on. The Federal Heights police finally took the cuffs off of MacFarland's wrists. "My prints should be on the back door, the front door inside handle, and the light switch," he told the sergeant. "Otherwise, I haven't touched anything."

Iverson looked around the crime scene. He spoke to the sergeant. "I realize this is your crime scene," he said, "but it may be related to a murder we are working on in Denver." After lukewarm promises to work together, Iverson turned to MacFarland. "Let's get you out of here."

As they left Boyce's house, MacFarland stopped Iverson. "Was Boyce really a person of interest in the Picket case?"

Iverson nodded. "Yeah, it turns out that Murphy had an alibi for the time of the murder. He was in Wyoming on a hunting trip with three other men. He only got back Sunday morning. We just released him an hour ago. So it is unlikely that he did these murders either."

MacFarland nodded. "There's one other thing this murder shows, Iverson."

"What's that?"

"You were right about Boyce. He probably isn't the guy who killed Picket."

Iverson shook his head. "There you go again, jumping to conclusions. That's why you never were a good cop."

CHAPTER SIXTY-SEVEN

MONDAY, MAY 9, 1420 HOURS

"THE MURDER WAS MADE to look like a murder-suicide, though no one believes that," said Lockwood, lowering his voice and trying his best to sound professional. "But Forensics found no powder residue on Boyce's hands. The angle of the bullet was at an awkward angle to be self-inflicted. The gun had no serial number on it. We're checking with the FBI to find out if the gun has been used in any other crime, but my gut feeling tells me they won't find anything useful. The gun is old--I heard someone say that it was probably manufactured in the '40's, so even if they find evidence that the gun has been used in other crimes, I am not sure they will help us with this one. Oh, they did find a suicide note on Boyce's computer which supposedly supports the murder-suicide theory."

"What did the note say?" asked MacFarland.

"I'll get a print out of it later for you, but the gist of the note was that Boyce regretted killing Brady, Hightower, and Picket, and rather than subject his family to having to live with his disgrace, he was going to end his life. And theirs."

"You're convinced it was not a suicide?" asked Pierson.

Lockwood shook his head. "A Magnum .357 is a pretty big gun. Why point it downwards at the top of your head? I would just put it under my chin and shoot upwards. I think someone murdered the people mentioned in the suicide note, and then murdered the entire Boyce family."

Pierson nodded. "My conclusion exactly. So the real murderer is still out there. He's just trying to frame Boyce for the three deaths." She looked over at MacFarland. "You're awfully quiet, Mac. What's troubling you?"

"I agree with all of Benny's and your conclusions except one. I don't think Hightower was killed by the same man who murdered all these others."

"Why not?" asked Lockwood.

"I think the man who murdered all these people made sure that the victims actually died. Even the first victim, Mike Brady, his death was set up in such a way that it was unlikely to fail. On the other hand, the hit and run death of Louis Hightower, that was sloppy. Hightower didn't die right away. I think we have two different murderers. One person killed Hightower. Someone else killed Brady, Picket, and the Boyces." MacFarland looked at Pierson. "Have they found the person who loaned Boyce a red truck? A relative of some sort. Shouldn't be hard to find that guy."

Pierson shrugged, glancing at Lockwood for confirmation. "We gave the lead to Iverson, but I don't know what he's done with it."

Lockwood got a disgusted look on his face. "When he arrested Murphy, Iverson stopped looking into the red truck lead. Tell you what. I'll get right on it. Now that Boyce is dead, we have reasonable cause to start investigating the rest of the family. What are you two going to do?"

MacFarland glanced at Pierson and smiled. "I had two

suspects in mind. It now seems that my primary suspect is dead, so that leaves my other suspect as the only real contender."

"Who is that?" asked Lockwood.

Both Pierson and MacFarland answered at the same time. "Vogel."

Pierson and Lockwood headed back towards the police headquarters building. MacFarland closed his hot dog stand early and drove it home. He then went out to Vogel's house to see if Riley Vogel had returned home. From the street, the Vogel house looked deserted. He went into the yard and looked inside several windows. No sign of any activity. Just to be sure, he checked with a neighbor who said she saw the wife and children getting into a taxi with luggage and their dog. The neighbor did not recall seeing Riley Vogel with the family.

As he drove back towards Denver, MacFarland called up Pierson. "Can you get Iverson to issue a BOLO for Vogel? It looks like he's running."

"Don't worry, Mac, he won't run far."

CHAPTER SIXTY-EIGHT

TUESDAY, MAY 10, 2230 HOURS

WHEREVER RILEY VOGEL WAS, he had found a good hiding place because no one could find him. Early Tuesday morning, uniformed officers checked with Norm Pelligrini to see if he had any idea where Vogel was.

If Wilson and Sykes were around, the uniforms did not report encountering them. According to their statement, Pelligrini expressed shock that one of his employees was capable of murder and vowed that he would do everything in his power to help the police bring the man to justice, but no, he had not seen Riley Vogel, and yes, he would call the police the moment Vogel came into the office.

MacFarland pestered both Pierson and Lockwood most of the day with queries on any progress regarding Vogel's location. When Pierson finally arrived home late in the evening, she held up her hand, stopping MacFarland from approaching her.

"Don't even ask," she warned. "We haven't seen either him or his car. We did check with the taxi that picked up his family. The Freedom cab company said that the driver took them to a house in Commerce City. We checked the house, but it was vacant. No one has lived at that location for at least a year. The location is a bit isolated, though there are some manufacturing plants located nearby. We checked with the sites, but no one recalls seeing a taxi or any activity at the house. So, dead end. We don't know where the Vogel family went. But we do suspect that they probably had their dog with them."

"How do you know that?"

"Because Lockwood stepped in fresh dog shit and got it in my fucking car. Now, if you'll excuse me, I have to go clean out my car."

MacFarland was finishing up the evening cleaning of his hot dog cart equipment when his phone buzzed angrily at him. He wiped off his hands and looked at the contact name. Wanda Warren. He looked at the clock. Ten-thirty was pretty late for her to be calling him.

"Wanda, is anything wrong?"

"I'm gong meetum!" mumbled Wanda, her voice garbled with urgency. MacFarland had problems understanding her because she seemed out of breath.

"Say again, I can't understand you!"

"I said, I'm going to meet him. I'm going to get the bastard to confess," she said, still breathless but trying to speak more slowly. "I'm going to the construction site. Hurry! Meet me there!"

"Who? Who are you going to meet? Vogel?" There was no answer. He shut down his phone, grabbed his keys and raced out to his truck.

Pierson looked up from where she was scrubbing a floor pad with a brush and soapy water. "Where are you off to in such a hurry?"

"Warren. I think she's in trouble."

"What kind of trouble?"

"Don't know. She said she's going to try to get someone to confess. I think it might be Vogel."

Pierson threw the brush into the bucket of water. "Where?" she asked, as she pulled out her phone.

"The construction site," said MacFarland. He didn't wait for Pierson to respond. Wanda Warren sounded desperate. He wondered if he would arrive downtown quickly enough to help her.

"Wait for me," yelled Pierson, but MacFarland didn't wait.

CHAPTER SIXTY-NINE

TUESDAY, MAY 10, 2300 HOURS

MACFARLAND DROVE his truck right onto the construction site. Ahead of him, parked at odd angles, he could see Warren's car, and near it, Vogel's yellow Tercel. The guard ran out of his shack and tried to wave MacFarland to stop. As MacFarland jumped out of his truck, he shouted to the guard, "Where did they go?"

The guard seemed to know who MacFarland was looking for. He pointed towards the west tower. "They went over there," he said. "What's going on?"

"Call the police," said MacFarland. "Tell them that Vogel is here."

The guard rushed back to his shack to make the call and MacFarland hurried over towards the tower that soared upwards on the western side of the building. This structure would eventually be thirty stories tall, according to Warren, as would the eastern tower. The central northern section of the building would climb even higher, with two sections reaching forty stories and the catty-corner sections reaching sixty stories. The crane that Warren operated was still situated in the open central area that would eventually be an indoor, four-story shopping mall and atrium.

MacFarland wasn't sure where Warren and Vogel were located, so he searched for a work elevator that would take him to the upper levels under construction. He pushed the "Up" button on the elevator, and it rose noisily higher and higher. It didn't have floors marked on it, but wooden boards on each floor indicated the level. When he got to the highest floor, he released the button and the elevator stopped. He pushed the gate open and jumped onto the floor. He estimated he was about twenty stories up. Steel girders climbed still higher, but the construction crews hadn't yet finished the floors and walls of the last ten stories.

He looked around, searching for any sign of Warren or Vogel. Dim, yellow safety lights provided barely enough light to see the clutter on the floor of the building. Damn, had he gone too high? He saw a stairwell and hurried over towards it. He rushed down to the next floor, then checked it for any signs of activity. He did that for another three floors before he saw someone moving in the shadows near the western side of the building.

The outside walls of the building had not yet been put up. As he approached the place where he had seen movement, he could look out over the western side of the city. He cautiously approached the edge of the building. Looking down, he could see Speer Boulevard stretching out below him, two rivers of red and white lights. He stepped hastily back from the edge, feeling a bit giddy. *This is why I never climb mountains*, he thought. This floor was filled with stacks of building materials, probably intended for the outside and interior walls. He heard a scuffle towards the north side of the tower, then he heard Warren scream. He ran in the direction of the scream as fast as he could.

He bounded past a pile of paneling and saw Vogel trying to push Warren towards the outside wall of the building, threatening her with a knife. MacFarland yelled in rage, and leapt towards Vogel, tackling him around his legs. Vogel turned away from Warren, who scurried back from the edge of the building. MacFarland and Vogel struggled, each trying to incapacitate the other. Vogel kept trying to stab MacFarland with the knife. MacFarland grasped his wrist and tried to dislodge the knife. In the close confines of grappling each other and rolling around on the rough floor of the building, MacFarland was not able to gain an advantage, while Vogel's heavier weight did give him a slight edge.

But Vogel was not a man used to fighting, and once he realized he would not be able to wound MacFarland with the knife, he switched his primary objective to getting away from MacFarland. Vogel dropped his knife, then tried to ward off the increasing number of punitive punches MacFarland was able to land on the older man's face. Finally Vogel pushed MacFarland away and struggled to flee.

What happened in the next minute occurred so quickly that MacFarland was not entirely sure of the exact sequence of events. MacFarland saw Vogel get up and grab a piece of lumber as he got to his feet. Vogel started to swing the lumber at MacFarland's head. Before the wood smashed into him, however, Wanda Warren screamed wildly and shoved Vogel backwards. Vogel staggered, lost his balance, then fell towards the edge of the building. Vogel tried to regain his balance, but wavered unsteadily, and with a scream of terror, he fell over the side of the building.

MacFarland jumped to his feet and hurried over to the side of the building and stared down, all the while fighting off dizziness. Vogel was spread out on the ground, right in front of the entrance to the future underground parking lot.

As MacFarland turned to see if Warren was hurt, he could hear the screeching of police sirens, all racing towards the building. Considering that the construction site was right across the street from the police headquarters, he wondered why it took them so long to get here.

Of course. Police inefficiency.

CHAPTER SEVENTY

TUESDAY, MAY 10, 2305 HOURS

WANDA WARREN WAS SHAKING VIOLENTLY as MacFarland reached out for her. He put his arms around her, trying to offer her comfort and protection. She looked up at him, her expression hidden in the shadows. He felt something wet, then realized it was Warren's blood.

"You're bleeding," he said.

"He caught up with me," she said. "He tried to stab me, but I managed to avoid the worst of it. I didn't even know he had cut me."

"What were you doing? How did you two end up here?"

"I wanted to get him to confess," she said. "I called him and told him I had the pictures that Mike had taken."

"You have the pictures?" asked MacFarland in surprise.

"No, no, I never got to see them. They are still on his phone, as far as I know. But Vogel didn't know that. I told him that I would give him the pictures if he would give me some money. He wanted to know how much, and I told him five thousand. He said he would bring it to me, but we needed someplace to meet. He wouldn't tell me where he was hiding, so I said here. But he never intended to pay me. He started cursing me, saying I had caused all his troubles. That's when I realized that he was going to try to kill me, so I started running up the stairs. I was getting tired, so I came out here, hoping to hide from him. I wasn't far enough ahead of him, and he knew I had gone to this floor. He tried to overpower me, but I can kick pretty hard. That's when he tried to stab me. I thought I could get away, but he was really enraged." She looked up at him. "If you hadn't arrived, Mac, I think he would have pushed me off the side."

MacFarland could hear the police climbing up the stairwell, and soon he saw lights from their flashlights. He called out, "We're over here! We're not armed. We need an ambulance."

Within a minute, they were surrounded by a dozen policemen. "Vogel is on the street below," said MacFarland. "Elati Street."

One of the policemen spoke into a microphone. "We've found his body. What happened?"

"First, notify Detective Iverson that Vogel has been found. He will want to know about this as soon as possible. Vogel was in the process of assaulting Miss Warren here. He had already stabbed her, and I am sure he was trying to kill her."

One of the officers called out, "We have a knife over here!"

A medic arrived, along with Pierson and Lockwood. Someone had managed to get a floodlight lit and the area was bathed in a bright light. Pierson spoke briefly with the policeman who was interrogating MacFarland, then came over to him.

"Vogel's dead?" she asked.

MacFarland nodded. "We struggled, and when he heard

the sirens, he panicked and fell off the building." He looked over to where Warren was being looked at by the medic. The wound looked superficial, not much more than a scratch. The medic was cleaning it and putting bandages on the wound. When the medic tried to get Warren to go down to the ambulance, she refused.

"I'll take her home," said MacFarland.

"I need to get her statement first," insisted Iverson. "Then you can take her."

MacFarland looked at him. "Can't you get that tomorrow, Iverson? I'll bring her into the station myself."

Iverson stared at MacFarland. "It's my investigation, MacFarland. I'll call the shots."

CHAPTER SEVENTY-ONE

TUESDAY, MAY 10, 2355 HOURS

IT WAS ALMOST midnight when Iverson finished his interrogation of both MacFarland and Warren. MacFarland led Warren out of the police station, told Pierson that he would be home in a while, and helped Wanda climb into his truck. As soon as they drove out of the parking lot onto West Thirteenth Avenue, she began to relax.

"I wish he had actually confessed," she said. She laughed bitterly. "The only thing he kept saying was that he didn't kill Hightower. Strange, isn't it?"

"What else did he say to you?" asked MacFarland.

"As I told that detective, I got him to meet me because I said that I had the pictures that Brady had taken. Whatever those pictures were, Vogel was concerned about them, or why else would he come out of hiding?"

"Did he mention where he was staying?"

"No, only that he sent his wife and family away. He wouldn't say where he sent them, though."

"What else did he tell you?"

"He didn't actually confess to killing anyone, but he did

say that Brady's death was all because of Pelligrini. He said he wasn't going down all by himself, he was going to bring Pelligrini down with him. He said he had proof."

"Where is this proof?"

Warren shook her head. "I don't know. He didn't tell me that. Just that he had it." Warren paused for a moment. "We didn't really talk much, since I realized that he wasn't going to pay me. And even though he intended to kill me, I sort of feel sorry for him. I don't think he wanted any of this. The killing I mean. I get the impression that he just wanted to get money for his family, and the killing was something he fell into."

"That still doesn't justify killing someone," said MacFarland.

"I know," said Warren. "It's just that he wasn't a bad person to work for. He was actually a pretty nice guy. He just ended up on a slippery slope and had no way to get off of it."

"He might have been a nice guy at some point in his life, Wanda. But it looks like he did cause Brady's death. He probably killed Picket. And he killed Boyce and his wife and two children."

Warren looked at him in surprise. "Boyce is dead?" She shook her head in wonder. "I can't say I'm sorry to hear that. It's a shame about the rest of his family though. Who could kill a kid?"

"Somebody who's lost all humanity," said MacFarland. Yet somehow that didn't sound like Vogel.

CHAPTER SEVENTY-TWO

WEDNESDAY, MAY 11, 1400 HOURS

MACFARLAND DID NOT TAKE his cart downtown Wednesday morning. He called his sponsor, Hector Spinoza, and said that he wouldn't be at the AA meeting that night. Spinoza wasn't happy to hear the news. Spinoza didn't seem to think that solving murders was as important as going to the AA meetings.

Although MacFarland was convinced that the news of Riley Vogel's death would create a lot of buzz, his own participation in the man's death gave him an uneasy feeling. He didn't want to be seen profiteering off of the man's death and being out on the street selling hot dogs seemed to do just that. So he also informed Pierson that he would stay home most of the day. He asked her to keep him up to date on any developments.

He spent a large part of the morning reviewing his index cards, trying to find what he had missed. He had no proof that Boyce had killed Hightower. He was still waiting for someone on the police force to determine if one of Boyce's relatives owned a red truck. He wondered who, if anyone, was actually looking for the red truck. With Iverson in charge of the case, MacFarland had little hope that the lead would be pursued. Maybe MacFarland needed to talk to Chamberlain about what needed to be done. But why would Chamberlain listen to him? MacFarland was, after all, no longer a cop.

The issue that most vexed him was whether Vogel acted alone. Yes, there was evidence that someone besides Vogel might have run over and eventually killed Hightower, but despite what he had thought earlier, MacFarland could not be certain that Vogel didn't also commit that murder. And who killed Picket? Was that another one of Vogel's crimes? He couldn't even say that Vogel wasn't also responsible for the deaths of the Boyces. That's the problem with dead men. They can't confess their sins.

And finally, what was the role of Norm Pelligrini in all of this? Did Pelligrini order the series of murders? Or was Pelligrini's role limited to running an embezzlement scheme in which everyone who was involved was simply trying to protect their own interests? Was Vogel involved in that scheme and was merely covering his own tracks?

When his phone rang at two o'clock, MacFarland had finally concluded that he might never unravel all the deaths. He picked up the phone and looked at the caller ID. It was Lockwood.

"What have you got, Benny?"

"Hi MacFarland. An interesting development. You're aware that yesterday we went over to Pelligrini's office to see if he had seen Vogel, right? It seems that after our visit, Pelligrini flipped. Went totally wacko! His secretary says that he started rummaging through his desk and filing cabinets and burning files. He tried to burn everything in a waste basket, but the fire set off the sprinkler system and prompted a visit by the fire department. Then, sometime after he left work, Pelligrini went home and tried to kill himself."

"What? Really? How?"

"Apparently he went out to the garage, turned his car on and tried to die of carbon monoxide poisoning. He disconnected the catalytic converter and flooded the garage with fumes. His wife thought he had gone back to the office, so he wasn't found for a couple of hours."

"Is he still alive?"

"So far. They got him into a hyperbaric chamber, but he is still in critical condition. He probably won't die, but we are not sure what his mental condition is. Until he is conscious, they can't tell whether or not there was any brain damage."

"Did he leave a note or anything that might explain why he tried to kill himself?"

"We haven't found anything so far, but the detectives are still looking. Since he figures so prominently in your case, I thought you should know."

"Thanks, Lockwood. I appreciate it."

He was about to hang up when Lockwood spoke up. "Hey, got some other news for you. The tire iron Iverson found in Murphy's car. Forensics says that it didn't have either Murphy's prints on it or any of his DNA."

"I didn't think it would," said MacFarland.

"But they did confirm that the partial prints on the tire iron did belong to Vogel. Probably not enough to get a conviction, but enough to make him the primary suspect."

"I'm not sure they could convict a dead man, Benny," said MacFarland bitterly. *But enough to close that murder file.*

CHAPTER SEVENTY-THREE

FRIDAY, MAY 13, 0859 HOURS

MACFARLAND WAS STANDING beside his cart, just finishing up making a pot of coffee. Rufus had found a discarded folding chair in some nearby dumpster and was setting it up in the shade of one of the decorative trees that lined the street. He was having problems with the chair collapsing.

"Boss, we need to get some chairs to sit on. This piece of junk just won't work."

MacFarland nodded indifferently. He wasn't really listening to Rufus. He was watching Pierson and Lockwood drive up to his corner.

MacFarland had tried to get back to work on Thursday, but business was light and he still had his mind on the case. He had finally broken the case into a series of related crimes.

First, the death of Mike Brady. The young man was killed, possibly by accident, but looking more and more like a deliberate act of sabotage. The motive for killing him was that he had uncovered evidence of fraud by senior management at Forrester Equipment and Construction. This linked the killing of Brady back to Pelligrini, and it would also explain Pelligrini's inexplicable presence at the time of the accident. He wanted to make sure that the threat to his scheme was silenced.

Pelligrini wouldn't set up the accident himself. He would get someone else to do it, someone he controlled. Vogel fit that bill very nicely. They had been working together for several years. Vogel had been observed on the job site early enough that he could have rigged the accident. Vogel had been in financial trouble. MacFarland had found evidence that Vogel had been taken to court by his creditors back in 2011.

Who had bailed him out then? Pelligrini? For what purpose? Back in 2004, Vogel had been implicated in another construction site death--Stephen Barry. Was this Vogel's only other accident, or had there been others?

Vogel still needed money. How much was he involved in the fraud scheme? *He has to be deeply involved*, thought MacFarland. But Vogel also had a side scheme going on--selling tools through the homeless people who hung around the area. This scam probably had nothing to do with the major embezzlement scheme. Selling tools didn't seem like the kind of crime Pelligrini would get into. No, the major scheme was run by Pelligrini and Peterson--he mustn't forget that. Norris Peterson was involved in this somehow, despite his protestations to the contrary. Yet, where was the evidence of that involvement?

MacFarland had no doubt that the embezzlement scheme was real, even though there was no accounting forensic proof of such a scheme--yet. Just let the police get hold of the company's books, and the numbers guys would find it. They were very good at this sort of thing. Besides, Brady had found some evidence of the fraud. He had pictures of suspect pages on his phone and possibly his computer, which is why they were stolen. A Chicago-based gang had engineered that break-in. Both Pelligrini and Peterson had strong connections to Chicago. Had one of them brought a gang out to Denver to provide muscle?

This same group had provided muscle for intimidation--attacking Wanda Warren, casing out Hightower's house, vandalizing MacFarland's cart, even trying to threaten Vogel himself. Wanda had thought that Forrester Equipment and Construction had mob connections, but perhaps they only had gang connections. Norma Sykes, an FBI agent investigating Peterson's holdings for RICO violations, was well aware of the Sons of BPSN gang from Chicago. Was that just a coincidence, or did Peterson have some connection with this gang?

The more he reviewed that line of reasoning, the more convinced he became that Peterson brought the gang to Denver to try to clean up Pelligrini's messes.

Unfortunately, where was the proof?

Second, the death of Louis Hightower. Hightower was the patsy in the accidental death case. Did someone want to kill him to make sure that he couldn't shed light on what really happened to Brady? Did Vogel try to eliminate Hightower? There was certainly no love lost between them.

Vogel had insisted to Warren that he didn't kill Hightower. Perhaps that was true. MacFarland was fairly certain that it was Ryan Boyce who had tried to kill the safety inspector. Why had Boyce gotten involved? Was he involved in the embezzlement scheme also, and so had a vested interest in making sure no one looked too closely into Brady's death? Or had Boyce realized that there was a cover-up going on, and taking care of Hightower was his price of admission? As Iverson would say, that was just speculation.

Third, the death of Picket. Picket had seen Vogel around the crime scene prior to the accident. Had Picket inadvertently also seen Vogel commit the crime and thus became a threat? Had Picket tried to shake down Vogel? Vogel's prints on the tire iron were conclusive enough for MacFarland, even if they wouldn't stand up in court. MacFarland also remembered the yellow paint on the tire iron, probably a good match for the paint on Vogel's yellow Tercel. He wondered if Iverson had asked the Crime Lab to compare the tire iron paint with Vogel's car.

As MacFarland reviewed the murders in his mind, he began to form a picture of Ryan Vogel, trapped into doing something he didn't want to do, but getting drawn deeper and deeper into the morass he had made. Did Vogel kill the Boyce family? Was that one more attempt to eliminate people who could link him to the original murder?

And then finally, the attempt to kill Wanda Warren. This seemed to be Vogel's last final act of desperation. It was the kind of illogic that many panicked people fall into. Get rid of the person who instigated the investigation and that would solve the problem. It didn't solve anything, but perhaps served as a form of retribution.

He walked to the curb as Lockwood pulled up. Pierson opened the passenger window. "We might have a break," she said. "They found a lockbox key on Vogel's body. Lockwood here, our star detective, was able to find the bank the lockbox is in."

"It wasn't difficult," said Lockwood, trying to sound modest. "The name of the bank is engraved on the key."

"That sounds good," said MacFarland.

Pierson smiled. "Chamberlain said that since you've been on this case for so long, you should be there when we open the lockbox."

MacFarland was surprised. After all, he wasn't a cop; merely a hot dog vendor. Hell with that! He wasn't going to say no to this opportunity! "Really? Let's go then." He got into the back seat of the car, and Lockwood raced over towards Lincoln to drive to the financial district.

An hour later, MacFarland, Pierson, and Lockwood, along with Iverson, were sitting around a table in a small room conference room at Police Headquarters, going through the contents of the lockbox. The contents, all carefully wrapped up in evidence bags, were spread out on the table between them.

One pile of cash, mostly twenties and hundreds, amounting to more than one hundred seventy thousand dollars.

One micro-cassette tape.

One burgundy-colored journal.

One detailed materials list.

Three passports, one each for Annette Vogel, Riley Vogel, and Lynnette Vogel.

One copy of a Last Will and Testament for Riley Vogel.

"Holy crap!" said Pierson, holding up the materials list. "Will you look at this? This is a detailed listing of all the materials taken from the construction site and sold back again. This is the fraud that Brady was killed for."

Iverson was perusing the journal. "This is even more spectacular," he said. "That little fucker has kept a journal of all the things he's done. Listen to this.

"'*The Journal of the Repairman.*'

"'*It is up to me. Norm Pelligrini has given me a new job. Nothing formal. In fact, quite secret. He wants me to be his clean-up man. I'm no fool. I made a recording of his request, in case he ever turns on me.*'

"Here's another section, much later.

"'*Feb 8 - Norm asked me to take care of Brady. The kid has been nosing around and even had the ~~timeroty~~ balls to confront Norm about the materials situation. Norm knows the Repairman can fix anything. I just have to figure out the right time and place.*'

"This is from a few days later.

"'*Feb 17 – At first I didn't want to do it. I even told Pelligrini that I wouldn't kill Mike. He wouldn't take no for an answer. Then, the Repairman figured it out! It was so easy! It is almost like I become an entirely new person when I put on the Repairman's black pants and shirt. I should get a mask. A creature of the night, danger hidden in the shadows. I even asked Norm to come over and see how his problem is eliminated.*'

"Um...let's see. Oh, here's one.

"'*Mar 12 – Told Norm that Wanda is causing problems over Mike's death. He wanted to know if Mike had any real evidence, but I said I didn't think so. Did he? Maybe I can find out from Shirley. She's starting to open up to me. You know, with a bit of makeup she would be rather pretty. Wouldn't mind porking her. Oh, Boyce has been bugging me too. Wants to be part of the action. The twerp! What makes him think he can cut in? Maybe I can get Boyce to shut Wanda up.'"*

Iverson scanned through the pages, then stopped.

"'April 4 – Fuck! That damn security guard knows something! Ryan overheard him talking to Wanda and he said he saw me. What did he see? Can I take a chance with that? No fucking way!'

"'Apr 11 – That asshole Ryan Boyce has been bragging about how he has put that hot dog guy in his place. Ryan knows something is going on, wants in. I need to talk to Norm about this. I don't know what to do.

"'Just got off the phone with Norm. He says to get Boyce to do something about Hightower. That way, we have something over him. Need to give this some thought.'

"'April 24 – Marty P tried to blackmail me. I was forced to take care of him. I hid his body in the tower form. I got to get them to pour tomorrow. Damn!'

"Brady. Hightower. And Picket. We got him by the balls!"

"Except he's dead, Iverson," pointed out Lockwood.

"And," added MacFarland, "it implicates Boyce in killing Hightower."

Iverson ignored MacFarland, but gave Lockwood a look of disgust. "I know he's dead! Doesn't matter. It means we can close out all those murders, you asshole."

Lockwood ignored him. "Any idea how much the embezzlement scheme was worth, Cynthia?"

She rummaged through a bunch of papers. "I am hardly

the expert on this, but I have to figure it was for at least three or four million dollars."

"That's a pretty strong motive for murder," muttered MacFarland. "If only Brady had gone to the police in the very beginning. Seven people might still be alive."

"Eight, if you count Vogel," added Pierson.

CHAPTER SEVENTY-FOUR

MONDAY, MAY 16, 0830 HOURS

AFTER THE EXCITEMENT of the previous week, MacFarland spent Sunday with Stefanie and Randy, watching a boring baseball game between the Braves and the Dodgers. Kaitlyn and Randy sat in the shadows of the man-cave, texting on their phones.

"What's the score?" asked Stefanie as she brought in some finger food for the two men to munch on.

"This is remarkable," said Randy excitedly. "Two pitchers, both with a chance for near-perfect games!"

"What does that mean?" she asked MacFarland. He shrugged in ignorance.

"It's the eighth inning, Stef! Both Robertson and DeSilva are pitching no hitters! I am not sure whether Robertson will be able to make it through the ninth. It looked like he really pulled a muscle on that last pitch. God, I hope they leave him in."

Kaitlyn stared at her father. "How can a game with no score be exciting?"

MacFarland got up. "Well, I've got to go. Need to get my product ready for tomorrow."

Randy stared at him in shocked disbelief. "You're not leaving now! History is about to be made! Mark, where are your values? What is wrong with you, man? This is a phenomenal game. Ah, shit, Lopez just got a home run."

MacFarland had grabbed a handful of the finger food, pecked Stefanie on the cheek, waved good bye to the kids, and raced home.

Monday morning, MacFarland pulled two folding lawn chairs out of his truck, replacing the broken one that Rufus had been trying to use. He sat down next to his friend and handed him a cup of coffee.

The morning was warm, pleasant, and quiet. Even the street smells were pleasant this morning. There were no sounds coming from the construction site down the street. Most of the prospective jurors were hurrying over to the courthouse. Although one or two of them stopped by for coffee, MacFarland just pointed to the temporary sign he had posted:

"Monday Special--Free cup of coffee!"

MacFarland brought Rufus up to date on the case.

"Pelligrini was still in the hospital on Friday when he was arrested for fraud and conspiracy charges. I don't know if he was conscious, but I am pretty sure he was wishing he had been more successful at committing suicide."

"He's the guy what owns the construction company?" asked Rufus.

"Yep. Reports to Peterson, too! I am sure hoping that the embezzlement case gets Peterson arrested. I'd sure like to see that bastard in jail."

"And this Vogel guy, he did all the murders?"

"Well, most of them. You remember Hightower, the black dude who did the safety inspections?"

"Yeah, he got fired for drinking on the job."

"It was all a setup, Rufus. Hightower might drink a bit, but he didn't cause the accident. He was wrongly accused."

"But Vogel didn't kill him."

"Correct. It was Boyce who did it. Lockwood told me on Saturday that they found the red truck. After reading Vogel's journal, Iverson finally got off his ass and started looking for the damn truck. The bumper had blood and DNA evidence that proved it was the vehicle that hit Hightower. The guy who owned it, a cousin of Boyce's, says he had loaned the truck to Boyce. Lockwood is checking out the guy's story, but I think it will hold. It was Boyce who ultimately killed Hightower."

"And then Vogel killed Boyce."

"They're still working that one out," said MacFarland. "It's entirely possible this Chicago gang killed Boyce and his family, but I don't buy that."

"Why not, boss?"

"They wouldn't bother trying to make it look like a murder-suicide. These gang-bangers just come in, make their kill, and leave. They don't even care if the police know it was them. It's a badge of honor to waste someone. There is no way they would try to make it look like a murder-suicide. Just not their style."

Rufus shook his head and finished his coffee. "Don't think I'd wanna run into them," he said. "They sound worse than Charlie."

MacFarland smiled. "They're probably back in Chicago by now. I think we've seen the last of them." He looked up and saw Pierson approaching him. "Detective Pierson," he said jovially as she neared his cart. "What brings you out here so early this morning?"

"Bad news, Mac."

Rufus got up and let Pierson sit down in his seat. He hurried over to the coffee pot and poured her a cup. Rufus knew how to get on Pierson's good side.

"Bad news? What do you mean?"

"Where to begin? Okay, let me start with the FBI. It seems that Wilson and Sykes stormed into the squad room on Saturday, waving a friggin' court order. They then swept up all of the files and evidence we had from the lockbox and all the files we got from Pelligrini's office. That bastard said that we were interfering with their fucking RICO case. We're investigating seven murders, for crying out loud!"

MacFarland could understand Pierson's outrage. If he had still been on the force, he would have felt equally violated. There were times when you wondered whose side the various state and federal agencies were on.

"That's it? Anything else?"

Pierson nodded grimly. "It seems that late Saturday night, something went wrong with the respirator that Pelligrini was on. He died during the night."

MacFarland's eyes widened. "What could have gone wrong? In the hospital? Where were the nurses and doctors?"

"They were there, but there was an unruly patient down the hall. The cop who was guarding at the door was called to stop a man from trying to stab one of the doctors. The cop and a nurse looked in on Pelligrini when they got back, and he seemed to be alright. Then, at eleven o'clock, when the nurse went in to do her scheduled check, she found that he had suffocated. That's when they discovered that the respirator had failed."

MacFarland stared at her without saying a word. With Pelligrini dead, what chance did they have of finding a basis to arrest Peterson? Was it possible that the scumbag was going to escape again?

CHAPTER SEVENTY-FIVE

TUESDAY, MAY 17, 0845 HOURS

MACFARLAND SMILED as Wanda Warren approached his wagon. Rufus had just left a few minutes earlier, and MacFarland was certain that his friend would kick himself for having missed her. "Good morning Wanda, how are you today?"

Warren smiled grimly. "I still have flashbacks to Vogel trying to push me off the building. I guess it wasn't a very good idea of mine to go there to meet him."

MacFarland shrugged. "Hindsight is always so accurate," he said with a short laugh. "Let's just be thankful that I got there in time."

Wanda bit her lip. "That's what I wanted to see you about, Mac."

MacFarland cocked his head. "What?"

"I wanted to thank you. For finding Mike's killer. For solving this whole thing."

"A lot of us were involved in closing this case. I didn't act alone."

Warren laughed. MacFarland was surprised at how different she was when she didn't put on the gruff exterior. "You don't need to be modest, Mac. I know what would have happened if you hadn't believed me. Brady's death would have remained an accident. All those bastards at Forrester would have continued ripping off the customer. And Vogel would have gotten away with murder."

"What's going to happen to the construction job now?"

"Oh, I think we're going to finish the job. They will just put new management in charge of the company and we will all go on as though nothing has happened."

MacFarland was not so sure that would happen, not if there was a RICO investigation going on. He wouldn't put it past Wilson and Sykes to confiscate the whole damn company. "If the company does have problems, can you find other work?"

Warren smiled and waved at the city around her. "This is Denver! Everything's happening here! There's lots of construction going on here," she said. "I won't have any problems finding another job." Wanda crushed her coffee cup and tossed it in the waste receptacle. "I heard that Pelligrini tried to kill himself."

MacFarland nodded. "Yes, he did. He didn't want to face the music, I guess. And he got his wish."

Wanda raised her eyebrows.

"They haven't mentioned anything at the job site? Pelligrini is dead. He died in the hospital. So he won't stand trial after all." He didn't bother mentioning that the Federal agents had confiscated most of the evidence that might be used to convict Pelligrini.

Warren whistled. "Damn, that's a shame. How did he die? Did he shoot himself?"

"No, he tried to die of carbon monoxide poisoning."

"That's a pretty sissy way to go," said Warren. "If I ever decide to off myself, I am going to do it like Thelma and Louise--drive off a cliff into the Grand Canyon. That would be spectacular!" She got a wistful look as she imagined that ending. MacFarland wondered who she would have as a companion.

"He didn't actually die from the C-O-two poisoning. Something malfunctioned at the hospital and he suffocated."

Warren turned her head sharply and stared at MacFarland. "That sounds awfully suspicious to me. I wouldn't be surprised if he wasn't silenced. Someone didn't want him going on trial."

MacFarland nodded. "You'd make a good detective, Wanda," he said as he thought about her observation. He had the same idea. Pelligrini's death by accident was just too convenient.

Wanda Warren stood up and prepared to go back to work. "I guess in the long run, it only matters that Brady got justice. His killer is dead. That's all that counts in my book. Thank you, Mac MacFarland. You did a great job." She paused, then leaned towards him. "Don't tell anyone that I did this. I got a reputation to maintain, after all." She kissed him on the cheek, then turned away and headed back towards the construction site.

As MacFarland watched her go, a bemused smile on his face, he thought about something else she had said. She mentioned that the embezzlement ring at Forrester was ripping off their customer. He hadn't really given much thought to the client, but then he realized that Norris Peterson was the customer. He owned the building. Yet hadn't Vogel said that both Pelligrini and Peterson were involved in the embezzlement? Why would Peterson be stealing from himself?

MacFarland suddenly realized that there was more to the embezzlement scheme than he had initially suspected. And as he had first suspected, Norris Peterson was deeply involved in it.

CHAPTER SEVENTY-SIX

TUESDAY, MAY 17, 1115 HOURS

AFTER WARREN LEFT, MacFarland put on his headphones, turned on his Spanish language CD, and started muttering the responses to the language prompts. As he practiced his phrases, he handled the occasional customer that came by. He prepared for a large lunch rush, since he knew that there were a lot of trials going on this week, and the juror pool would do anything to get out of the courthouse.

He waved a greeting to Sidney Morgan, who was featuring Texas Wieners today. Morgan had explained that Texas Wieners didn't come from Texas, but from Paterson, New Jersey. The Texas sobriquet came from the piles of chili sauce that smothered the dog.

"Isn't that the same as a chili dog?" MacFarland had asked.

"A chili dog is $2.50," said Morgan. "A Texas Wiener is $4.95."

Just before the lunch crowd broke through the doors of

the Lindsey-Flanigan Courthouse, Norma Sykes strolled up to his cart. "Hello, Mac," she smiled in greeting.

He raised his eyes to look at her, but kept his head down. He wasn't sure if his reluctance to face her directly was because he felt annoyed that she and her partner had interfered with the DPD's case or because he was afraid that he would find himself enjoying what he saw too much.

"Did Grey send you here to confiscate something?" he asked, trying to sound surlier than he really felt. "All I have is hot dogs."

"No, I've come because I wanted to see you." She hesitated, a bit flustered. "I guess I will order a hot dog, though."

He tried to relax. "What would you like?"

"Oh, one of your foot longs. And a diet drink."

MacFarland pulled a foot long dog from the heating pan, got a warmed bun, and wrapped it up for her. "Any particular type of diet drink?"

"Diet Coke would be fine."

He handed her the order, then shook off the ten dollar bill she held out. "It's on the house," he said.

She smiled hesitantly, then put the bill back in her purse. "We are going to get Peterson."

MacFarland looked up. "Really, is that so? When? How many more people is Peterson going to get killed before you Feds decide that he is a danger to society?"

"Mac, the case we are working on is a lot bigger than the murders you've seen."

MacFarland glared at her angrily. "Nothing is bigger than the murder of Nicole," he hissed.

Sykes winced at the depth of his anger. "I didn't mean that. I know that your loss is a terrible one. But trust me, Peterson is part of a much bigger picture. We are using him to bring down a huge syndicate. I promise you, Mac, we will get him. You will get justice."

MacFarland snorted. "I don't think the justice you are promising will come soon enough for me. I am not going to wait for you Feds to make a deal with Peterson that only puts him in witness protection. I will find a way to get my own form of justice."

Norma Sykes stared at him, her expression one of concerned sadness. "Are you after justice--or revenge?"

MacFarland looked over at her, his face grim with determination. "Is there a difference?"

EPILOGUE

TUESDAY, MAY 17, 1200 HOURS

"DR. EVEREST, I really appreciate all of your help," said Norris Peterson. "Here is a little something for your efforts." He handed the doctor an envelope.

The doctor flipped the envelope flap up and looked at the small stack of hundred dollar bills. "I don't like doing that sort of thing, Mr. Peterson. I don't want ever to do that again."

Peterson smiled and leaned back in his chair. "I think it's a bit late in the game to be worrying about moral correctness, Doctor. You should have thought of that before you had your little fun."

"It's blackmail," said Dr. Everest quietly.

"Actually, Dr. Everest, it's simpler than that. You can make your lifestyle public and weather the consequences, or you can graciously accept our help in keeping those indiscretions out of the public eye. I think we are just providing you a service that helps keep your medical practice the success it currently is."

Dr. Everest shook his head. "Well, your problem's taken care of. As far as anyone is concerned, it was an unfortunate equipment malfunction. The hospital's lawyers will sort everything out with Pelligrini's widow. Are you satisfied?"

Peterson didn't respond to that. "Thank you again for your services, Dr. Everest. Now, I have work to do, so if you'll excuse me?"

Everest got up, his shoulders slumped. He turned slowly and headed for the door.

Peterson watched the doctor leave his office. He wondered if Everest was going to be a problem in the future. *One more problem that I will have to handle,* he thought. A few minutes later, his intercom buzzed.

"Those four gentlemen are waiting for you in the Continental Divide conference room, Mr. Peterson," said Joyce Hill in a pleasant voice. If the men in the conference room disturbed her, it didn't show in her voice.

"Thanks, Joyce. I'll go see them now."

As he entered the conference room, he thought to himself that it was remarkable that he felt so calm. The four men he was about to meet--really, two boys and two young men--probably had already killed fifteen people among them. By any stretch of the imagination, they were dangerous men. Psychopaths, who could not be trusted.

Yet, they were his tools. He controlled them. While average men might fear these four men, Norris Gilbert Peterson knew that he was superior to them. After all, they did his bidding.

The four gang members were slouched around the room. One was playing with the video presentation equipment, probably with the intent of destroying it. None of these men had any respect for private property.

"Good afternoon, gentlemen," said Peterson. "I am sorry to have kept you waiting, but now I am ready to deal with you."

The youngest of the group, known in the gang as Bullseye, laughed. "What kinda deal you gonna make? What're we still doing here? We need to get back to our own turf."

Peterson held his hands out, palms down. "Your leader has made it clear that he wants to expand the Sons of BPSN to this city, Bullseye. This is your turf now." He turned to face the oldest of the group, a man barely older than twenty-five. "Mex, how many recruits have you gotten?"

The man known as The Mex counted on his fingers. "We have eight so far," he said. "But they ain't proved themselves yet."

Peterson knew that in order to prove themselves, the new recruits would have to kill someone. Peterson smiled. That might be one way to make sure the doctor wouldn't talk. But that was for later. "You know, it's getting kind of hot here in Denver," he said. "How about the four of you to taking a little vacation?"

The other youngster, a nineteen year old known as Slice n Dice, looked annoyed. "We been on a fucking vacation, man. When we gonna see some action? I mean real action."

"Soon enough," said Peterson. "But in the meantime, you need to stay out of sight. We've got Feds breathing down our necks, and I don't need you gentlemen getting caught up in their dragnet." He wasn't sure if any of them would recognize his dragnet reference. That was the problem of dealing with doped-out punk kids. They were just so ignorant. "I have a nice place up in the mountains where you can stay. It's next to a camp for homeless kids that I sponsor. My only request is that you stay away from the kids. Is that clear"

Mex furrowed his brow and gave Peterson a look of annoyance. "Yeah, man, what the fuck do you think we are? Monsters?"

ALSO BY MATHIYA ADAMS

Novels

The Avid Angler

The Busty Ballbreaker

The Crying Camper

The Desperate Druggie

The Eager Evangelist

The Freaky Fan

The Groping Gardener

The Impetuous Intruder

The Jaded Jezebel

The Kitchen Khemist

The Lazy Lawyer

The Morose Mistress

The Naughty Neighbor

The Obnoxious Oilman

The Paranoid Patient

The Quibbling Quartet

Novellas

The Christmas Corpse

The Easter Evader

ABOUT MATHIYA ADAMS

I've lived in Denver for more than thirty years, but my job as a corporate trainer often kept me away from the city I loved. Finally I got the courage to follow my dreams and stay home and write about a character who has lived inside my mind for several decades: a disgruntled detective who runs a hot dog stand and studies foreign languages (both of which I have often dreamed of doing).

Mark MacFarland is my idea of the ultimate hero. Not the kind who can save the world single-handed, but the kind who cares about what he is doing and does his best. He makes mistakes, often because he acts without thinking. Fortunately, he has Cynthia Pierson to do his thinking for him. He just needs to come to his senses and realize that.

You can contact me at mathiya.adams@gmail.com.

Made in the USA
Columbia, SC
14 September 2023